Montana Snowfall

Other Books by Caroline Fyffe

McCutcheon Family Series

Montana Dawn
Texas Twilight
Mail-Order Brides of the West: Evie
Mail-Order Brides of the West: Heather
Moon Over Montana
Mail-Order Brides of the West: Kathryn
Montana Snowfall
Texas Lonesome

~~~*~~~

Prairie Hearts Series

Where the Wind Blows
Before the Larkspur Blooms
West Winds of Wyoming
Under a Falling Star

~~~*~~~

Stand Alone Western Historical

Sourdough Creek

Montana Snowfall

A McCutcheon Family Novel

Book Seven

Caroline Fyffe

Edited by Pam Berehulke
Beta Reader Kandice Hutton
Cover design by Kelli Ann Morgan
Interior book design by Bob Houston eBook Formatting

Proudly Published in the United States of America

ISBN # 978-0-9861047-2-5

Dedicated to my Dear Readers, with love

Chapter One

Heart of the Mountains Ranch, Y Knot, Montana Territory, September 1886

Roady Guthrie exited the bunkhouse, his overstuffed saddlebag thrown over his shoulder. Excitement mixed with a good dose of restlessness tumbled around in his gut. He stepped off the porch, strode to his horse tied at the hitching rail, and hefted the burden over the sorrel's hindquarters, securing it behind the saddle. Next, he picked up his bedroll and tied it on top. Finished, he sucked in a lungful of fresh morning air and let it ease away his disquiet.

Across the ranch yard, the door to the main house opened and Luke McCutcheon stepped out. He crossed the distance between them, scattering a handful of chickens. "You ready to head out?"

"Reckon so." Roady ran his hand down the rifle scabbard at his mare's shoulder, then checked one more time to be sure he'd packed enough ammunition. His gaze strayed to the other rifle, the one that would stay in its case, the one he brought along just because.

"Sure you don't want to go, Luke? Bear hunting's a good diversion, especially when there's a baby in the house. I'll hold off if you want to grab a few things and saddle up."

Luke chuckled, then gazed longingly at the mountains. "I'd ride along, but Faith just might come hunting me if I did."

"The joys of bachelorhood," Roady said with a cocky smile. "I can go and do as I like. No one to ask permission." He gave his horse a firm pat on the neck. "Actually, I prefer going alone. It's the only solitude I get all year. Living in a bunkhouse don't afford much privacy—or thinking time. A few days in the woods puts things into perspective, and rights my soul."

Luke arched a brow. "Talking pretty deep, aren't you?"

He shrugged. "Who knows? Maybe this'll be the year I bag Behemoth."

"I wish you'd let the past go. Let me take that rifle to Waterloo with me when I go, consign it in the gun shop."

"You know I can't do that."

Luke's brows rose. "Can't or won't?" The moment stretched out. He grasped Roady's shoulder. "Be careful. That man-hunting grizzly has earned his name. It's been a handful of years since he's been spotted. I'm thinking maybe he's dead."

"Could be, but I don't believe so. He's just playing it safe by staying up in the high country since he mangled his front paw in Taylor's trap. He's a clever one. Knows he's easier to track."

Francis came out of the bunkhouse, pulling his suspenders over his shoulders. He gazed around with eyes still dull with sleep and hair resembling the bristles of a broom. "Thought I heard you out here, Luke."

Luke nodded.

Francis ran a hand over his lightly stubbled jaw as he took in Roady's horse and camping gear. "I'd sure like to go along, Roady."

"You're needed around here, Francis," Luke said. "Especially when I go to Waterloo next week."

Francis's chest puffed out, and he missed the thankful expression Roady sent to Luke. It wasn't that Roady didn't like Francis—because he did. A lot. Thought of him as a younger brother, and cared about him mightily. The fact that they had no blood ties didn't matter. But going alone was important. There was just something about being in those mountains all by himself. He'd meant what he'd told Luke.

A gleam of interest lit Francis's eyes. "I hear Matt and Mark are going to Waterloo with you, Luke. Should be an eventful trip."

Luke nodded. "That's why Flood will depend on you more than ever with most of the men gone, as will the women."

The sounds of deep male voices and laughter filtered out from the bunkhouse. The hands who weren't out on watch were waking up.

Francis glanced at Roady. "How long you staying out?"

"That's tough to say. Probably about ten days."

Francis leaned back against the hitching rail. "You're not heading straight to the hunting cabin?"

"Not this time. Going to spend a day or two in the high mountains first."

Luke's face darkened. "Keep a watch on the weather. It can change in the blink of an eye this time of year."

The bunkhouse door opened again and Lucky limped out, carrying a pail of water. He pitched it off the porch opposite the men. "Breakfast is ready. You best come get it before it's gone."

When Francis headed in, Roady turned back to Luke. "Care to join us inside?"

"Thanks, but no. I ate with Ma and Flood." He patted his stomach but his smile faded. "I mean it, Roady. I want to see you back here in ten days, or a few days after. Don't take any undue chances with that hide of yours."

Luke's concern touched him. They went back years; were best friends. They didn't mollycoddle each other, either. This bear-hunting trip was something he did every year. To clear his head. Get back to his roots. But mostly, to try to collect on a debt long overdue.

"You know I won't, Luke. I have too much to come back to."

Really? Like what? A bunkhouse full of smelly men?

Roady pushed away a seed of loneliness, not letting it take hold. He'd been working for the McCutcheons so long it was darn difficult to remember when he'd started. He wasn't complaining for the good life he'd been handed, it was just that he was starting to believe a man needed something more. Something to leave behind after he'd passed on to show he'd been a part of this world. The notion had started a year ago, and with each passing season the yearning grew. "Spring roundup will be here before we know it."

Luke chuckled in his dry way, making Roady smile. "We have winter to get through first. Last year was a doozy."

"You're right about that." He shrugged and headed for the bunkhouse door. He was hungry and intended to stuff his belly past full, enough to keep him stoked up most of the day. After which, he'd subsist on jerky and the other items he had packed in his saddlebag until he arrived in the mountains and set up camp. When his beans and biscuits ran out, he'd hunt for fresh game. The thought of a mouthful of fresh venison or a big fat turkey cooked by his own hands made his mouth water.

"You remember what I said," Luke called as Roady went through the bunkhouse door. "Two weeks at the very most. If not, I'll come looking."

Chapter Two

Ruined! The horrible word rolled around Sally Stanford's head like a hot coal. She stood on the scarred wooden platform of the train station surrounded by her family, dressed in her best eggshell shirtwaist and her periwinkle grosgrain skirt. She was the picture of decorum; she just wished she felt it as well. Even her new small-brimmed straw hat, a gift from her mother, couldn't calm her disquiet.

She gripped her mother tightly, wishing she could go back in time and change so many things. Turning her face away from the others, she corralled her burgeoning emotions. She'd not divulge the scalding heat of fear that burned within. If she could manage to get through the next few minutes without giving herself away, she'd board the train and be safely on her way to Waterloo, Montana Territory, no one the wiser to the secret she carried.

"Five minutes," a porter in a jaunty uniform and hat called out.

She pulled away, loath to leave the warmth and security of her mother's embrace.

"What in the world has you looking so serious?" her mother crooned, and laid her palm on Sally's cheek, her thumb gently caressing. The gesture of love was almost Sally's undoing.

"You've been planning this visit for weeks," her mother said. "Have you changed your mind?"

Sally's gaze roamed the beloved faces of her family before her. "Of course not. I'm just a bit melancholy. Three months is a long time to be away."

Her mother's concerned expression eased into a smile. "Is that all? With the cost of a ticket, it's prudent you stay for a good long while. I'm sure Heather is over the moon, waiting for her baby sister to arrive. You be sure and write with all the news."

"Tell us about Hayden," Anita chimed in.

"Yes, Mother. And you know I will, Anita."

Someone tapped her arm. Sally glanced down into Melba's anxious eyes.

"Be sure to tell Heather I'm coming out next year," Melba said with resolve. "I'll be fifteen then and able to make the trip alone—if she meets me in Waterloo like she's meeting you. It's so exciting you get to ride in a stagecoach."

The youngest of the family was bundled to the hilt in a long fur-lined coat, woolen scarf, and hat. Her tenuous health had steadily improved until she was able to make small excursions from the house on rare occasions. Everyone knew her plans to go to Y Knot were just wishful dreams.

"You won't forget, will you?" Melba asked, her thin voice sounding like a bird's. "That's why I'm getting better and not going to heaven. I want to see a real live Indian, and the blue Montana sky filled with puffy white clouds."

Sally smiled and chucked her baby sister under her chin. "You should be the writer, Melba, instead of me. That was beautiful." After so many months of worry, it was lovely to almost have her back. "I won't forget to relay your message to Heather. It will be the first thing out of my mouth." She winked, feeling her mood lighten. "And you tell Aunt Tillie good-bye for me. I'm sorry she didn't feel up to coming along this morning. But it's wonderful she made such a quick recovery from her illness."

Her mother ran a soothing hand down Sally's arm. "She was disappointed but didn't want to chance a relapse. Not with having to care for little Frankie. Now, you be careful, my beautiful little bird. You may be eighteen and think you're grown, but you're naive of the ways of the world. Three days alone on the train…" Her mother gave a long-suffering sigh. "I don't know what I was thinking to give you permission."

If you only knew! I'm not inexperienced of the ways of the world, or of men. She pushed her troubling thoughts away, knowing they would break her mother's heart. Sally would do anything to spare her *that* humiliation. Even move away to a place she'd never seen and never come back.

"I badgered you."

Her mother laughed. "That you did. Truthfully, I can't begin to express how proud I am of you, Sally! First your job at the newspaper, starting your novel, and now your fearless, independent spirit."

Sally glanced around at the nodding faces of her siblings, tendrils of shame threatening to choke her.

"We all are," her mother went on. "I wish your father were alive to see what a lovely woman you've become. He'd be very proud as well. Now, don't forget to send me a telegram as soon as you meet up with Heather and Hayden in Waterloo. If you don't, I'll worry."

"I will." The fabrication about her sister meeting her at the train station in Waterloo seared shamefully in her chest, but that was the only way to gain her mother's permission. Not only was she ruined, but now she was a liar as well.

They all moved together for one large family hug.

"I love you," her mother called softly as Sally turned and stepped up onto the train.

Sally took one last look. *I may never see any of you again.* "I love you too, Mother. All of you," she amended quickly.

What would Heather do when she found Sally at her front door? And again, when the baby started to show? She didn't want to disparage her older sister's good status in her new town, but she didn't know where else to go.

Chapter Three

The rough-riding train travel from St. Louis to Waterloo, the dank air thick with coal dust, together with all the starts and stops had triggered Sally's motion sickness and taken the starch right out of her sails. All her good intentions about continuing on the same day she arrived at the Waterloo station had evaporated like a drop of sweat landing on the red-hot coals in her brother's forge.

Yesterday, the moment she'd stepped off the passenger car and onto the train platform, her queasy stomach had almost made her run for an outhouse. Boarding the stagecoach to Y Knot had been unthinkable. Even though she hated to spend a penny of her precious savings, she'd searched out an affordable boardinghouse after taking in a bowl of soup in a nearby restaurant. Once in her room, she'd collapsed on the quilted bed, sleeping the time away from then until now.

Today, though, Sally was eager to head to Y Knot. She was rested and bathed, with her whole life in front of her. Optimism swirled within. With her resourcefulness, she'd figure out some way to support herself and her child. So what if she remained a spinster for the rest of her life? Her lot had been chosen by destiny—and there was no changing it now. Having sent the promised telegram to her mother, Sally exited the telegraph office. She stopped and looked at the Wells Fargo stagecoach across the street in front of the Oyster Hotel. The sight of the long, fuzzy ears of the mules hitched to the front actually tugged a smile onto her face.

She opened her satchel. *Only ten Premium soda crackers left. I need to find more before it's time to board. Without something to nibble on, my stomach will sour up and the trip will be miserable.*

The door behind her opened, and the three men who had entered just as she was leaving came out.

"I'm glad to have that taken care of, Matt, Luke," one of the tall cowboys said to his two companions. They smiled at her and doffed their hats as they passed by. The three stopped a few feet away. "Now all we have to do is ride out to Boucher's, collect the horses, and return. If we don't have any complications, we'll have a day or two in Waterloo to enjoy our time unfettered."

She glanced at the guns strapped to their thighs, then averted her eyes.

"Hey, McCutcheon," a man called from a wagon passing in the street. Filled with hay, it looked like a muffin top as the fodder almost overflowed the sides of the rickety dray.

All three men smiled in acknowledgment. "Tarkington, it's been years," one called back.

"You stayin' in town? I'd like to get together. Chew some fat."

The cowboys nodded. "We're riding out today, but we'll be back with six head to stable, as well as our saddle horses. You have room?"

The wagon was almost gone. "Sure do. I'll be lookin' for ya!"

The wagon passed and the men started away. "What say we head over to the saloon and wet the back of our throats before we get a meal? We can ask around for the best establishment to get a steak and potatoes," one said as they ambled off.

At the mention of food, Sally discreetly covered her mouth, and her face felt heat. Thoughts of the cold, greasy eggs she'd forced down this morning flicked through her mind. The boardwalk seemed to tilt dramatically to the left.

"I need crackers—*now*," she mumbled. She grasped the pole in front of her and rested her forehead as she waited for the feeling to pass. "I wonder if the Willow Tree Restaurant has some I can purchase?" She gazed across the street at the eatery next to the Oyster Hotel. "If not, maybe they'll have a loaf of bread to sell."

"What's that, my dear?"

Surprised, Sally whirled around, the quick motion making her head spin even more. She briefly closed her eyes as her world continued to tilt and bob.

"I'm so sorry," a tall, elderly woman said. "I didn't mean to startle you, but I heard you speaking and thought your words were directed to me." She held out a hand in supplication, the other rested on top of a tall cane.

"That's all right," Sally responded quickly. "I was muttering to myself, wondering where to find some soda crackers to nibble on for my trip to Y Knot. I guess I'll try the restaurant across the street."

Kindness radiated from the old woman's eyes. "Do you need some help crossing? Dodging the traffic can be tricky."

"Thank you, but I'm from St. Louis. Streets are quite busy there as well."

She dashed across the wide street in front of the St. Louis News, *jumping the puddles made by the rainstorm. Hurrying into the lobby, she shook the rain from her coat and hat as if she didn't have a care in the world.*

Sally's breathing faltered at the memory. Those were wonderful times. Writing for the newspaper. Earning a wage.

Mr. Greenstein emerged from his office, a wide smile on his face. "You're bright, Sally. You have a talent for stringing words together to paint a picture…"

Another wave of dizziness threatened to topple her. "Oh—"

She hadn't realized she'd made a sound until the old woman stepped forward and peered into her eyes, then steadied her with a gentle hand. "You come here directly and sit a spell. I won't take no for an answer. Your face looks like a freshly laundered sheet."

Sally took hold of the woman's arm with one hand while she fanned her face with her other. Moisture slicked her mouth as the queasiness doubled, then tripled. Breathing heavily through her nose, she sank down onto a bench in front of the telegraph office, feeling hot and prickly. She lowered her head toward her knees.

How? How had it happened? How did he fool me so easily?

Mr. Greenstein—no, *Eric* as he insisted she call him when they were alone in his office—had been so kind, so caring, so dedicated in seeing her hopes and dreams come true. She had thought him the most wonderful man in the world. He was different—refined and intellectual compared to her brothers, who worked with their hands and muscles all day, forging and bending iron over searing coals. They came home smelling of sweat and manure, while Mr. Greenstein always seemed clean and pressed, with perfectly manicured hands and nails.

He asked her questions that made her think. So instrumental in her writing career, he insisted on meeting her family, and she his. His wife was a wonderful woman, one Sally admired greatly. What had Sally done to lead him on? She couldn't fathom. She'd thought of him as a mentor, a father figure. Still, what happened must be her fault somehow. Even now, the guilt was enough to steal her breath away.

Gathering her emotions, Sally sat up.

Compassion shone in the older woman's eyes. "Can I get you a dipper of cool water? There's a barrel right over there."

Sally did her best to smile. "Thank you. That's very kind."

Leaning heavily on her cane, it took the woman a few minutes to return with the water. She sat next to Sally and held up the long-handled dipper to make drinking easier.

"How far along are you?"

Sally startled when water splashed onto her lap. She quickly brushed it away. "Pardon me?"

The kind smile was back on the woman's face. "I had three children of my own, albeit a long time ago. I recognize the signs."

"What? I'm…" Heat scorched Sally's face. "I'm not in the family—"

"You don't have to say another thing, my dear. I was watching you before we met. You're filled with anxiety. You looked like a hen that has lost her clutch." She took Sally's hand and held it between her own. "Do you have somewhere to go?"

Sally stared at her.

"It's all right."

Finally, Sally nodded. "I do."

"Good. I'm glad to hear that. But just in case that doesn't work out, I have a large two-story home on the other side of town. For years, it's just been me rattling around inside all by myself. My husband's passed on, as did my two boys. But last month another young woman moved in, and I haven't been happier. She's expecting, as well. If you ever need a place to stay, you have it with me."

The woman handed her a small square of stiff paper. Sally glanced down at the name and address.

"My name is Mrs. Mary Margaret. Everyone here in Waterloo knows me. If you want, come back and we'll work this out together."

When Sally opened her mouth to respond, Mrs. Mary Margaret shook her head. "Don't say a thing, my dear. I just want you to have the comfort of knowing you have a place to go."

Chapter Four

Roady rolled from his bedroll on the ground, still wearing the thick leather coat he'd slept in, a buffer against the cold morning wind. He took a moment to study the sky as he worked the stiffness out of his back. The mass of dark clouds didn't bode well. The tall pines swayed and his mare looked over from where she was tethered, her mane and tail alive with the wind.

Five days hadn't produced one bear track. Plenty of elk, turkey, a good-sized cougar, and other game, but not what he was looking for. Grizzlies in the high country didn't go into hibernation until November, so they were out there, he'd just not seen any. The top of the ridge was still a day's ride away. He planned to camp there next, but the crispness of the air today had him on guard. He couldn't afford to get snowed in. Not without some sort of sturdy structure for shelter. The Montana clouds were known for dumping several feet of snow in no time at all, even in the fall—*especially* in the fall. All the way up here, that could be deadly.

A cold breeze, heavy with the scent of snow, tickled his face already covered with dark whiskers.

He ran a hand over his jaw, then picked up the coffeepot from his supplies and headed for the stream. Squatting next to the bank, he was careful not to wet his boots. Having cold, damp feet was one thing he couldn't abide. Reminded him too much of when he was a lad, and his pa made him walk behind their peddler's wagon filled with bottles of whiskey spiked with rainwater, turpentine, and mint. Weather didn't matter.

Roady's stomach soured.

"Ain't no room for ya inside the wagon, boy. You know I'd let ya ride if I could. The old nag cain't take much more. We gots to make 'er last. If I didn't have this bum knee, I'd walk and let ya drive." Reaching down, his old man rubbed his leg, letting go a loud moan. "It's painin' somethin' fierce these days."

Funny how his limp disappeared the second they reached a town where his pa wanted to sell his concoction. They'd roll down the street until they found an empty nook or cranny to stop. Once they were set up, Roady went around town and put up notices of when his pa would be peddling his wares. It usually took two or three days before they were run off.

The painful memory was one he rarely let himself ponder. He'd never had a ma. As a boy, he'd lain awake on his worn-out blanket under the stars, his stomach chewing the backside of his belly, pretending that the man who claimed to be his pa had stolen him away from his rightful parents. Ones who were clean and decent, parents any boy would be proud to call his own. His pretend ma had warm eyes and soft hands. His pretend pa was knowledgeable and kind. And proud of him. Just as soon as Roady was old enough, he'd set out one night and never looked back. Promised himself he wouldn't end up like *him*—the swindler he lived with. He'd have honor in his words and deeds. Whatever he chose to do, it would be in goodwill and honesty.

Water splashed over Roady's hand. He stood, then started back to camp with a pot filled with clear mountain water, letting the concerns of his past life fall away.

His mare nickered, gazing at him expectantly.

"Patience, Fiddlin' Dee."

She pawed the ground forcefully. She'd cleared away the spare mountain offerings in a perfect circle.

"Just as soon as I get this pot on a fire, I'll feed you and move your stake. Can you wait three minutes?"

He stopped, looked at her, and a staring contest ensued. "No? Didn't think so. All right, you win."

Roady set the coffeepot down and closed the distance between them. He unscrewed the tethering stake and led the horse over fifteen feet. Once she was secure, he went to his pack of sorghum. She pushed her muzzle into the small amount he scooped onto the ground, eating hungrily.

"There. That should do you fine for a little while. At least until I get something hot in my belly, and guzzle down that pot of coffee I'm dreaming about."

With his mare taken care of, he started a fire. He cupped his hands around the small flame, not wanting the wind to snuff it out before it caught. The ember glow grew, and a few of the smaller twigs began to pop and then burn. He blew gently on the infant flames, their delicious heat licking his fingers and face.

He sat back when a snowflake settled on his hand. Watching it melt, disappointment stabbed him. Weather would cut this trip short, ruin his chance to kill that bear that had caused such damage, as well as lay a heavy blanket of guilt across his own shoulders. These few days in the fall each year were the only opportunity he had to try to even the score. The mauled body of the stranger was as fresh in his mind as if the attack had happened yesterday, not eight years back.

The day had begun like any other. He'd ridden out to check the herd settled in the pasture by Covered Bridge. A gunshot in the hills startled him, but he figured someone was hunting. It wasn't until the third and fourth report that Roady galloped off to investigate. The giant grizzly, known around these parts as Behemoth, had a man backed into a narrow crevasse of a massive granite outcropping. Trees were dense, and house-sized rocks were everywhere.

Roady pushed his frightened horse forward. The screams of the fellow could still bring Roady out of a dead sleep, covered in sweat. Roady had pulled his Winchester, but with the dense forest and the moving target, he couldn't get a clear shot to the bear's heart. He shot till his rifle bullets were gone, then he'd emptied his handgun, but the bear had hardly noticed.

If only he'd gone to investigate sooner. Maybe he could have distracted Behemoth while the man got away. By the time the male grizzly finished playing with his prey, the man was unrecognizable. Roady waited until the grizzly lumbered away. The fellow had no identification, and any recognizable feature was gone. The only thing left was his rifle. Roady retrieved it, then dug a grave with the folded shovel he carried on his saddle.

Since then, the man-killer had been spotted every few years, usually coming out of the mountains to lay claim to some easy stock. What Roady wouldn't give to at least see a sign that Behemoth was still alive. If he was dead, so be it—at least Roady would know. But if the bear still walked this earth, Roady had a score to settle. He wouldn't rest until it played out to the end.

But for now, it was the snow that concerned him. Roady glanced at the top of the pines. He'd give it an hour. If the snowfall didn't stop, he'd have to start down for the hunting cabin off Placer Creek where he would wait out the storm. It was either that, or head directly back to the Heart of the Mountains, which would mean forfeiting the rest of his hunt until next year. He wasn't quite ready for that.

Chapter Five

"We'll be stoppin' shortly to water the mules," the shotgun messenger said through the window of the moving stage. He grasped a long rifle in one hand and held on to the rollicking coach with the other. Even the fast clip of the conveyance didn't seem to discourage his interest in the passengers. He smiled amiably.

Sally jerked her gaze away. He was young and handsome, and came to talk with them often, which made her wonder at his intentions. He was simply being friendly and doing his job, she chided herself. She wouldn't let Mr. Greenstein tarnish her feelings toward all men.

He chuckled. "And also to give you ladies a few minutes to stretch your legs. I know how stuffy it can get inside this contraption." He touched his hat and was gone.

"If it's like last time, we'll hardly have a moment before it's time to climb back in," the elderly woman across from Sally said. Mrs. White held her grandson on her lap, even though he looked too old for such pampering. The boy's mother, on Sally's side of the seat, kept her eyes closed for most of the trip. According to the grandmother, she had some malady that wasn't infectious, but made her weak and tired.

"Yes. The fresh air will be nice," Sally replied. She glanced outside at the branches dancing in the wind.

"I want out now!" the boy screeched, making his mother open her eyes and look around. "I'm tired of this place."

"Hush, Fredrick!" his grandmother commanded. "You know you can't get out yet. The man said we'd be stopping in a minute. Be patient and count to one hundred. Your mother is trying to rest. Be a good boy, please."

Sally gave silent thanks when she felt the stage begin to slow. The inside stayed warm and stuffy, even though the temperature outside had dropped more than several degrees. She closed her notebook and tucked the novel she was writing away in her carpetbag. She'd started it before the incident with Mr. Greenstein had happened. Since then, she'd not been able to add a single word.

Yes, a lungful of fresh mountain air would do her a world of good. Even though she was starving, she didn't dare extract a cracker from her carpetbag now. Not until Fredrick was out of the coach. The first time she had, his eyes had lit up like the sun. Under normal circumstances, she'd be happy to share, but her dwindling supply needed to last until they reached Y Knot. Once Fredrick knew what she carried, he'd begged relentlessly until he'd eaten the majority. Some even ended up on the stagecoach floor.

"Finally," Mrs. White complained when they rocked to a halt. "I can't wait to feel earth beneath my boots."

The door opened and the young man—Mr. Slater—put out the stool so they could disembark. He reached for Fredrick and lifted the child out, and then helped his grandmother. When the boy's mother waved him off, he turned toward Sally.

"I can manage on my own, thank you," she said as she stashed several crackers into her pocket.

"It's a good step down, Miss Stanford. I don't mind."

But I do.

"The Wells Fargo Company wouldn't want you to fall." He gave her a charming smile.

Even though she knew it was unreasonable, she couldn't bring herself to put her hand into his. When she waved him away as well, his eyes dimmed, and she felt like a crotchety old mule. What had happened to her wasn't his fault.

Sally took a deep breath of crisp air as she looked up and down the narrow, deserted road. She pulled her shawl more closely about her shoulders, noting the black clouds blocking out the sun. In a clandestine move, she slipped a cracker into her mouth. The salty goodness was heaven. She'd be relieved when they finally reached town.

Childish laughter rent the air as Fredrick ran circles around his grandmother, who looked like a worn-out dishtowel. The woman's hair straggled into her face, and the growing wind blew it here and there.

The poor woman, Sally thought, just as the boy dashed off into the forest.

"Fredrick! Come back here this instant!" Mrs. White cried. She made her way to the edge of the woods where he'd disappeared. "Mr. Slater, can you please fetch my grandson for me?" she called to the shotgun messenger, who had his hands full with watering the mules. "He's playing hide-and-seek in the bushes, and I can't find him."

The driver, overweight and red faced, nodded at his younger helper.

It didn't take long for Mr. Slater to drag Fredrick out by the collar. The child's overly mischievous behavior made Sally want to tweak his ear. He knew he was running his grandmother ragged, and didn't care a whit.

"You better mind your grandma, little tyke!" The tall cowboy glared at the boy when his grandmother wasn't looking. "Wouldn't want a wolf or bear to gobble you up."

The boy's eyes went wide, but Sally didn't feel sorry for him at all. Most children she knew minded their elders. That child needed a firmer hand.

"Load up," the driver called in a raspy voice. Mr. Slater let Fredrick climb in first, and then assisted the lad's grandmother.

Reluctant to leave the beautiful scenery for the stuffy interior, Sally stole one long last look around, hoping Mr. Slater would take the hint without her having to hurt his feelings again. Thankfully he did, stepping back. She couldn't stop a small smile of appreciation.

"All comfortable?" he asked after she was settled.

"Yes, thank you."

"You may want to spread out your lap robes. It's gettin' cold. We may even get a few snowflakes before long. And the road ahead becomes a bit more narrow and rocky as we climb in elevation. Our pace will slow down some, but not much. We still have a few hours to go."

Mr. Slater disappeared and the coach lurched forward.

"I guess we should have our lunch," Mrs. White said, reaching for her carpetbag. Unwrapping a cloth-covered sandwich, she handed it to the child and repeated the process for herself. "I don't think your mama is hungry," she whispered to Fredrick, who was gobbling up his food. "Maybe she will be later." The sadness in her voice was impossible to miss.

Sally reached for her own travel bag and tore off a chunk of bread from the large loaf she'd purchased at the Willow Tree Restaurant in Waterloo, knowing she needed to keep something more than crackers in her stomach, for the baby's sake.

As Mr. Slater had mentioned, the coach began an uphill climb. They were going along at a nice clip when the stage jerked violently, sending Sally's heart lurching up her throat. The bread on her napkin-covered lap tumbled to the floor, and her carpetbag skittered to the opposite door. The sleeping woman by her side let out a loud shriek.

Gasping, Sally grasped the edge of the seat to keep from falling to the floor. Outside, a large cougar dashed into the bushes. A shout from the driver was followed by a string of unintelligible words.

The coach tilted precariously, as if the wheels on one side had dropped off the road where the earth fell away a few feet. It jerked to a stop almost on its side, and then a loud screech was followed by a crack that rang out from underneath.

Sally's scream was drowned out by the old woman's and the child's. She gripped the windowsill and struggled to keep from sliding onto the others below her.

Chapter Six

Sally couldn't hold on much longer. A few frightening moments passed before she heard Mr. Slater's voice over the wailing of the little boy.

What had happened? Were they under attack?

Mr. Slater appeared at the window, on the upside of the tilted coach. A gash split his forehead and blood flowed down his temple, but he brushed it away from his deathly white face. He yanked the door open. The frightened mules' braying filled the air, and a loud scraping sound made her grimace as the coach moved forward a few inches.

"Let's get you out!"

He took Sally under her arms. She had no option than to let him, even though a hot lance of fire raced up her spine at his touch. She stifled a groan and scrabbled with her feet to find something solid. Once she found purchase with one toe, Mr. Slater hefted her out. She grabbed onto anything she could find to keep from falling. He climbed down, making it look easy, and then assisted her to the ground.

"Go wait over there." He pointed.

"You're hurt."

"Go on. I'd need to know you're out of the way. Don't argue."

Sally backed away. Worried about the driver, she started around to the front, giving the conveyance a wide berth as sounds inside said Mr. Slater was hefting someone else out the door.

She gasped and covered her mouth. The driver lay crumpled on the ground, his sightless eyes staring into the heavy gray clouds. She'd never seen a dead person except at a funeral. Wide eyed and numb, she took a step back.

Fredrick's head appeared through the door of the crippled stagecoach. Sally rushed back to the side of the contraption and put out her arms, thankful for anything to get her mind off what she'd just seen. "Come on, Fredrick. Don't be scared."

Mr. Slater's head popped out the door. He kept hold of the lad until she could get a grip on him, helping him climb off. Once she had him, Mr. Slater disappeared back inside.

"Don't cry," she crooned, struggling to lift him into her arms. Tears streamed down his jelly-smeared cheek. As she rocked him, his grandmother's head appeared in the doorway. Mrs. White was disheveled, and blood covered her chin.

Sally set Fredrick on a rock. "Sit here and don't move a muscle. Do you understand?" she said sternly. "I don't have time to worry about you right now. I need to help Mr. Slater. If you run off, it's to your own peril." She felt a twinge of guilt being so stern after the harrowing situation they'd just been through, but there was no help for it.

The child nodded, and she hurried away.

Mr. Slater was having a difficult time getting the older woman through the small door. Sally edged up the outside of the coach, praying it wouldn't tip any farther. She reached up until her fingertips touched Mrs. White's arm.

"Come on, ma'am. Can you climb out? I can help you once you're through the door."

"I don't want to leave Gertrude!"

"You need to come out so Mr. Slater can help Gertrude."

That seemed to sink in. The woman scrambled, and Sally figured the shotgun messenger was pushing from below. Sally assisted her to the ground. Once Mrs. White's feet hit the dirt, she rushed over to Fredrick, who was sitting on the rock where Sally had left him.

Sally cupped her hands around her mouth and leaned into a burst of cold wind. The temperature had dropped even more. A few snowflakes floated in the air. "Mr. Slater, what do you want me to do now?"

"Not sure."

Several moments ticked by. Surely he couldn't carry Gertrude's deadweight and climb out with her.

"Fetch me the coiled rope tied to the back of the coach," he called.

With trembling hands, Sally worked at the tether until she had the rope in hand. Gathering her skirt, she scrambled up the side of the leaning stage and gazed inside. "Here."

"Good. Hand me the end." He tied the rope around Gertrude's body.

"Do you want me to pull?"

"You're not strong enough. I'll have to hoist her out. You wait with the others."

"Would it be better with me pushing from behind?" Sally asked.

"I'd rather do this myself. You've helped plenty." The bleeding on his temple had stopped, but his face was still pinched with pain. Blood had dried in a long streak from his temple to his chin, and an egg-sized lump was forming.

Sally climbed down, being mindful of the fabric of her skirt. The last thing she wanted to do now was fall from clumsiness. After a few minutes of work, Mr. Slater had Gertrude out and cradled in his arms. He carried her off the road and laid her under a tree. Her mother and son gathered around.

Sally joined them as well. The poor woman looked horrible, but she was alive and awake.

"I'll have to go for help," Mr. Slater said, wavering on his feet. "We can't risk waiting for another stage. With the weather turning, they'll hold them on either end. Y Knot is closer, so I'll go that way."

"What about the driver?" Mrs. White asked in alarm. "Can't he go and you stay with us? I'd feel better with you standing guard." Her face tightened and she began to shake. She gazed at her daughter, and pulled her grandson protectively to her side. The boy was conspicuously quiet.

"He can't go, ma'am. He's dead," Mr. Slater said.

"Dead! What happened?"

"A cougar spooked the mules. Jimmy fought to keep the stagecoach on the road, but something happened. He took a big gulp and went stiff. Before I realized something was wrong with him, he'd flopped off the side and hit the ground. He said he had a bad ticker, but I thought he was saying that to get attention. Guess it was true."

"That's horrible," Sally said. "The poor man. Can we get the coach out of the ditch? I don't much like the thought of spending the night out here in the wilds."

He shook his head, looking younger than he had before. "'Fraid not. The axle is broke. That coach isn't going anywhere."

"Oh my." Mrs. White wailed, bringing a round of tears from her grandson.

"We'll just have to wait until help arrives."

The grandmother pointed to the dark clouds. "We can't wait. We'll freeze to death by the time help arrives. Someone has to go and let them know we're out here."

Wheezing, the old woman eased down on the ground by her daughter, and gathered her body in her arms. Her eyes were larger than the saucers of Aunt Tillie's best tea set.

Fear snaked through Sally as well. "Mr. Slater can't go. I think he has a concussion, ma'am. He wouldn't make it very far."

Mrs. White's eyes darted around, looking for a solution. "Miss Stanford, you're as fit as a fiddle. Yesterday, you told me how you used to ride through the park with your sisters. Surely you can handle a mule for a few miles. You go for help."

Sally blinked when Mr. Slater looked at her. It was true; she did know how to ride. Quite well, actually. Not only Sundays in the park, but sometimes the animals her father and brothers had shod before their owners picked them up. She was no wilting violet. It was early enough in her pregnancy that it wouldn't hurt the baby—unless she fell off.

"I don't know…" Mr. Slater's expression was doubtful.

"She's correct, I can ride."

"Bareback?"

Sally nodded. "How far is it to Y Knot? You'd said a few hours, but won't it be faster riding?"

"Not unless you gallop the whole way. I can't see you doing that without a saddle. You still won't make it before dark."

Or before the storm hits.

Chapter Seven

At the sound of Cinder's small voice jabbering away from her bedroom, Amy McCutcheon knew her toddler had awakened from her afternoon nap. Any thought of Cinder always brought a smile to her face. Amy set aside the rolling pin in her hands and removed her apron. If she didn't hurry, Cinder would become impatient and start to fuss.

"Mommy? Mommy!"

Her daughter's singsong voice reminded Amy of the tiny golden bells dangling from the tips of the Christmas stockings Mrs. McCutcheon hung each year on the fireplace mantel. The McCutcheons were such an incredible family. Her years married to the second-oldest McCutcheon son had been the happiest of her life.

"Nappie wet. Nappie we-e-e-t."

Amy hurried up the stairs and through the child's bedroom door, ignoring the ache in her back caused from the new child she carried. She scooped her daughter from her crib and into a hug, and breathed in the warm aromatic blend of soap, apples, and powder. "How's my little sweet pea? Did you sleep well?"

Cinder nodded, her two middle fingers planted firmly in her mouth. With the other hand, she patted her soaked diaper.

"Wet," she whispered, her brow pulling down in consternation.

"Don't you worry about that. We'll take care of it zippity-quick."

Amy carried her over to the small bed on the other side of the room, the one Cinder would move to once the new baby was born. Laying her on the multicolored log-cabin-patterned quilt, Amy quickly unfastened the safety pins and stripped off the soaked material, then dropped it into a tin bucket. Diapers soiled with more than urine were marched straight out back immediately—much to Cinder's amusement.

In moments, Amy had a new diaper firmly in place and pulled on a snug pair of wool pants. She hoisted Cinder up by her arms.

"Would you like to help Mommy with the pie? I'm rolling out the crust now."

Cinder's eyes brightened. When she nodded, her wispy black hair floated around her face like feathers.

"Auntie Charity is coming over tonight for supper, as well as Auntie Faith, Auntie Rachel, and Grammy. We're going to start planning the Christmas social. December will be here before we know it."

"Da?"

Amy kissed her daughter's head. "No, sweetie. Remember, Da's gone to Waterloo. But he'll be back soon enough—and he's bringing you a surprise."

Mark's return couldn't come fast enough for her. She'd had to convince him to go, promising she and Cinder would be fine in his absence. He watched over her like a mother hen now that she was again expecting. She'd seen the excitement in his eyes whenever the men talked about the six new mares they were buying, and didn't want him to miss out. As much as the brothers had protested against going, the three had been happy for their time away. She stifled a smile. But why not? Most of the ranch work was completed, and Mark hadn't had any time away for over a year. At least going together, they could keep each other out of trouble.

Cinder scrunched her legs and tried to bounce.

"Oh no, you don't." Amy laughed and picked the toddler up, heading back to the kitchen. "After the pie is in the oven, we'll go catch and pluck—"

Amy snapped her mouth closed. Cinder loved the hens, all fifteen of them. *I should have taken care of the butchering while Cinder was asleep.* Well, she'd just have to think of something to distract the toddler while she got the job done. Perhaps she'd bring in the mama cat and her three kittens.

"Here you go," she said, setting Cinder down. Amy reached for her apron and put it on, tying the bow behind her back.

"Up, Mommy," the child said, lifting her arms.

"All right." Bending, she lifted Cinder but gasped as a white-hot pain zipped through her abdomen. She all but dumped Cinder next to the piecrust on the flour-sprinkled countertop. Alarmed, she pressed her hand to her stomach as the pain quickly subsided.

She knew *that* pain all too well. She'd lost her and Mark's first baby several months after they'd married. The heartrending experience was one she never wanted to go through again. The whole family had been devastated. As much as she tried not to think about the miscarriage, the possibility of the same happening again was never far from her mind.

Chapter Eight

"You'll take Dolly," Mr. Slater told Sally, unhitching one of the front mules from the team, then leading her forward. "She's gentle and rides well. She won't give you any trouble."

He took out his knife and sliced off the long reins, leaving enough length that he could tie them in a knot at the mule's withers. The rim of his hat was buffeted by the afternoon wind that was gaining momentum.

He threw a small blanket he'd fetched from the driver's seat over Dolly's back. "Stay to the main road and you won't get lost."

Indecision shone in his eyes. He was obviously as unsure of her going on alone as she was, but what other option did they have? Weather was changing. They needed to get over this mountain and into Y Knot.

Sally glanced at the others huddled under a blanket at the foot of the tree, the small boy clinging to his grandmother's side.

She'd changed into an extra pair of Mr. Slater's pants and made a makeshift belt from a short piece of rope. Mrs. White, looking apologetic for having suggested Sally for the job, wound her own wool scarf around Sally's neck and then kindly patted her cheek.

Mr. Slater packed some food into a saddlebag, as well as a gun with a handful of bullets after showing her how to load it and pull the trigger.

"I don't need a gun, Mr. Slater. I can't even shoot."

"Take it anyway. Just in case."

"Are there any other roads I should be careful of?" Nervous energy rolled around inside her. "Different ways to go?"

He thought for a minute. "Not really." He took off his hat and scratched his head. "Actually, there is a split or two, now that I think about it."

"Are they marked?"

His long delay made her swallow.

"Not that I recall. Just take the first split to the left…"

"The first split to the left," she repeated, making a mental note.

He looked down at Dolly's hooves for several seconds. "No, that's wrong. Take the first split to the *right*."

Filled with alarm, she gaped at him. "This is important, Mr. Slater! Do you even know? I don't want to get lost." *I have my baby to think about.*

"I don't want you to get lost either," he said stiffly. "It's just I'm always riding shotgun, you know, keeping watch around, forward and behind. I've never paid much attention to the route. But don't worry, Miss Stanford, I'm sure it's the first split to the left."

"You just said *right*!"

"That's what I meant! You've got me muddleheaded with your questions. I'm absolutely positive on my pappy's grave you take the first split to the right, and the second split to the left. Once you do that, it won't be but an hour before you come to the outskirts of Y Knot. You may even see a traveler or two. For now, you'll be climbing steadily until after you've passed the two splits." The mule turned her head and looked at them. "And don't let the saddlebag slip off." He gave Sally a quick once-over, then added, "If you have to dismount to fetch it, you might not be able to get back on."

She nodded. Anxiety swirled within. It wasn't only the issue of the route that had her worried, but all the other dangers she knew Mr. Slater wasn't mentioning. Like outlaws, Indians, and wild animals. Hadn't a cougar frightened the mules and caused the crash in the first place?

Her brother's face popped into her mind. *"Don't let fear stop you from doing anything, Sally. Always do your best, with a strong heart. You're a Stanford."* Travis had been giving her a talk after he'd found her crying over the math problems she couldn't figure out, not preparing for a ride through the wilderness. Still, his words fortified her. She *was* a Stanford, and she'd make it through and get her baby to safety. She would be like him—and Morgan! And Heather. Her sister had traveled this same road herself.

"And you'll be sure my trunk gets on the wagon as well?"

"Yes, don't you worry about that."

Even with the extra clothes Mr. Slater had made her layer on, as well as the dead driver's thick leather jacket, the chill in the air couldn't be denied. It would snow tonight. She had to make it to Y Knot before that happened. The small leather gloves her mother had given her for the trip were of little protection, and her fingertips were already cold.

"Now, up you go." He cupped his hands together, and Sally slipped her boot inside.

Once situated on the animal's back with the saddlebag set behind her, she tried to smile. This felt wobblier than she remembered. "I'll get there, Mr. Slater. You can count on me."

He looked up at her, his crooked smile endearing. "I know you will, Miss Stanford. Just keep riding. Y Knot's not that far away. Tell the sheriff our quandary, as well as the stage office. Go on now, and don't dally. You don't want to spend the night alone in the woods. You'll make it to town right after nightfall, so that won't be too bad."

Not too bad? She hoped he was right. It had been almost a year since she'd ridden, and about six since she'd ridden without a saddle. She felt timid on this rangy animal. The fuzzy gray ears rotated front to back, and when the mule swished her wiry tail, it was long enough to slap Sally on the foot.

When she tugged on the reins, the beast turned its head, but nothing else happened. Sally thumped her heels into the mule's side several times, but Dolly just stood there.

As if to punctuate the dire situation, a gust of wind almost took the hat Mr. Slater had plunked on her head, and she grasped at it to keep it from flying away.

She gaped at Mr. Slater. "She won't go."

He hurried to the side of the road, and with his knife, cut a switch from a tree. He quickly stripped it of its leaves, but left several on the end. "You're going to have to use this whether you like it or not, Miss Stanford," he said, handing the skinny branch to her. "She won't want to leave the others."

Sally took the sinewy piece of aspen, not liking the way it felt in her hand. "Mr. Slater—"

"Can't be helped. Go on now."

Chapter Nine

Dolly brayed loudly, then pulled on the reins as she tried to look back the way they'd come some two hours ago. Time after time, the mule brayed, and by now Sally was beyond caring that she'd alert any ruthless characters or hungry animals to their whereabouts. Persuading the mule to keep quiet had been impossible. Just getting her to plod up the road was exhausting enough.

Sally's head hurt from the noise, and her arm throbbed from switching the cantankerous creature on the behind. Stubborn wasn't the half of it!

"Hush, now," Sally said sternly, glancing at the shadowy underbrush alongside the road. A few feet ahead, some kind of small animal darted off the dirt road into the grass. "I don't like this any more than you do, girl."

She thumped her heels into the mule's sides, hoping for a trot. They'd accomplished that once, and only for a short amount of time. Thank goodness this particular mule had a nice thick mane for support.

With the passing of time and increased elevation, the temperature had dropped. Dampness chilled her to the bone. She wished she'd thought to ask how soon to expect the first turnoff. "Everything is going to be fine," she said aloud.

"When we reach Y Knot, I'll make sure they feed you a double portion of oats."

Hee-haaaw, hee-haaaw.

Sally tried again, pounding her boot heels into Dolly's vibrating sides, and gave her a switch to her butt. If only she would move a little faster. It was amazing how slowly the animal could walk, considering when harnessed to the stagecoach the team galloped on for miles at a time. You'd think she'd packed a heavy load of rocks in her saddlebags that weighed five hundred pounds.

Sally's stomach burned with hunger, and her thighs quivered with fatigue. She should have stored some crackers in her pocket where they were easy to reach. Was her baby hungry? Could it tell her mama was riding a mule? She supposed she could try to dig the saltines out of the saddlebag, but she was so cold, falling was a good possibility.

Her baby. Would it have her fawn-colored hair, or be fair, like his or her father?

Sally glanced up at the darkening sky, a myriad of feelings swirling inside. At first, after *it* had happened, and pretending she wasn't with child was no longer possible, she'd been angry, scared...*hurt.* She'd wondered if she would hate the baby once it was born, especially if it looked anything like Mr. Greenstein.

How would she ever be able to forget that horrible afternoon? Her boss, ever so solicitous, had asked her to stay behind after everyone else had gone home for the day so they could go over a part of her article that needed clarification.

Once they were alone, he'd said there was a reference he needed in the upstairs storeroom, where they kept the broken-down equipment and archived newspapers. If she wanted to come along, he'd show her where it was, in case she ever had to access anything herself. It had sounded strange to her, but she had no reason to distrust him. He'd been her friend and champion for over a year. He'd come to her house twice, to drop off an assignment. Her brothers all thought him nice. *"It will only take a moment. Then you can be on your way."*

She gasped, almost overcome with grief. Angry at herself, she pushed the frightening memories away. They had the power to crush her, to steal every ounce of air from her lungs. Now was not the time for regrets. She touched her tummy, thinking of the tiny babe nestled within. She had to protect her baby, get it to safety. She could never hate something that was part of her. The child wasn't guilty of its father's sins. She needed to keep a clear head and find her way to Y Knot. Everyone's safety depended on it.

Snowflakes drifted down before her eyes like tiny fairies in a quiet wonderland. Sally huddled deeper into her coat as they moved up the road, rutted from the passage of the stagecoach. Again she thought of the food in the saddlebags. Could she get some out without falling? What would she do if she came upon an outlaw?

"Don't go looking for trouble, because enough will find you on its own."

Sally had never felt as alone as she did right now with the dark gray clouds churning above her head and tiny snowflakes floating before her face. She imagined her mother's comforting arms around her, and indulged her imagination for a moment that she was once again a little girl. She wished she could go back. She'd change so many things.

The dense forest foliage transformed to an expanse of rolling hills, and the snow a silent white wall.

Startled, she took in the sight of a road up ahead on the left. *What? We're still climbing uphill. Mr. Slater said the split would come later after we reached the crest.*

At the fork, she pulled Dolly to a halt and sat there. How she'd love to dismount and stretch her sore muscles, to walk out the stiffness.

With a sigh, she took in her choices. Both roads had wagon ruts and looked well traveled. There were no markers or other indications as to which was the correct way to Y Knot. As she pondered her dilemma, Dolly let out an anxious bray, then swished her tail unhappily.

Which way? Sally shivered, the cold biting at her hands and face, seeping deep inside her. *Which way to Y Knot?*

Chapter Ten

A feeling of accomplishment washed through Amy as she admired the side dishes lined up on the counter. The table, set with her best linen and dishes, looked inviting. Thankfully, the worrisome pain had not repeated itself. She'd stay confident, and would not let any undesirable thoughts tarnish the rest of her pregnancy. Even though Cinder didn't really understand what was happening, she seemed delighted to hear they were expecting a baby, like her tiny cousin Holly. History would not repeat itself. She'd delivered Cinder with no problems, and she would this baby too. Still, she'd be thankful when Mark returned. Their home felt empty without him.

Amy went over the evening's menu in her head one more time. Mashed turnips, sprinkled with nutmeg. The last of this year's garden vegetables, sliced and lightly steamed. Celery and pickle salad. All she had left to do was cut the still-warm loaf of bread, cream some honey into the fresh butter, and pull the chicken out of the oven and let it cool.

The girls would be arriving anytime.

Amy glanced out the window in the fading light, still amazed at the turn in the weather. Light snowflakes drifted about, covering trees, fences, and the expanse of land running out into the back pasture.

Three distinct knocks sounded on her front door. Humming a little tune, she removed her apron and left Cinder playing with a couple of pots on the floor by the warm kitchen oven. "Mommy will be right back, honey. Stay away from the stove."

When she was almost to the door, an uncharacteristic loud rapping sounded again.

Puzzled, she hurried all the faster to pull open the door. Surprise reverberated through her. Amidst the snowflakes on the wind stood her older brother behind a scruffy beard and mustache.

"Cade!" That was all she could get past her constricted lungs. It had been years since he'd left their family home in Pine Grove, taking her younger brother, Alister, with him. She hadn't known he was even aware of her marriage to Mark McCutcheon. She took a quick glance around, but didn't see his horse.

"Amy," he said, the cold air rushing into her warm house. "Don't you have a word of welcome for your kin?"

"I'm sorry. Come in." She grabbed his arm and dragged him inside, closing the door behind him. He set his pack on the floor with a *whump*.

What does he want? He'd made it clear the day he and Alister had ridden out that they were leaving the territory and never intended to come back. They were off to see the world.

"My stars, Cade, it's good to see you," she said, brushing snow from his shoulders and back. She thought she detected the scent of whiskey, but then it was gone. Her mother had cried the day her sons left home, only to discover the can that held her savings had vanished along with them. As much as Amy felt guilty for being suspicious of Cade's motives, he'd given her ample reason.

"Are you in trouble, Cade?"

His quick dark eyes had the power to drill right through a person when he wanted them to. That, mixed with his unkempt black hair, reminded her of the wanted posters Brandon had at the jailhouse. He wasn't wearing a hat.

"You're just like our old man. Always thinkin' the worst of me." He shrugged away his irritation. "No, I ain't in trouble—at least, not that I know of." He chuckled. "Relax, I'm only kiddin' you. I just needed to get out of the cold for a while. Heard you married up and thought I'd come say hello. See your big, fancy house and meet my brother-in-law." He offered her a charming smile. "This is a social call, sister."

His tone was contrite, but her wariness remained.

"Well, Mark's not here at the moment. I guess you went home to Pine Grove since you knew where to find me. You swore you'd never set foot there again."

He nodded. "People change."

"You know then that Mama passed away last year."

"I do. It was a shock for sure."

His words didn't move her. His lack of compassion his last few years at home had changed her feelings for him. "Where's Alister? Did he stay at home with Pa?"

Cade sniffed, then pulled out a handkerchief from his pocket and blew his nose. "No, he didn't. He stayed back in some Podunk town about a year ago. I told him it was time to move on, but he didn't want to come. I think he'd taken a cotton to some woman. Anyway, I have no idea where he is now."

Poor Alister. Always looking up to the wrong person.

Grief for her younger brother squeezed her heart—as well as anxiety over the situation at hand. "You were supposed to look out for him."

A pained expression crossed Cade's eyes, but she'd dare not soften to him. He was a good actor.

Cade put his nose in the air as he began unbuttoning his coat. "Somethin' sure smells good."

"I have dinner guests on their way."

Cade's family. You should invite him.

His gaze never stopped wandering the room. "Who?"

"All my female in-laws. We have some planning to do."

You should invite him. It's probably been days since he's had a good meal. Perhaps he's really changed. Who am I to judge? I should at least give him a chance.

"Cade, would you like to join us for supper? There's plenty."

His eyes lit up. "I sure would."

She hoped she wouldn't regret this. "Fine then. Upstairs, in the last bedroom, you'll find all you need to clean up. Take the water pitcher from my room next door. I'm wondering, though, did you walk all the way here? I didn't see your horse."

And how is it you got past the other houses on the ranch without being seen?

"I didn't think you'd mind," he said, "so I put him up in your barn."

Of course you did. "Well, the others will arrive any moment, and I have things to finish up."

A noise, like a pot hitting the floor, clanked out. Cade drew his gun and pointed it at the kitchen door.

"Cade!" Amy lunged forward and pushed his arm down. "Pack that gun away if you want to stay here! I *mean* it! That's just my daughter." They stood toe-to-toe, and she jabbed a finger into his chest. "Be warned, Cade—any minute the sheriff from Y Knot will be here dropping off his wife. If you're lying and you're in trouble, you best ride out now while you still can. I won't stand for one second of tomfoolery from you! I won't lie or protect you! Is that understood?"

"Just calm down. I'm sorry for drawing my gun. I've been cold for a month, and I need rest and vittles. Can I please stay?"

Amy wished Mark were here.

"Amy?" He rubbed his hands together, warming them.

She hoped she wasn't making a big mistake. "All right."

"Thank you." Her brother started for the stairs, but the sight of Cinder appearing in the doorway stopped him. "Well, would you look at that. Ain't she cute." He smiled warmly. "And you're expecting again. Pa didn't tell me I was an uncle."

Probably hoped you'd ride by without stopping.

"The last room in the hall," Amy said again, hurrying over to Cinder. She lifted her and pressed her next to her heart. Cade wouldn't harm any of them, would he? It was horrible to think such thoughts about her own brother. Was the story he'd told about Alister true? Mark's return couldn't come fast enough to suit her.

Chapter Eleven

Dolly stopped, seemingly for no apparent reason. The animal's head bobbed once, and then it lowered so the mule could sniff at the snowy trail.

"Go, mule." With great effort, Sally uncurled her icicle-like fingers from the animal's snow-covered mane and tried to move her arm, to switch her on the behind with the stick still clenched in her fist, but she was too cold.

Dolly brayed loudly at the dwindling light, as if she knew they were in dire trouble. It wouldn't be much longer and darkness would prevail.

My baby. How can I save my…

She desperately needed to reach Y Knot where she could warm up and get some food to nourish the child nestled inside. She didn't want to perish out here alone.

What should she do? Look for some dense trees to wait out the storm? How long did it take a person to freeze to death? She held back a sob to conserve her energy. Crying wouldn't help.

Far off, a cougar, or some animal that sounded like a cougar, snarled. Frightened, Dolly shied to the side, and turned a quick half circle. Frozen stiff, Sally was unable to stop herself from sliding to the ground, followed by the leather saddlebags.

When her feet hit the snow, pain radiated up her legs and into her back. Frozen, and tingling from lack of circulation, she almost collapsed. She moaned and clung to Dolly's mane, trying to take the weight off her frozen extremities.

If she stopped now, they would surely die. Reaching deep for fortitude, she forced herself to bend over and heft the heavy saddlebags out of the snow. Her arms shook so violently she could barely get the leather bags back on the mule.

"As much as I hate to say it, Dolly, we have to go back." She hugged the mule's cold, wet neck. Somewhere, they'd taken the wrong road, perhaps even two wrong turns. The current one had led from a split, one Mr. Slater hadn't mentioned. In her desperation, she'd turned right and kept going when her heart said to turn around. Hope and fear had moved her forward even after the road had narrowed and then turned into a path.

She wished she could feel some of the animal's heat through her thick coat. "I don't know how we'll make it in the dark, but we have to try." She hugged her again, emotions overflowing. "Thank you for bringing me this far."

For the first time Sally noticed how the foliage had again thickened and the terrain had changed. She must have been in a trance as Dolly plodded along.

Unable to mount until she could find a rock or log, Sally slipped the reins over the mule's tall ears and started slowly back down the way they'd come. She chose her steps carefully as she squinted through the falling snow. When had the flakes gotten so large? The last she remembered, they were little white specks.

They'd only gone a few steps when the mule halted again, the jerk of the reins almost yanking Sally off her feet.

She turned around. "What now?" she asked, and tugged the reins.

Dolly refused to take another step. Sally held the switch in front of her face. If they stopped now, they'd never get going again.

The quiet wall of white surrounded them as if they were in a soft cocoon. Before she knew what she was about, a chuckle burbled out of her mouth. Then another and another. She laughed to keep the desperation that clawed at her insides from coming up her throat.

"Dolly, *please*. We have to find the road to town." Such silliness. They would never find the right path. They were lost and would freeze to death this night, even in a few hours.

She reached out and halfheartedly switched Dolly's front legs, but the mule just blinked and looked away.

Please, Lord. Make Dolly move. I can't make it without her.

The hot prickles behind Sally's eyes were the only thing in her that was warm. Bewildered, she turned in a half circle. Hunger stabbed her belly like knife points, and a dull ache squeezed her forehead. She hoped Mr. Slater and the other passengers had been found and were safe in one of the towns.

A gust of wind sent the branches in front of her swishing back, revealing a dark structure that stood on the far side of a small clearing. Sally blinked, thinking it a dream of her longing. Dare she pray it was real? It wasn't that far away, but in the twilight was difficult to see. She squinted, trying to make it out.

Yes! A cabin! Some sort of dwelling. A jolt of happiness almost sent her to her knees.

Shelter. Safety. Life!

"Come on." Sally tugged on Dolly's reins, but the animal refused to move. Stepping to her side with a new conviction, Sally raised her arm and gave the mule a swift lash to her hindquarters. The mule stepped forward. "Good girl. We can't give up now. Not ever! God has given us a place to stay until the storm passes, Dolly. We're saved!"

Sally slowly walked forward, feeling the empty pain in her stomach from going so long without food. Her nausea had long since passed, and the pangs of hunger disappeared over an hour ago. Her insides felt like an empty cavern. She rolled her frozen lips over her teeth and struggled to lift her exhausted legs through the surprisingly heavy snowdrifts.

She glanced back at Dolly plodding along behind. "If there's a cabin, girl, there has to be a lean-to for you. It must be around back where I can't see it." She studied the area. "And if there's not, you're coming in with me."

The fresh snow was undisturbed, the shutters closed. The place appeared deserted.

If someone is in there, I'd see some light through the logs. They wouldn't sit around in the dark waiting for cold, unsuspecting girls.

As Sally got closer, a guarded giddiness swirled within. Soon she'd be able to eat and warm up. With each moment that passed, she expected the door to fly open. For an outlaw to step out and give her an evil grin as he beckoned her inside. If a man did step out, she'd take him on. She was getting inside that cabin and no one, not even an outlaw, was going to prevent that from happening.

The thought almost made her smile, but that would take too much energy. Only the muted thud of Dolly's snow-filled hooves and the wind's howl in the trees disturbed the all-encompassing silence.

"It's up to us, Dolly," she said, the sound of her voice deadened by the snowstorm. "No one will even know if we live or if we die."

Chapter Twelve

Cursing the storm and the clouds that looked as if they'd never stop dumping, Roady dismounted in front of the hunting cabin and peeled the wet leather gloves from his hands. Cramming them into his pocket, he clenched and unclenched his frozen fists and then held his fingers inside his mouth, blowing hot breath around them. Crystals of ice and snow fell from his whiskers. The howling wind drowned out the equally loud rumble of his empty stomach. A hot fire and warm food was all he could think about.

Fiddlin' Dee dropped her head and waited to be unsaddled. Long torrents of breath streamed from her nostrils. Stepping to the door, Roady pushed it open. The welcome scent of musty air hit him square in the face, like the kiss of an old friend. *Shelter.* He couldn't wait to get inside.

Back at his horse's side, he slipped his rifle from its scabbard and leaned it against the cabin wall, leaving the second rifle in its scabbard. Lifting the carcasses of the four large grouse tethered together by twine, he tossed them in the snow next to the door, thinking how good they would taste once he cooked them up over a hot flame. Fumbling because of his stiff fingers, he unlaced the leather ties that held his gear in place, then hefted the heavy, snow-covered bedroll and saddlebags off his mare's back and flopped them inside the dark interior.

With a swiftness born of repetition, he had his horse unsaddled in moments. He set his rig inside with the rest of his things and took up his rifle. He'd spotted wolf tracks twice since he'd reached the high country, as well as cougar, and wasn't taking any chances. He and his horse waded through knee-deep snow as they headed around back to the small corral and lean-to.

At the gate, he stilled. The skin at the back of his neck prickled.

There was something in the lean-to.

He felt the presence, but in the darkness of night and with the low overhang of the shed roof, he couldn't see. Had Behemoth come looking for food before he settled into hibernation?

Roady stepped back and raised his gun, thankful that even half-frozen, he'd had the presence of mind to bring it along. It was too dark to use the sight on the end of his rifle. He'd have to do this by feel.

Definitely not bear-like sounds. In fact, the thuds were familiar from the barn back home. He lowered the rifle and watched in disbelief as a horse—*no, mule*—emerged, clearly happy to have company. The animal's large ears rotated forward, then it let out the most god-awful sound. Relieved beyond measure, Roady released his pent-up anxiety in a large cloud of white breath as the animal ambled over, eager to see who would be joining it in the compound.

Roady's gaze darted to the cabin. Was the owner of the animal inside? Why hadn't they made their presence known when he opened the door? He studied the way back to the front, now seeing places where the snow had been disturbed and then covered over.

Quietly, he opened the gate, pushed back the mule, and led his horse inside. He slipped off her bridle, exited, and closed the gate.

Whatever came to be in the next few minutes, *he* wasn't leaving this cabin and going back out into the storm. That wasn't an option. Lifting his rifle at the ready, he returned in his own tracks. Whoever it was might be outside by now, waiting to shoot him down.

He arrived at the half-opened door unmolested, then stood there with his back to the wall, listening. All was quiet except for the loud swish of blood in his ears.

Maybe they'd gone out to hunt for food. But wouldn't there be a fire in the hearth, or at least the smell of smoke of one recently lit? Someone had put that mule in the corral.

Confused, he slowly inched inside. With the two windows shuttered tight, only a tiny amount of light from the cloud-covered moon filtered in through the door, and ended halfway across the room.

He didn't feel any danger. In fact, didn't feel anything at all except curiosity, the blessed absence of the frigid wind, and a burning desire to get a fire built.

Roady hoped he wouldn't regret this, but he quietly set his rifle on the table, then dug inside his coat pocket for his matches. That took some doing through his damp clothes with frozen hands, and made plenty of noise. Confident now he was alone, he lifted the glass globe of the lantern on the table, and touched the wick with the small glowing flame.

Amber light chased away the shadows.

The one-room hunting cabin was vacant. He saw a saddlebag against the wall. As he stepped toward it, something in the shadows by the hearth shifted, and he pulled up short.

So much for not letting down his guard. A moment of panic had him thinking of the bear, even though the outline was much too small. He stood there and stared. Was it a child, engulfed in a large leather coat, asleep by the cold hearth?

Stepping forward, he squatted, then lifted the lapel away.

A woman! What? A thousand thoughts crashed through his brain. He stared, poleaxed, trying to figure out how and why a woman would be all the way up here—*alone.*

She was small-boned, and the profile of her face, beautiful. He wondered why it pulled at his heartstrings. Maybe it was the vulnerable way her cheek rested on her folded hands, as if she'd fallen asleep in prayer. She had thick, dark lashes and a straight nose. A smattering of very light freckles across the bridge reminding him of a quail's egg. Her hair, still wet from being out in the storm, appeared frazzled. She must be exhausted to sleep through his arrival.

He glanced over his shoulder and up to the rafters at the cot and a stack of blankets cinched to the underside of a crossbeam, out of the way of any little critters resourceful enough to find a way inside.

Without another thought, he pulled the bench over, stepped up, and quickly released the cot and coverings. Setting them next to the wall, he scooped her into his arms. Even when he laid her down on her back, she didn't awaken, but her head lolled to one side and she whispered something in her sleep.

He knelt by her side. "Miss?" Her lashes quivered against the flushed peach color of her face. At the sound of his voice, her brow scrunched momentarily, but she drifted back into slumber.

He needed to remove her wet clothes. The last thing he wanted was for her to come down with a fever. He'd seen a man suffer paroxysms once caused by a high temperature. It wasn't a pretty sight.

Not wasting a second, he carefully unwound the soggy scarf from around her neck, the scent of damp wool sweeping over his senses. Completely relaxed in sleep, she reminded him of a slumbering lamb in the arms of its shepherd as he lifted her limp body and removed the man-size leather coat. He tossed it to the side. Off came another damp layer that looked to be a castoff of some man's shirt as well.

Finally, he stopped stripping her garments when he came to her fitted shirtwaist with puffed sleeves. The garment was dry and looked much too fine to have been homemade. Impossibly tiny buttons in narrow buttonholes fastened the two sides of her bodice together.

His gaze roamed lower. He hesitated at the damp pair of extremely baggy britches, held up by a rope, wondering if her dignity was worth the possibility of her catching the chills. He'd wait on those in hopes she woke up soon.

Was something other than the obvious going on here? Was she already sick? Passed out? He shook out several blankets and covered her

Who was she? And how did she make it all the way up this mountain by herself in such a hellish storm? A gust of wind buffeted the shutter over her head, reminding him he'd better get a fire started. It wasn't all that much warmer inside. Was she alone, or would someone come crashing through the door at any moment?

Chapter Thirteen

Nervous energy raced through Amy when she heard Brandon and Charity's laughing voices outside. In moments they'd come through the door. What would they think of Cade? Her brother had yet to come down from upstairs.

They knocked and then opened the door, calling out, "Hi, Amy, we're here."

Amy came out of the kitchen, forcing a smile. She hoped it didn't look as fake as it felt. Brandon and Charity laughed and stomped the snow from their boots.

"You should see the weather out there." Charity peeled off her gloves, then went about unbuttoning her coat with shaky fingers. "It's going to be a whiteout before the night is over. I hope the girls and Mother arrive shortly, or it might just be you and me for your dinner party." She looked around at the floor. "Sorry about this mess. I'll clean it up."

Amy brushed away the comment with her hand. "Don't worry about that. How was the ride from town? Must have been cold."

Cinder rushed for Brandon, who had already divested himself of his coat and hung it on the rack. Cinder held out her small arms, and he gently lifted her high. Bending his knees, he gave her a few dramatic swoops, eliciting a round of giggles.

"A winter wonderland—*in September*," Charity gushed, watching her new husband swing Cinder. "This is the earliest storm I can remember. Now that I'm living in town, I appreciate the beauty of the land even more. It's like I'm seeing it for the very first time each time I ride out."

Amy clutched her hands together and glanced out the window. "It's coming down pretty hard."

"More please, more please," Cinder jabbered between laughs each time she thought her uncle was slowing. Her cheeks turned a pretty watermelon pink, and her baby-soft hair flew away from her face, her eyes bright.

Amy appreciated Brandon's astuteness. Although strong and healthy, Cinder was the smallest of the cousins and had a delicate frame. No one ever mistook her for a little boy, even when she was wearing hand-me-down britches from her male cousins. She was all girl, through and through.

"You're heavy, Cinder*ella*," Brandon said with a chuckle, emphasizing the special pet name, "my arms are about to fall off. You must have gained a good two pounds and grown four inches since the last time I swung you. Now, hold on, here we go."

Charity peeked into the kitchen area. "Your table is beautiful. I love all the fall-colored leaves in the centerpiece. Good thing you gathered them before the weather turned. Thank you for thinking of this evening. It'll be fun with just us girls making party plans without the men around."

Brandon looked at her. "What do you mean?" He slowed to a stop and set Cinder onto her feet, then patted her head. "Us men always come up with the best ideas. I don't know what you're talking about."

Charity drilled him with a no-nonsense stare. "You want a shooting contest at every single event."

He shrugged. "Can't blame us for trying. Besides, you do well enough at shooting, Charity. Last July in Rio Wells makes my point quite nicely."

She buffed him playfully on the arm, unaware that her nose, red from the cold, made her look like a child who'd gotten into some paint. She shivered. "Maybe so, but this is a Christmas barn dance, Brandon. Maybe we'll have a singing contest, or poetry recital."

When he scrunched up his face, everyone laughed, including Cinder, although she clearly didn't know what they were talking about.

"Or a marathon waltz," Amy added, trying to get into the spirit of things.

Charity's eyes brightened. "I like that idea. I love waltzing in my husband's arms. Even better if it's for hours, and a prize is involved."

"Her competiveness rears its ugly head. But did you say hours?" Brandon looked between the two women, his expression crestfallen.

"What? Don't you like waltzing with me?"

"Of course I do. But I like shooting contests too."

Amy shook her head. "You're outnumbered, Brandon."

"Well, I wouldn't be outnumbered if Mark were here."

Amy couldn't stop a laugh. "You may as well get your dancing boots all spit-shined now. Only about three months to go." She put her hand on Brandon's arm and nudged him toward the door.

"Won't you miss me, darlin'?" he said to Charity. "We've been hitched less than two months. I was disappointed when I heard the invitation was only for the women." He cocked his eyebrow at Amy as he put his arms around Charity's waist, pulling her close.

Charity pushed away when he nuzzled her neck. "You behave! You and Pa have an evening planned at the bunkhouse, playing poker to your hearts' content. And you'd best be on your way. The others are probably anxious to ante up."

"I'd rather stay here and have supper with you. Whatever you have cooking smells real good, Amy. What time should I be back to fetch you, charming wife?"

She crossed her arms. "How about I fetch you when *my* night is over?"

He tweaked her nose. "No doin'. You stay put until I ride into this yard. I'll stable your horse before I leave." Brandon shrugged back into his coat.

"I hope this weather doesn't delay the boys' return from Waterloo," Charity said.

Brandon hoisted Cinder one last time. "The first storm of the year usually doesn't last long. It's Roady I'm thinking about." He set Cinder down and finished buttoning up, then pulled on his gloves. "If he failed to make it to the hunting cabin in time, he'll have to find shelter somewhere to wait out the worst of it." Brandon chuckled. "He's not going to like that one bit."

A shout sounded from outside.

Recognizing Francis's voice, Brandon yanked the door open. The women followed. Francis rode up through the wall of white.

"What's wrong?" Brandon shouted before the cowhand could even dismount.

"Nothing. Just wanted to get here before you left. Mr. and Mrs. McCutcheon want all the women and children to bundle up and come over to the big house for a night or two because of the weather."

"Why?" Amy asked from the doorway, the cold air biting her face and hands. "It's just some snow."

Francis rode closer to the door, his hat and shoulders white. Charity ran back into the house and stood by Amy, clinging to her arm to stay warm.

"They feel antsy because Mark and the other men are gone." He glanced around at the snow that was coming down thicker by the moment. "No telling how long this'll last. They want you and the grandkids under their roof." He sat there looking at them. "And I was told to tell you, there is no discussion on this, so please come."

Amy lifted Cinder into her arms when the child wandered over to the door.

"Frans," she said in her childish voice, and bumped up and down in excitement.

"But I've cooked dinner for everyone," Amy said, looking back at the kitchen where the chicken was ready to come out of the oven. "What am I supposed to do with all the food?"

"I'll take care of that, Amy."

Everyone turned at the unfamiliar voice. She wondered again what had prompted Cade's unexpected visit.

Brandon came back inside. "Who're you?"

"This is my brother, Cade Morrow. Cade, meet my sister-in-law, Charity Crawford, and her husband, Brandon Crawford, the sheriff of Y Knot. That's Francis out on the horse."

Thank goodness Cade had cleaned up, combed his hair, and looked presentable. His face was clean-shaven, and his guns weren't anywhere to be seen. She couldn't miss Brandon's suspicious perusal of her brother.

Brandon put out his hand and Cade grasped it. "Mr. Morrow. Good to meet you."

Amy went over and stood by Cade, giving her unspoken support. "I haven't seen Cade in years. This is his first time to our home."

A few uncomfortable moments ticked by.

"You're not coming with us?" Brandon directed his question to Cade.

"Naw, it wouldn't feel right bargin' in on Amy's in-laws since I don't know anyone yet. 'Sides, I can surely take care of myself here alone, if Amy needs to go." He looked around the room, at the sturdy beams running the ceiling, the warm woolen throw lying across the back of the settee. "It's the best place I've ever seen. But it's understandable the others are worried about Amy—her being in the family way and all. I'll be happy to set up here and watch over the place, keep it safe. That is, if you trust me, Amy. It's a sight better'n campin' outside."

What could she say? That she didn't trust her own brother in her home? Anything of real value was locked away in Mark's safe.

"Of course you can stay, Cade," she said quickly, mad at herself for such thoughts. "Eat supper and make yourself at home."

Cade chuckled. "I'll even do the dishes."

"Y Knot's not that far, Amy." Brandon sent her a sidelong glance. "If you'd rather, he can get a room at Lou and Drit's while you're away."

Seemed there was something her brother-in-law didn't like about Cade. For all she knew, Brandon's feelings could be correct. A lot of things could have happened during the years

Cade had been gone. Hadn't she been thinking the same thing about him not half an hour ago?

Amy gave herself a mental shake. But what if he *was* just hungry and cold? How horrible of her not to be charitable to family.

Everyone waited for her answer. "No, Cade can stay, if that's what he wants to do."

"Fine." Brandon's nostrils flared. "Then your food problem is taken care of. But you're still coming with us to the big house." She dared not argue with his stern expression. "Go pack up a few things for you and Cinder while I hitch your wagon. Francis, am I supposed to pick up the others on the way there?"

"Naw. Smokey went out with a wagon early enough to catch the others before they set out here. He's takin' care of them."

The snow was so thick Amy could barely make out Francis still waiting on his horse. "I'll be ready in a minute. I'll just pull the chicken out of the oven."

"I'll do that," Charity said, eyeing Cade as she hurried by. "You just get your things. I can tell Brandon is anxious to get going."

"Of course." Amy turned back to Brandon and set Cinder on the floor. "Will you put her coat and hat on her for me while I go pack?"

She pulled back, surprised at the wariness in Brandon's eyes. His fun-loving uncle role had been replaced with the no-nonsense lawman.

"Never mind, I can do it as soon as I gather our things. Come on, Cinder," she said, picking up her baby girl and hurrying to the stairs. Brandon wasn't letting down his guard with a stranger in the house, family or not.

Confused, she kissed Cinder on the cheek as they ascended the stairs. "Guess what, sweetie? We're going to see Grandpa and Grandma."

And I hope your Uncle Cade behaves himself while we're gone.

Chapter Fourteen

Mr. Greenstein stood on the other side of the room, lurking in the shadows. The expression in his eyes turned Sally's blood to ice. Instinct told her to run, to get away quickly. Suddenly he was on top of her with his hand painfully crushing her mouth.

"I know you like me, Sally. I can tell by the way you watch me work, watch me work, watch me work..."

"No!" Sally cried out. Her eyes jerked open to darkness all around. She searched for safety and snagged a small stream of light coming from somewhere, and then the amber glow of a fireplace. A noise made her turn her head.

A man sat on a bench not three feet away. When he saw that she was awake, he stood and came over.

She tried to pull away but the wall was at her back. When he sprang forward and grasped her shoulders, she screamed.

"Shhh."

His firm hold made her struggle all the harder. "No, let me go. Let me go!"

He didn't let go, but held her down. She wished she could see his face, his eyes, but the darkness of the room made that impossible.

"Easy now, Miss, you don't want to fall. This contraption isn't that sturdy. Lie still. You're safe with me."

His large hands were what frightened her most. They were strong—like Mr. Greenstein's. Able to do anything he pleased.

Where was she? It was deathly cold. The instinct for survival fueled her flagging energy, and she pushed at his arms for all she was worth, thrashing her head back and forth. She sensed his bulk by her side and knew she was defenseless to him when he decided to attack. Despair threatened to choke her.

"No, *please*." She tried again, knowing her attempts to stop him would be futile. "Please don't do this. Let me go."

Scents of snow and pine brought a fleeting memory of being outside. Of being wet and cold. She tried to sit up, get away, needing to put space between her and this person, but he easily held her in place as if she were no larger than a flea.

"Don't be scared," he said calmly, but didn't take his hands away. "I won't hurt you."

She swallowed, and her gaze roamed the edges of the dim light as she tried to figure out where she was. She couldn't remember. Where was her family?

"If I fetch the lamp, will you stay put? Stay calm?"

His deep, steady voice whispered through her consciousness, soothing her. She didn't have any other option except to nod.

He stood, went to the table, and returned with a lantern. "This'll make you feel better," he said, placing the light on the floor close by. "No woman I ever met is a friend of the dark." His smile brought a lightness to his eyes.

The area opened up and she could see sturdy beams over her head, a window across the room and another over her cot, both tightly covered by well-made shutters, currently rattling in the driving wind. On the far wall was a large rock fireplace with a blazing fire. Iron tools leaned against the stones, and two pots hung over the flickering flames. Several more pots were stacked on the side. A bench situated close to the hearth was draped with some clothing, apparently being dried. There was a table, a bedroll in the corner, but not much else, other than lots of blankets piled on top of her.

The man held out a canteen and gently raised her by her shoulders. "Take a few sips. I'm sure you're plenty thirsty by now. It's been almost twenty-four hours since I found you."

The cool water was a blessing as it flowed down her throat. She *was* thirsty and ravenous. The water tasted good.

She dared a glance up at his face. "How long have you been here?"

"I arrived last evening 'bout seven. You've been fast asleep ever since. I got to wondering if you'd ever wake up."

He wasn't as old as she'd first thought. The sound of his voice was like warm molasses. When he went to take the water away, she reached out quickly and grabbed it back, gulping down several large mouthfuls.

He chuckled. "Go on and drink to your heart's content. There's more where that came from," he said as he glanced at the door.

Sally remembered the snow piling up outside. Then realizing she'd been staring at his whiskered jaw, she quickly averted her eyes.

"Helps keep me warm," he mumbled as he laid her back. "My name's Roady Guthrie. Are you alone? Or is there someone else out in this storm that I should be looking for?"

She glanced at the ceiling where the fireplace rocks met the wood, thinking. Her disconcerted thoughts tumbled in her head. What was he talking about? When was the last time she'd seen her family? Was Anita or Melba outside in the storm?

"Well, you think on that for one minute. I have to add some more snow to this bucket I'm melting for my horse and your mule." He nodded. "You understand?"

His voice was surprisingly kind and patient—different from what she'd expect from a mountain man. But that didn't mean he wasn't an outlaw, or a disreputable type of man just the same. She'd best try to get her wits about her. When he walked away, she pushed up on her elbows, feeling completely discombobulated.

A gust of wind shot through the room when he opened the door and scooped a bucket full of snow.

"I'd say you made it in just in time," he said, glancing at her as he crouched in front of the fireplace and scooped handfuls of snow into a large pot.

The hours since departing Waterloo slowly crept back into her mind. The broken-down stagecoach. The snowstorm. The agonizing hours astride Dolly's bony back. Her frozen fingers and toes.

"As it is, you're darn lucky you don't have a nasty case of frostbite."

Sally stretched out her legs and her muscles protested. Pain shot up her back, then back to her feet. Oh, it hurt. She held back a groan, not wanting to draw any more attention to herself than she already had. Apprehension sliced through her when she glanced under the blanket and realized she had been partially disrobed. Those clothes by the fire—*the pants*—must be hers!

He saw the direction she was looking. "Couldn't be helped," he said. "I waited for you to wake up, but…" Even with a fire, his lips were tinged blue from the cold. "Sensibilities are no nevermind when a life is concerned." He offered a small smile. "You stay put while I gather more firewood from out back." He slapped at his arms several times, then stomped his feet as if to get the blood flowing. "It'll get plenty drafty once I open the door a few times. Lie back and stay under the covers." He reached over and felt her clothes lying across the bench. "Your things are almost dry."

"I remember," she said, stopping him. "There *are* others out there. The other passengers on the stagecoach."

He came back and hunkered down again by her side, his eyes serious. "Where?"

She tried to think, but her thoughts were still a bit muddled. "Back there," she said, looking at the door, as if back there made all the sense in the world. "On the way from Waterloo, the stagecoach went off the road and broke an axle. I need to tell the sheriff in Y Knot so he can send a wagon for them."

He stared at her for several long moments. "They sent *you* for help?" His voice was incredulous. "On a *mule?*"

She nodded. "The driver was killed. Mr. Slater, the only other employee, was injured. Besides, he had to stay with the others. Two women and a little boy. I was the only one able to ride."

"But the road to Y Knot is miles away."

Sally laid back and closed her eyes, suddenly feeling very tired. Her stomach pinched painfully from the lack of food. "I know." She shook her head at all the bad decisions she'd made. "There were too many forks in the road. We got mixed up."

"We?"

"Dolly. My mule."

He bit out a few choice words.

Surprised, she pushed back against the cold logs of the wall. Were his true colors finally showing?

"I'm sorry. I'm sure you're not used to hearing such. But whoever was stupid enough to let you ride off was a fool of the worst kind! You would have died if you hadn't stumbled onto this cabin."

"Mr. Slater and the others need our help. Can we go back?"

He shook his head. "One night's come and gone. Nothing we can do for them now."

Regret welled up inside her. She'd failed. What had happened to Fredrick and the others?

"Someone will find them." His mouth was a thin, hard line when he muttered, "Sending a girl off to find help." His gaze softened. "You're not at fault."

She nodded again, feeling ten years old. The fact that he was taking charge felt good after all her hours of indecision and worry.

He stood and went to the pegs by the door and began layering on more clothes.

"You never told me your name," he said as he wrapped a scarf around his neck. Once his coat was on and buttoned up, he pulled on his gloves. All bundled up, he looked like a woodsy Santa Claus, although his legs were long and his shoulders wide.

"I'm Miss Sally Stanford from St. Louis."

His hands stilled. A quirky smile pulled his mouth and a quiet chuckle slipped through his lips. "Miss Sally Stanford, you say?" His tone was one of astonishment.

"Yes."

"Well, I'll be."

"I'm pleased to make your acquaintance, Miss Sally Stanford. Any chance you're related to Heather Stanford? Or should I say Heather Klinkner? As well as Morgan Stanford?"

He shook his head in disbelief. "I'm a fool not to see the resemblance right off." He chuckled again, still shaking his head. "I know Heather. As a matter of fact, I was one of the bachelors who courted her for a short spell."

Heather? This tough-looking mountain man had courted her sister? That must have been when Hayden had refused her as his mail-order bride and she'd moved out of the Klinkners' home to the boardinghouse in town. Surely if he'd courted Heather, he was a good, honorable man, and she was safe with nothing to fear.

She managed a smile. "Did you write her a courting letter like all the other men? Heather said she didn't open a single one."

He doesn't seem like the scholarly type to me.

He chuckled again. "I wouldn't know about what she opened and what she didn't, but I can tell you I wasn't one of the heartsick swains to go as far as put my feelings to pen and paper for all the world to see. I did take her on an outing to visit the fossil bed—which she liked very much. And I escorted her to a concert."

A wide smile split his face as he reached for the door. He glanced at her again, and then pulled his scarf up over his nose. "The firewood will take a few trips, so stay under those covers, like I said." The words came out muffled. "When I get back, I'll serve up my supper concoction. You must be plenty hungry after not eating for so long."

At his mention of food, her mouth watered. "I am. Thank you."

"Don't expect anything fancy. And, if you're interested, there's a chamber pot underneath your cot."

Anxiety gripped her. She'd planned to tell her sister and brother, and all the folks in Y Knot, that she was a recent widow. That she came west to try to escape the hurtful memories of her dearly departed husband—which she'd kept hidden from her family. Even though her strategy was totally farfetched, she didn't know what else to say. Heather would eventually guess the truth, and maybe Morgan too. But without thinking, she'd told Mr. Guthrie she was unmarried. Now she didn't know quite what she'd say once they reached Y Knot.

Mr. Guthrie picked up his rifle and opened the door to a blast of wind that almost pushed him back into the room. The flames in the hearth crackled and popped, and the small flame of the lantern was nearly extinguished. He looked back at her, and if she wasn't mistaken, saw him wink.

Relaxing, she returned his smile. His easygoing way was quite endearing. Thank goodness she'd ended up with a man who knew how to survive in the elements, because she certainly didn't.

Chapter Fifteen

Roady pushed his way through the knee-deep snow as he took in the darkening forest that surrounded the cabin. He made several trips between the woodpile out back and the front of the house. His body heated even in the below-freezing temperatures. Releasing the last armful of firewood, he let the logs drop to the stack that had accumulated beside the door.

No telling how long he and Miss Stanford would be stranded up here together. She looked young, around Charity's age. He could tell she was intelligent by the words she used and how she said them. He'd tried to ignore how her eyes drew him in. They were watchful and a bit wary, but the kind that could move a man to distraction.

The thought of her riding up here by herself in such a hellish storm made him furious. Any number of calamities could have befallen her—Behemoth, for one. The thought of the old grizzly brought the usual surge of guilt. Maybe Luke was right; maybe the animal was dead. Or maybe he should give up his vendetta and forget about the beast altogether. But that didn't feel right either.

Off to the north a wolf howled, the low timbre of its voice echoing through the trees.

Warm now from the physical exertion, Roady opened the door and brought the wood inside, stacking the logs on the stone hearth.

"I couldn't find any matches."

He turned around to see she was watching him work. "Matches?"

She shook her head. "When I first arrived. I scarcely made it inside at all, the snow was coming down so thick and fast. And I was cold."

He stood and went over to the counter, looking through the crates below. He pulled out a small wooden container and then another, then began searching through them.

"I'll bet you were plenty glad to find a cabin way out here." He chuckled, still digging through the belongings that remained in the dwelling for everyone to use, then turned and held something up. "Here they are."

"You didn't get them out before?"

"I brought some of my own."

She sat on the edge of the cot, her blanket clutched tight.

"I didn't see the crates in the dark." Her voice was a bit defensive.

"I wouldn't have either. Being frozen and hungry didn't help a'tall."

She thought on that for a moment. In the dim light, he thought he saw her lips twitch, but he couldn't be sure.

"When I first noticed the cabin in the trees, I was afraid it would be locked—or occupied by someone I'd rather not meet. Is it your place? Do you live here year-round?" She gazed up into the beams, then around the room and back at him. Her perusal didn't take long. "I scarcely think so. It's quite sparse."

"Nope, sure don't. This place doesn't actually belong to anyone, per se," he said clumsily. He was pulling out his whole arsenal of words to impress her. Didn't want her to think she was holed up with a country bumpkin. "It's a hunting cabin. The rule is to replace what you use. In the spring, I'll come back and set in more wood."

"You're hunting then?"

He nodded.

"For what?"

When he didn't answer right away, her eyes narrowed. He saw her suspicion return.

"Mr. Guthrie?"

"I'm hunting bear."

She sat up straighter. "Are there a lot of bears in these mountains?"

He nodded. "As many as the next place, I suppose. But I'm not hunting just *any* bear. I have a particular one in mind." He was surprised she was talking so much. Now that she was awake, she'd probably like some privacy. He'd been thinking on that. Maybe he could string one of the blankets kitty-corner, and close off her bed.

"Why?"

Roady thought about that. Why, indeed? "Because he taught me a lesson the hard way, and I owe him. A man died because of me."

Sally's intense gaze made him fidget. Going to the fire, he squatted and poked around in the coals with the iron tool just for something to do. The heat felt good on his face. He picked up a wooden spoon and stirred the grouse stew simmering in the pot, hoping it would be to her liking. "This is ready anytime you'd like to eat. Since I'm still bundled, I'll finish the chore of watering the stock first, though—if that's good with you. It's bad enough they're going without food."

Her eyes widened. "Of course."

"They'll be okay for a few more days. I have a little sorghum I've been rationin'." He shook his head, sorry for the animals' plight. "It's really just enough to wet their whistles and get their stomach juices goin'. I don't know what's worse, nothing to eat or a hummingbird-sized meal."

"Is there anything I can do while you're outside? Set the table, maybe?" There was still an edge of distrust to her gaze, but at least she was awake and talking.

"Sure, you can. Over in those crates you'll find a couple of bowls and cups. Spoons too. Don't know how clean they're gonna be."

He stood. "I have a mind to hang a blanket so you can have some privacy. Would you like that?" Her bright eyes were his answer, and he chuckled. "Fine then."

From the crates where he'd gotten the matches, he retrieved a hammer and some nails. Taking one of the blankets, he tacked it on the opposite wall by the end of her cot, and a foot above his head. Pulling it tight, he tacked it along one of the ceiling beams, then to the other wall kitty-corner. It barely fit, but was better than nothing. Since she'd remained on the cot, now he couldn't see her.

"You still in there?"

"Yes." The blanket muffled her response.

"That's good. Just wanted to make sure you hadn't run off," he joked, feeling a bit self-conscious. "We'll just have to get you down the hill to Y Knot as soon as possible—to your sister and brother. They must be worried sick when your stage didn't arrive."

"Not really. They aren't expecting me."

"What?" That surprised him. He turned and looked at the blanket, wishing he hadn't put it up quite yet. "They're not expecting you?"

Sally pushed the blanket back and looked out. "No. I wanted my arrival to be a surprise."

That was strange. Was something else going on here that she wasn't saying? He felt her clothes. "Your things are dry. You can dress when I go outside. Desperate times call for desperate measures. No need to feel embarrassed." He gathered her garments and handed them to her. "Can you manage on your own, or do you need help?"

"I can manage." The words tumbled over themselves so quickly he was surprised they came out in order.

"Good. I won't be back for at least ten minutes." Going to the fireplace, he carefully took the pot of water off the iron rod and carried it to the door. "When I return, we'll eat supper."

The cold blast of air in his face was as welcome as a dip in the creek on a hot summer day. He might be a gentleman, but curbing his overactive imagination about Sally would take some doing. A few minutes outside was sure to help.

Chapter Sixteen

"I wonder what everyone will think once we make it into Y Knot?" Sally said softly, the quiet of the thick snow-covered forest blanketing the night.

The question was never far from her mind. To stay unchaperoned with a man in a cabin was just as damaging as shouting from the rooftops that she was with child. She let her hand fall under the table to caress her stomach, now delightfully full. It brought her peace of mind to know the baby had something to eat.

The fire popped, and a spark flew out. Mr. Guthrie reached out and squished it with his boot.

"Don't matter what *they* think. What matters is what *we* know. There'll always be folks who believe the worst—and that's a fact. Nothing you can do about that now, so you'd best prepare yourself." He scooped a spoonful into his mouth and chewed heartily.

The dinner was good, and warm. Sitting across from Mr. Guthrie, she tried not to watch him as he ate, but with little else in the cabin at which to direct her attention, that was near impossible to do. He was enjoying his meal immensely. The noises coming from his throat attested to the fact. Along with the good-sized grouse concoction, he'd managed to whip up some biscuits and cook them in a pan of drippings he'd saved while roasting the hens last night. He did know his way around a cooking fire, and for that she was grateful.

"What's Y Knot like?"

"You coming to visit or planning to stay?"

How strange. "Does the answer depend on a defining variable? I'd think the characteristics of a town wouldn't rest upon the visitor, but the hard facts." She scraped her empty bowl one last time, then licked her spoon.

His eyes widened in surprise. "Why, *sure* it matters." He took a moment to wipe his mouth, using the square of fabric she'd placed in the middle of the table for them to share as a napkin. She'd taken it from her saddlebag, where it had wrapped her loaf of bread. They were saving that treat for tomorrow.

His teasing expression made her smile. "A visitor'll want to see the sights, find out which eatery makes the best pot roast, and visit a place to pick up some trinkets to take home. Where a person who plans on staying a while starts to look for a place to nest, acquaints himself with the friendly and the cantankerous, so they can woo the one and avoid the other. They inquire to which side of town the water never runs dry, and which merchants are swindlers and which are straight shooters. All the important stuff."

She nodded, conceding that he had a point. She'd never thought about it in those terms before. "I see what you mean."

He eyeballed her bowl. "You want some more? There's plenty. It's been a while since you had a square meal." He put the rest of his biscuit into his mouth and chewed. "I can always go hunting."

She smiled again. "Yes, thank goodness for that. I think I'll pace myself." Her tummy felt full, and a sense of peace surrounded her. She was waiting for the queasiness to hit, but it didn't.

His brows arched in disbelief. "If you say so."

"When do you think we'll be able to leave?"

He looked up from spooning in the last of the broth from his bowl. "As soon as it stops snowing. I'm not sure when that might be."

"How long does it take to get to Y Knot?"

"A full day and into the night. But that depends on the snow as well. You climbed a distance into the mountains. The trip back down'll be tedious and slow. More difficult than traveling the road."

She couldn't imagine climbing back onto Dolly with her sore legs and aching back. Until she had to actually do it, she'd put that thought out of her mind.

He held out the last biscuit. "Eat this, Miss Stanford. You'll need the fuel in your belly to stay warm tonight when the temperatures plummet even more." He charmed her with his smile. "I insist."

"I'm much too full, Mr. Guthrie. You take it. Tomorrow we have my bread."

Reluctantly, he set it back in the pan he'd cooked them in. "We'll just save it in case you change your mind."

The coffeepot set deep in the coals had been perking for a good five minutes. Roady grasped the handle with a folded cloth. With jerky movements, he set the scalding pot down quickly on the table, then snapped his hand away, shaking off the heat. A happy grin split his face. "Tomorrow, if the storm still hasn't let up, I'll go hunting. See what I can bring home."

Sally fingered the cuff of her once pretty eggshell shirtwaist that extended from her rolled-up coat sleeve. She'd saved her salary for three months to buy it at Conner Place Clothing, the most talked-about women's apparel store in her neighborhood. Thoughts of the newspaper made her heart squeeze, bringing to mind her home, her family—and the baby she'd have.

A surge of sentimentality rushed up into her throat, and she knew if she opened her mouth to speak, she'd embarrass herself. Heat scalded her face. Mr. Guthrie hadn't yet noticed, but he would. Nothing seemed to get past him. When she felt her eyes well with tears, she scooted down the bench to go to her cot, but he stopped her with one word.

"Miss?"

She turned and peered into his earnest eyes.

"Did I upset you? Sometimes I run my mouth like a thick-skulled youth."

Sally wanted desperately to be able to close her eyes and pretend none of this had happened, that she was back home in St. Louis before she'd ever thought of working for the newspaper. All she wanted was to lie down and rest.

"No, it's nothing you said. I'm just tired, and…well…" She glanced away. *Emotional. Homesick. And worried about my future.*

Chapter Seventeen

After checking on the animals one last time, Roady pushed open the door and stepped back into the blessed warmth devoid of any wind, then dropped the bar back into place.

Sally stood in front of the fire with her hands behind her back, clearly soaking up the warmth of the flames. Golden light from the lantern shimmered in her eyes. She looked so young, *was* so young. He often saw traces of Heather, as well as her brother Morgan, in her expressions. Especially her smile.

As if she'd read his thoughts, she smiled. "I was just going to open the door and call you. You've been out there a long time. You must be frozen."

"Just taking care of the stock." By the door, he stomped the snow from his boots, then started the arduous task of removing his snow-covered outer clothes. His hands were a bit unresponsive, and he fumbled several times.

"Are they all right? I hate to think of them going without food."

"So do I, but it can't be helped."

Her gaze followed his actions as he stripped off his coat. "Did you get any of the snow cleared away from the ground?" she asked, her brows still drawn together in concern.

"Tried, but the forage that was there before the storm hit has been trampled by their hooves. Looks like the snow's about run its course, though. It's barely coming down at all anymore."

She heaved a sigh of relief.

Actually, if the weather cleared, they could even head down the mountain tomorrow. He was worried about her family, and what they would think about the days they'd stayed together unchaperoned. With his wet clothes off, he went to his bedroll on the floor and picked up a blanket, tossing it over his shoulders. He glanced at the fire.

"There's room for you, Mr. Guthrie," she said, stepping to the side.

"You sure? I don't want to crowd you."

"I'm happy to share the warmth." There was kindness in her eyes.

"This is going to feel so darn good," he mumbled, stepping over until they were shoulder to shoulder. "Mmm." He closed his eyes and basked in the wonderful heat radiating through his pants and long johns to his cold legs. Feeling generous, he crouched down and tossed two more logs onto the flame.

"We won't run out, will we?"

He shouldn't have looked up. The flames and lantern light reflected in her eyes wove magic through the cabin. She must have brushed her hair when he was outside because it lay across her shoulders and down her back like a coffee-colored shawl. The wind had calmed into a light whisper, gently moving the branches against the side of the structure. The world seemed to close in around them.

He wasn't like Luke and Brandon and the rest of the men, needing a mate to plan a life with—a future. At least, he'd thought so up until this point. But now, looking up into Sally Stanford's trusting gaze, he felt a chink in his armor.

"No, there's plenty more where this came from." He jerked his gaze away and stood. "Are you warm enough?"

She nodded. "With the food and the fire, I believe I'm going to make it after all."

"Make it?" He laughed. He hadn't thought she'd been that worried. "That's mighty good to hear." He strode over to the counter and the crates stacked beneath it, willing the picture of her from his mind. Taking the top crate off the second, he shuffled through it, knowing he had her undivided attention. At the bottom, he found what he was looking for. He went back to the table and moved the dirty bowls aside.

"What's that?"

"Something to pass the time." He went about setting up the battered old checkerboard. "You want red or black?"

"Checkers?" Her voice rallied, bringing another surge of emotion within him.

"You betcha."

"I'll take red."

Sally seated herself across from him and began setting out the whittled wooden spheres. Some were cracked or chipped, then dyed to create a reddish tint. Her delicate fingers and well-tended fingernails kept drawing Roady's attention. He had to force himself to concentrate on what he was doing.

With his brownish-black pieces all lined up and ready, he glanced at her and smiled. "I didn't know you were such an enthusiast," he drawled slowly, still enjoying the heat from the fire as well as her excitement.

Her brow arched. "How do you know that I am?"

"Because you jumped at the chance to play. In my recollection, womenfolk don't much cotton to board games. Believe they belong in a saloon."

"I have six brothers and three sisters. At my house, there's always someone who wants to go a couple of rounds—the womenfolk included."

"Fine then." He waited for her to make the first move. "I won't go easy on you."

"You better not."

When she just sat there, he looked up. "Ladies first."

"Smoke before fire," she corrected.

So, she wasn't teasing about her abilities. He thought about the flask of whiskey he had tucked away in his saddlebag for cold nights away from home, but knew better than to bring it out.

With his finger, he pushed one of his men forward and waited for her to do the same. Several turns went by quickly as they moved closer to the opposite side. She got the first jump, and for some reason that pleased him. Her face was triumphant in the lamplight.

He smiled back. "There you go."

She nodded. Some strategic setting up played through the next few moves. When he jumped three of her men, her smile faded.

"King me."

She looked up in astonishment. "I didn't see that coming, Mr. Guthrie." She studied the board as if she wanted to remember what he'd done to surprise her.

"Call me Roady."

Her lips curled. "All right, Roady. And you can call me Sally."

A wolf howled from somewhere far off. When she lifted her gaze to his, fear shadowed her eyes.

"Just a wolf. Can't get through the door."

She pulled the blanket more tightly over her shoulders and went back to studying the board.

"Are you married, Roady?"

Surprised, he finished his move and glanced up at her.

"I'm sorry if that's too personal," she added quickly. "It's just that I've been telling you all about my family, and you already know Heather and Morgan, but I don't know much about you. Just worried what your wife, if you had one, would do when we got back."

"No, I'm not married, but I'm not opposed to the binds of matrimony. The opportunity just never presented itself." He leveled his gaze on her, thinking she sure looked pretty tonight after her long rest and a belly full of food. He liked her quick wit and her love of the game. "Guess I'll know when the right gal comes along."

Her brow drew down in consternation. "You sound like my oldest brother, Travis. He isn't married yet either, although he came very close this year. Since my pa's gone, my mother would like to see him settle down. Morgan too." She shrugged and then pushed her man onto the next square. When she talked about her family, her posture relaxed as her wariness seemed to fade. "I'm the third youngest, with two little sisters. Anita is sixteen, and Melba fourteen. We know exactly how to drive our brothers to distraction."

"And you're sixteen and a half?" he said in all seriousness.

She scoffed. "No. I'm *eighteen*." She narrowed her eyes. "You're kidding me again!"

Her laughter reminded Roady of a flock of sparrows in spring.

"How old are you?" she asked.

He raised a brow, wondering at her curiosity. "I'm twenty-eight. Not quite old enough to be your pa, but almost." He shifted uneasily in his seat, thinking he'd best steer this conversation in another direction. It was making him a mite edgy.

"Heather sure is proud of you, Sally," he said, jumping one of her pieces. "She always has something nice to say about her smarty-pants baby sister who works for the newspaper. Even said your boss has taken you under his wing and is showing you the ropes of being a woman reporter. That's pretty darn impressive."

Sally's hand jerked, and the piece she had under her finger flew off the board and hit the floor with a pop.

Roady bent over, searched around until he found it, then handed it back. "Here you go."

"Thank you."

"What's his name?"

Shadows lurked behind her eyes as she glanced up at him. "Who?"

"Your boss in St. Louis."

Sally put the piece back onto the board. "Mr. Greenstein."

Roady nodded and gazed back at his men. When he took another of her kings, she barely reacted. It took three more captures for her to perk up.

"I don't know how you're doing this," she finally said. "I'm usually much better."

He chuckled, although her mood had changed. Her smile was gone, as well as the light in her eyes. "It can't be that I'm just good enough to beat you?"

She quickly conceded the point as if she realized just how stuffy her statement sounded. "Of course it can—and you *are*," she replied. "Better than any of my brothers as well."

Roady stood and went to the counter to pick up the two mugs they'd used earlier. He returned to the hearth and poured them each some coffee, then settled back onto his chair.

As he lifted his own mug to his lips, he studied her over the rim for a moment, considering. She was hiding something. Whatever it was, she'd not confide in him, he was sure.

Obviously, she was out of his league. But that didn't stop him from enjoying her quick mind—as well as her pretty face.

Chapter Eighteen

Luke ambled to the parlor window of the Oyster Hotel, a mug of hot coffee in his hand. Large flakes of snow floated down to the already white streets of Waterloo.

He took a sip from his mug as he watched a fellow hurry into the telegraph office across the street. It had been months since he'd been away from the ranch, and Faith had to convince him that she and the children would be fine for a few days alone. That he should go and keep his brothers out of trouble. A smile played around his lips as he wondered if Amy and Rachel had said the same to Mark and Matt.

"You're up early."

He turned. Matt descended the stairs, with Mark right behind.

"As are you two." He cocked his brow. Both brothers were bathed and dressed. "Guess none of us are accustomed to taking time off and sleeping in. I'm glad the snow held off until we returned with the horses yesterday."

"Is the dining room open?" Mark looked around as he covered a yawn. "I've been dreaming about flapjacks with melted butter and maple syrup for hours."

"That's what I'm waiting on now," Luke said. "Coffee's brewed. If you poke your head in the kitchen, they'll give you a cup." He took a healthy swig from his mug. "It's good and strong."

Mark headed toward the kitchen.

"Bring me a cup," Matt called to his brother's retreating back.

Luke and Matt had barely turned back to the window when Mark returned.

"The cook hasn't arrived to work. The manager said the old-timer has a penchant for the bottle. He recommends we go next door to the Willow Tree Restaurant if we're in a hurry to eat." Mark glanced back and forth between his two brothers.

Luke set his mug on the side table and grasped his leather coat off the chair where he'd laid it, pulling it on. "What are we waiting for?" He opened the door to a gust of frosty air, then preceded Matt and Mark down the snow-dusted boardwalk already covered in boot prints. Ten strides later, he opened the door to the busy café and stood back so his brothers could enter.

"Polite of you," Mark quipped. They removed their Stetsons and shook off the small amount of snow that had collected on the rims, and then hung them on a rack of elk antlers.

"You're welcome, bro."

Standing three abreast with his brothers, Luke took in the noisy room of busy tables and smoky air. Every table visible was seated with customers, in one stage or another of taking their morning meal. A woman with a pencil behind her ear hurried here and there, a metal coffeepot in one hand and a cloth in the other. When she spotted them, she pointed with the pot to the back of the room.

Luke nodded, then wove his way through the congestion, past a warm potbellied stove in the middle of the room. Finding a vacant table snugged up next to the pink and green wallpaper near the back door, the three pulled out some chairs.

Mark sat beside Luke, leaving the remaining seat for Matt. His oldest brother looked none too pleased to have his back to the room. The three reached for the only menu lying in the center of the table.

Matt triumphantly whipped it off the red-and-white checkered tablecloth first. "I've got it, boys." He cleared his throat. "The specials are ham and eggs, a tall stack of flapjacks with bacon or sausage, a T-bone beefsteak with all the fixings, corned beef hash, huevos rancheros, Dutch-oven cinnamon rolls, oatmeal with all the fixings—"

Mark made an appreciative sound in his throat. "I'm liking this place more and more."

Luke nodded, his mouth watering in anticipation.

The middle-aged coffee pourer approached. At one time this morning, her apron must have been clean.

"Mornin', gentlemen," she said with a saucy smile. "Coffee?"

They nodded and replied in unison, "Yes, ma'am."

"I'm no ma'am," she said with a husky laugh, and began splashing hot coffee into each mug. "I work evenings at Blackstone Hall." Her direct look left little to the imagination with its bold invitation. "My name's Abigail, but you can call me Gabby."

Luke tried to imagine what Gabby would look like cleaned up and in a dress, but gave up. The possibilities were too distressing. "We surely will, Gabby," he said.

Finished pouring the coffee, she set the pot directly on the tabletop and pulled a scrap of paper from her apron pocket. "You know what you want to eat?"

"That's a difficult question," Luke said. "My head is still spinning with all the possibilities."

"I'll make it easy on you then, handsome." She smiled and winked.

Matt and Mark chuckled.

"We just run out of corned beef hash not ten minutes ago, and that gentleman directly behind me got the last beefsteak." Her eyebrow cocked when someone called her name, which she ignored. "How was we to know it'd snow and everyone and his brother would come hunting a hot breakfast?"

It had been that exact steak that Luke had been eyeballing. "Tarnation! That's what I wanted."

Gabby cleared her throat, her pencil tapping the notepad she held.

Luke grabbed the menu. "Fine then. Let me just see here." He quickly scanned the list. "Give me a double order of huevos with plenty of frijoles and tortillas."

"You got it." She looked at Matt.

"Ham and eggs with extra potatoes."

She scribbled furiously. "A cowboy after my own heart," she said with a smile. She looked at Mark. "You best hurry up 'fore all the favorites are gone."

"Gabby!" a man's voice hollered from somewhere in the kitchen. "Order up!"

"I'll be right there," she shouted back over Matt's head, making him wince.

Luke struggled not to laugh.

Gabby cocked her hip impatiently. "See what I mean? Food's flying outta here faster than a cat on a frozen pond."

Mark leaned forward as if he was afraid she'd actually leave without taking his order. "Tall stack of flapjacks with bacon. And add one order of Dutch-oven cinnamon rolls to split between us."

She hastily made a few more notes. "Got it, boys. You just sit tight and enjoy your coffee. We'll have this for you lickety-split."

Luke relaxed in his chair and stretched, enjoying the slow morning and the aromas wafting about. There was something good about breakfast in a warm café, about knowing everything was fine back home, and that he and his brothers could enjoy a few days to themselves. Everyone needed a change of scenery now and then. Just as soon as they finished up with their morning meal, they'd visit some old friends. Then tomorrow, when the shops opened up, they'd pick up some Christmas gifts. Unique doodads that they couldn't find in Y Knot or Pine Grove, and have them shipped to the sheriff's office to keep the surprise.

"What are you smiling about?" Matt asked, taking a draw from his mug. The typical mantle of responsibility that was common for the oldest McCutcheon sibling was gone, replaced with a relaxed humor.

"Just thinking about the family and Christmas, and what I want to bring home. Colton's due for a rifle. He's been using the one I had as a boy. I'd like to check out the selection at Stan Locke's gun shop while we're here, as well as get some special things for Faith and Dawn."

"And Holly?" Mark leaned back, taking in the room.

Luke chuckled. "Nope. I've got some grace time with her. At least a year. Faith's made her a doll."

Chuckles that sounded identical to his own came from both of his brothers. Thoughts of Christmastime when he was a boy traipsing after Matt and Mark, and John toddling after him, meandered slowly through his mind like good Kentucky bourbon. His ma, with baby Charity in her arms, made Flood promise the men of the family wouldn't return without a Christmas tree fit for a castle. It had to be at least ten feet tall, and well formed all around. The bundled-up McCutcheon boys had scrambled onto the buckboard seat next to their pa, their hearts full to overflowing to make their mama proud. The tree went in the living room, smack in front of the front window, for all the ranch hands to enjoy as well.

"I know about that," Mark added. "This will be Cinder's first real Christmas, where she's waiting for St. Nick. Putting out the cookies and milk. Even if she doesn't quite understand it all yet, she knows something wonderful is just around the corner. Dawn and Little Beth have made sure about that. Amy wants a new dress from the Red Door Dress Shop across the street. She dropped a few not-so-subtle hints, asking me to be sure to see what style dress was displayed in their window, so I can tell her all about it when I return home. I'll pick up something girly for her and Cinder."

The men nodded.

"Same with Rachel," Matt added. "I guess we've been had, boys. I didn't make the connection until now." He laughed.

Luke scratched his head and nodded. "I think you're right, big brother. But you know, I don't mind a bit. This time away is good. If John were here, it would be perfect. Come Tuesday, when we're headed back to Y Knot with the horses, rested, relaxed, with a few Christmas gifts on the way, we'll be ready to get back to ranching."

After a good half hour and two coffee refills, Gabby hurried toward them, her arms overflowing with large plates of food.

Across the chaotic café, the front door opened, and the sound of Sunday morning church bells followed behind a fellow as he tromped in. He brushed snow from his shoulders and looked around. When he spotted whoever it was he was looking for, he cut through the room and pulled up a chair one table over from the McCutcheons.

"Did you hear the news from Y Knot?" the man asked two others sitting at the table. "Friday's stage never made it to town. Sheriff went out around one this morning with his deputies, and Sheriff Crawford did the same last night."

Chewing a mouthful of eggs, beans, and tortilla, Luke exchanged a pointed look with Matt and Mark. It wasn't unusual for a stage to be late by an hour or two, but overnight was cause for concern. Especially if there were women aboard. This stage was coming up on a day and a half overdue.

"What do you think?" Matt asked after he swallowed a forkful of flapjacks.

"Hope it's just the weather that has it bogged down," Luke said quietly. "Or maybe one of the animals pulled up lame."

Matt gulped down the coffee Gabby had just refilled. "Yeah. But I don't like it in this weather. I was there when the stage boarded. Three women and a small boy."

The casual, happy-go-lucky feeling that had prevailed all morning evaporated. Luke sat forward, along with his brothers, not wanting to say good-bye to their holiday, but knowing full well none of them would turn a blind eye to people in need.

Mark picked up a strip of crispy bacon and stuffed it into his mouth. "Eat up. Looks like plans for the day have just landed in our lap."

Chapter Nineteen

With full bellies, Luke and his brothers saddled up and rode out, intending to help in any way they could. Only a few miles out of Waterloo, they encountered the sheriff and his two deputies on their way back to town. They reined up.

"What'd you find out?" Matt asked.

"Met Jack Jones, deputy of Y Knot, about six miles back," the sheriff said. "He'd come to tell us they found the stage and to send us back to Waterloo. Seems a cougar spooked the team. As the driver fought to keep the stage on the road, he suffered some kind of seizure. They went into the ditch, breaking the axle. He's dead. The shotgun messenger had the passengers huddled inside the coach to keep warm. Crawford has two buckboards on their way now with food and blankets to fetch 'em back to Y Knot."

Luke glanced up at the low, dark clouds. "That's good. He tell you anything else?"

"Naw. Jones was in one mighty hurry to get back to town and warm up."

Mark shook his head in disgust. "Sounds like Jones."

Luke reined his horse around, behind Matt and Mark. The three lawmen loped off, leaving them to return through the quiet countryside.

"I sure would have liked to speak with Brandon," Luke said. "Hear how things in town are managing since we left. As peaceful as Y Knot is, I'll sleep a lot better when Charity and Brandon get their new place built. I can't help but worry with her living in town."

"She's a married woman, Luke," Matt teased. "You can't be fretting over her like she was still a girl, but...I know what you mean. I do too." He chuckled. "I wish she'd hurry up and approve the house plans she's been mulling over for weeks. How long can it take to decide if she wants two bedrooms or three? Seems she changes her mind every day. Even Rachel is amazed, and getting a bit frustrated. And you know how my wife backs up everything that little sister of ours does."

Mark snickered. "Sure do. Amy too."

"And Faith."

Mark went on, his horse ambling forward through the snow between Luke and Matt's mounts. "At least Brandon is smart enough to keep out of it. Says he doesn't care if it's a shack or a castle, just so it has a place to rest his head at night."

The three looked between themselves and smiled.

"Or maybe a bit more than that," Luke said.

Mark's face grew serious. "You can't blame him for wanting to complete it before the onset of winter. Last week that thought may have been a possibility. Now they might have to wait for spring." He huffed out, sending a rush of hot breath in front of him. "He's obviously letting Charity handle everything so they don't end up in any arguments. The two have sure been getting along good since they tied the knot."

Luke raised his brow. "I always said she'd settle down once that happened."

Matt harrumphed.

Mark unfastened the top two buttons of his coat, pulled a watch out of his vest pocket, and flipped open the lid. "It's only nine. We have a whole day to kill."

Luke's mind was still back in Y Knot, or more specifically, his kitchen. Faith would be whipping up a batch of griddlecakes smothered in butter and huckleberry jam to serve Colton and Dawn while she tried to keep Holly happy and involved. That was *his* job. He missed them. Sunday morning without his family was a bit sad.

"Colton better not try to ride War Bonnet while I'm away," he said, trying to redirect his thoughts. The horse had not settled down as Luke had hoped. If the gelding didn't straighten out soon, he'd take him to the ranch and let Smokey ride his socks off. If that didn't work, he'd find a mount better suited. But he didn't want to do that. Colton had already come to love the horse. "That boy has started bucking my rules of late. I guess he's growing up."

"You just wait," Matt said, tipping his hat brim so they could see his eyes. "Billy and Adam think they're grown men. They're still respectful, but I can see in their eyes their ideas don't quite coincide with mine. Billy stands eye to eye with me, and he's only a year older than Colton. I'm starting to feel old, like Pa. I wonder what they're doing right now."

Luke pulled his mount to a halt, and the others looked back at him, then stopped.

"Why're you stopping?" Matt asked as his horse pulled on the bit, anxious to get back to the barn in Waterloo. He spun him around and faced Luke.

"Look at us! What a sorry lot of cowboys," Luke replied. "I'm sitting here thinking about Faith and the tykes, and wondering what they're up to. And it's as clear as these dark clouds over my head that the two of you are doing the same thing. This is the first time we've been away from the ranch together in years. I say we enjoy it while we can. We'll be heading back to Y Knot before we know it."

Chapter Twenty

Except for Cinder on her lap, Amy was alone in the ranch house dining room. The candles flickering in the wall sconces, as well as several lanterns scattered about, gave the room a cozy feel. Because of the heavy snowfall, they wouldn't be making a trip into Y Knot for church.

Reaching for her coffee cup on the white tablecloth, she couldn't keep from wondering about her brother Cade. Was he still at her house? What was he doing? After all these years, why had he returned?

"How're you feeling this morning, dear?" Claire McCutcheon asked as she descended the staircase. Her mother-in-law wore a flowing blue and green calico skirt and a fitted blue shirtwaist. She'd added a crocheted collar held together over her chest with a cameo pin.

"Very rested, thank you." Amy smiled at the woman who had become so dear to her.

Over the years, Claire had made a conscious effort to nurture Amy, to seek out her opinion on family matters, and just be her friend. Amy had shared her fear after having the intense pain the other day. Her mother-in-law, in her abiding wisdom, offered that as long as Amy did everything to her ability to take care of herself, and her new babe, all the rest was up to God. Worrying didn't help a thing.

Claire kissed Cinder on the top of her head, and at the same time ran her hand affectionately down Amy's arm. "I'm so pleased to hear that. And how is this little angel on your lap? I didn't hear a peep out of her all night."

Amy and Cinder had slept in Mark's old room, and Faith and Rachel had stayed in Luke's and Matt's. Claire was beyond happy having all her daughters-in-law to fuss over and pamper—along with all her grandchildren. Since the snow had let up, they all planned to go home later in the day.

"That's because she slept through until morning with no problems at all." The previous night, perhaps because of the unexpected and unsettling visit from an uncle she'd never seen before, Cinder had awakened several times in a puddle of tears. Her mother-in-law had come to check to see that everything was all right.

Esperanza came in from the kitchen carrying a large platter with scrambled eggs on one side, and rows of crisp bacon piled high on the other. She set the banquet on the side table, sending savory aromas into the air.

"Good morning, Señora Amy," the maid offered shyly. Her perfectly pressed dark blue dress flowed around her legs underneath a white lace-trimmed apron.

"Good morning, Esperanza. The coffee is exceptionally good this morning." She lifted her cup.

Claire pulled out the chair of her customary seat on the right hand side of Flood's. Settling herself, she turned her cup over and poured from the silver coffeepot in the center of the table. "I would have thought my hungry grandsons would be here already cleaning out the kitchen. I've hardly seen them since they arrived."

At the mention of her boy cousins, Cinder perked up and looked in the direction of the front door. "Adam!" she said enthusiastically. "Colton!"

Amy and Claire laughed.

"Actually, they were all here about ten minutes ago," Amy said. "Lucky fed them in the bunkhouse. They were preparing to ride out in the fresh snow with Pedro and a couple of the other men to check on the cattle. I didn't stop them. Perhaps I should have?"

Claire waved off her concern. "Oh no. They'll be perfectly safe with the ranch hands. I'm certainly glad to see the clouds clearing. I enjoy the snow each year, but not until December or January. There is still too much to accomplish before winter sets in."

Before Amy could respond, Faith, Rachel, and their toddlers appeared at the top of the stairs. "Good morning," they called out in unison.

"Morning, Grammy!" Dawn sang out with gusto. She struggled to get free of her aunt Rachel's restrictive hold so she could scramble down the stairs like a mountain goat—a common occurrence when the child was unattended.

A knock sounded on the front door by the time everyone was off the staircase and in the dining room, scooting in around the large rectangular table.

Francis let himself in, pausing in the entry, his hat dangling in gloved hands. He wore cream-colored chaps and a leather coat. At his neck, a glimpse of his usual red bandanna could be seen behind a turned-up collar.

"Good morning, Francis," Claire said. "Would you like to join us for breakfast?" She indicated several open seats at the end of the table next to Dawn and Beth. "I haven't seen Flood yet, but I'm sure he'll be down shortly."

"He's already in the barn, ma'am."

Claire's brows rose in surprise. "Well, he's a slippery one this morning, I didn't see him come down."

Dawn and Beth giggled, hiding their smiles behind their hands, clearly excited to see him. Amy almost laughed when Dawn fluttered her eyelashes at him. Poor Francis. He wouldn't dare accept Claire's invitation. The young man's face had already turned three shades of pink at the spectacle of so many female eyes trained on him.

Mark had told her Flood had found Francis in Butte as a child, after driving a herd north to the railhead. Flood and his crew had ridden all the way home with the boy taking turns behind their saddles. He'd been with the McCutcheons ever since.

As expected, Francis shook his head. "Oh no, ma'am, but thank you kindly. Lucky has me full to overflowing. Just wanted to let Miss Faith, Miss Rachel, and Miss Amy know I'm heading out to their places momentarily to feed the stock and check on things. " He dipped his head, then turned and secured his hat.

"'Bye, Francis!" Dawn called, making him turn back. She waved when she had his attention.

He smiled and winked. "'Bye, Miss Dawn. You be a good girl."

Amy watched with delight, but couldn't stop her thoughts shifting once again to her brother Cade, all alone in her house. People did change, she chastised herself. She should at least give him a chance until he proved himself untrustworthy.

Chapter Twenty-One

Sunday morning dawned to a cloudless sky. Sally stood in the doorway of the cabin wrapped in a heavy blanket, feeling truly optimistic for the first time since boarding the train in St. Louis. Maybe the beautiful snow-covered scene before her had changed her mood. Or perhaps it was a small reprieve from God. A heart could only take so much. She hoped Roady was right about the other passengers—that they had been found and were now safely in Y Knot.

Nestling deeper into the covering, she admired the view. Dazzling rays of sunshine glimmered through the stands of alders and pines. It was so unearthly it almost stole her breath. *I want to remember this place just as it is right now.*

Things *would* work out. Life *would* go on. Hers would change, but there was nothing she could do about that now. A giddy, sweet feeling made her smile. She'd warmed to the idea of being a mother, of having a child of her own. She hugged herself, thinking how wonderful it would be to hold her very own son or daughter in her arms.

"Good morning!"

At the sound of Roady's voice, she searched the far bank of trees until she found him emerging on his horse. His face was alight, and his smile stretched from cheek to cheek. It didn't take long for his mount to push through the snow and arrive at the door in front of her. He dropped a bundle of quail at her feet. "Rounded up breakfast."

"So you did. Would you like me to take care of them from here?" She could. All of her brothers were hunters.

Beneath the brim of his brown felt cowboy hat, one brow arched up in question. "Would you mind?"

"Not at all."

"Look at this weather," he said cheerfully. "Not a cloud in the sky for as far as the eye can see. A perfect day to make our escape." He extended his arm and gestured to the wintry wonderland. "Just as soon as we fill our bellies, that is. That should make you happy."

Y Knot. Heather and Morgan. It did make her happy, but unsettled as well. Her plan to arrive as a grieving widow wasn't possible anymore. She'd have to think of something else before she started to show.

"Sally?"

"Yes. It pleases me very much," she hurried to say. She hefted the string of birds in her hands. "Give me a half hour and I'll have these roasting over the fire."

By nine o'clock, with a stomach warm with sustenance and his spirits riding high, Roady had the animals packed and the cabin put to rights. He'd dismantled Sally's privacy blanket and folded it with the others. The cot hung in the rafters, the few pots scrubbed and stacked, the fireplace divested of ashes.

"Sally," he called into the cabin. Seemed to him she'd been dragging her feet. "You ready to mount up?"

"Here I am."

She stepped out the door, bundled to her chin. He repressed a smile of pride at the picture she made. Her scarf wound around her neck and up over her mouth. So caught up in her eyes, he forced himself to look away. They were dark blue and reminded him of a meadow full of bluebonnets he'd ridden through once in Texas. At the time, he'd thought it the most beautiful sight he'd ever seen. Now he knew different.

"I'm glad to see you're prepared for the cold. I'd rather not stop if we can help it. We should arrive at the McCutcheons' somewhere around eight or nine tonight."

He followed her around to Dolly's side.

The one saddle between them had been the topic of discussion all morning. And boy, did she know how to discuss. Every reason he had for her using it was met with a better excuse why she shouldn't. When he finally insisted, she'd flatly refused and wouldn't hear another word.

He leaned over and cupped his hands, easily boosting her aboard the folded pad he'd fashioned out of one of the blankets that belonged in the cabin. She grimaced in pain as she got settled.

"Still sore?"

She nodded.

"You sure about the—"

She waved him off. "If something happens on the trail, you're the one who'll need the saddle. So you can give chase after whatever tries to attack us."

He liked her spunk. In reality, there wasn't much about Sally Stanford he didn't like. "Attack us?"

She glowered. "*Yes*, attack us. Didn't you tell me you were hunting a bear? That you'd seen sign of a wolf pack and the prints of a cougar? We could encounter any one of those animals. I, for one, won't be doing the chasing, I'll tell you that right now."

He checked the door one last time to make sure it was firmly closed. Gathering his reins, he mounted up. "I guess I did. I better watch what I say from now on."

He clucked to Fiddlin' Dee and his mare dutifully started out of the yard, stepping through the knee-high snow. After a few strides, he glanced over his shoulder. Dolly still stood in front of the cabin door, Sally thumping her heels into the animal's side for all she was worth.

Roady circled back around. As he did, he unwound his rope and without dismounting, secured one end to the side of the mule's bit.

"I can do this," Sally said, her eyes snapping with agitation. "It just takes some effort at first."

"I 'spect you're right, but you'll use too much energy doing it." He sensed she was about to argue this out as well. "We have a helluva long day ahead of us, Sally. Let's just cut to the chase and say I won this one. It'll be much easier that way."

Was she worried about their arrival? He was. He didn't want her reputation to be ruined on account of the stage accident, something she had no control over. Didn't matter that she'd acted a perfect lady the whole time. There would be people in Y Knot who would judge her wrongly no matter what.

Chapter Twenty-Two

Roady reined up in front of the bunkhouse by the light of the moon. All was quiet. A welcoming glow emanated from a lantern Lucky kept burning on the far side of the porch. Snow had begun to melt in the common areas at the lower elevation, but plenty still remained around the trees, outcroppings, and pastures.

He looked down at Sally cradled in his arms and took a moment to study her sleeping face, the gentle slope of her brows, her rosebud lips. A deep ache filled his chest, and he felt a sad smile play around his lips. He'd miss their time in the cabin. Too bad they were so unsuited. Her with her highfaluting vocabulary, and him just a plain old cowpoke.

In his push to get off the mountain and back to the ranch, he'd opted for carrying her when she'd become so cold she could barely hang on to Dolly's back. Her chattering teeth hurt him all the way down to the soles of his boots. Of course, she'd resisted his suggestion, but after an agonizing ten minutes of debate, he'd finally won out.

Getting her aboard had been awkward. Her limbs were stiff with cold and wouldn't cooperate. He scooted back in the seat and put her sidesaddle in front of him, where he could make sure she didn't fall. She'd been embarrassed when there wasn't anywhere to put her arms except around his middle and lay her head upon his chest. That done, he'd folded his coat around her ice-cold body, then covered that with a blanket the best he could.

To her credit, she'd complied without too much of a fuss. It didn't take her but a minute to snuggle in and fall asleep. That had been hours ago. His own back ached painfully, but he pushed that aside. It was Fiddlin' Dee and the extra weight she had to carry through the snow that had him worried. All that, in addition to his horse's empty belly. She'd done well. The Heart of the Mountains was a truly welcome sight.

He pursed his lips and softly whistled. A moment later, the bunkhouse door opened.

Francis came out. "Roady, that you?"

"Yeah," he responded softly. "Come over here and take Miss Stanford. Try not to wake her." Even in the dim light, he was able to see Francis's eyes go wide.

"Did you say *Miss Stanford?* We've been searching for her all day. Her sister is 'bout crazy with worry. And Morgan. They didn't know anythin' about her comin' to Y Knot." He glanced about. "Some men are still out searchin'. Flood sent me back to the ranch to feed the animals and do the night chores around here, then I'm supposed to go back out. How'd you find her?"

He came around to the left side of Roady's horse and held up his arms.

Roady hesitated. "On second thought, you run over to the big house and knock on the door. Ask Mrs. McCutcheon if Sally can stay overnight. There's no way she can make it all the way into town."

"It's past midnight, Roady."

"That won't matter."

Francis just stood there.

"She can't stay in the bunkhouse, Francis." Roady tried to keep the irritation out of his voice. He was tired, cold, and past starving. His stomach felt like a crater. Claire would be annoyed if they *didn't* ask on Miss Stanford's behalf. "Of course, Mrs. McCutcheon will welcome her. She welcomes everyone! Or do you plan on putting her in your bunk?"

"'Course not! Just let me get my jacket."

In the blink of an eye, Francis darted into the bunkhouse and was back out again, striding across the ranch yard toward the house.

Dolly stood peacefully by Roady's side, her big eyes blinking in the moonlight. He rocked back in the saddle, holding Sally like a baby. He liked the feel of her in his arms.

"Wake up, sleepyhead," he whispered, memorizing her face. He reached up and stroked her cheek, something he'd wanted to do since he'd first seen her asleep on her pillowed hands in the cabin. "We're here, Sally, although I don't mind holding you a little longer. You're only a mite bit heavier than a baby bunny soaking—"

"Who're ya talkin' to?"

Roady had been so lost in Sally's sleeping face, he hadn't heard Lucky limp out the door. Apparently Lucky hadn't yet noticed Sally in his arms.

"Don't go sneaking up on me like that," he barked testily, embarrassed he'd been caught sweet-talking a sleeping woman.

"I ain't sneakin' up on no one, and I'll ask you the same damn question I just did. Who's that?"

The sounds of a conversation at the house floated over on the night air. He glanced over and Mrs. McCutcheon, dressed in her night robe, waved him over.

"Gotta go, ol' man. I'll be inside in a few to answer all the questions busting your craw."

He reined Fiddlin' Dee around and started for the ranch house with Dolly trailing dutifully behind, even though Roady had dropped her tether. Francis met him with outstretched arms. Roady could hardly refuse with Mrs. McCutcheon looking on. He handed Sally over, dismounted, and then took her back.

"Is she all right?" Mrs. McCutcheon asked with concern, trying to see Sally's face. Esperanza stood at the threshold of the door with a lantern.

"She is, Mrs. McCutcheon. Just cold and tired, " Roady replied. "Francis, would you mind taking care of Fiddlin' Dee and the mule? They haven't eaten for several days, so don't give 'em any grain, just hay and water. Take extra care of their legs. Rub 'em with liniment and double wrap both."

"What about me going back out?"

"Ask the next cowhand you see to ride into Y Knot and leave word to call off the search."

"Will do."

"Thank you, Francis," Mrs. McCutcheon said with a warm smile. "Bring her in, Roady. My daughters-in-law have been staying for a couple nights and only left today. But John's room was undisturbed. We'll put her there."

He carried Sally through the door and across the darkened living room. The large house was quiet, with just the sound of Esperanza following behind. "They were staying here, Mrs. McCutcheon? I didn't know. Has there been some kind of trouble while I was away?"

She offered him a soft smile as they ascended the stairs. "Flood and I just wanted to have all of them close during the snowstorm. With the boys gone, we felt better having them here."

He followed Mrs. McCutcheon through the hall and into John's room. She pulled back the cover on the bed, and Roady laid Sally down.

"I can take it from here," Mrs. McCutcheon said. "You be sure to come by in the morning for breakfast, so you can tell us how you found her. The whole town has been abuzz since the rescue party returned and they learned there was a woman who'd gone for help."

"You sure you don't need any help?" He looked at the door. Felt a responsibility to see things through to the end, even as ridiculous as that sounded. "She's pretty tuckered out, ever since—"

"Roady?" Sally opened her eyes and looked around.

Before he thought it through, he picked up her still-cold hand and held it between his own. He leaned over to get closer. "I'm here, Sally. We made it to the ranch. You're upstairs now with Mrs. McCutcheon. Tomorrow, just like I said, we'll get you to Y Knot and into the arms of your family."

He looked up to find Mrs. McCutcheon watching him with a perplexed expression. "Why, Roady. It's very sweet of you to want to make sure Miss Stanford isn't frightened."

Carefully setting Sally's hand to her side, he straightened.

Sally sat up. "Are the other passengers safe? Little Fredrick, his mother and grandmother…"

"They're fine, dear," Mrs. McCutcheon said. "The sheriff of Y Knot retrieved them and they're in the hotel right now. I heard say they're traveling on as soon as they can. Rest assured, everyone came through in one piece."

"And Mr. Slater?"

"Him too."

The small smile that appeared on Sally's face was a balm to Roady's heart.

"I apologize for being so sleepy. I can't seem to make my eyes stay open. "

She began to stand, but Roady stopped her with a touch to her arm. "You stay put. Today's ride would sap the strength out of most men I know."

"Roady, you've turned into a regular chatty squirrel," Mrs. McCutcheon said, all smiles as she looked between the two. "I think I can handle things from here, though. You go get yourself something to eat, and we'll see you in the morning."

He nodded. They *would* see him bright and early. Just as soon as the sun came up.

Chapter Twenty-Three

Some ranch hands were just riding into the yard when Roady closed the door to the main house and headed for the bunkhouse. A few more men loitered on the porch, and called to him as he drew closer. Smokey and Ike slapped him on the back when he was within reach.

"Heard ya found the girl," Smokey said, nodding toward the main house. "How's she doin'?"

"Fine." *What am I supposed to say now? The minute I speak the particulars, everyone's minds are gonna gallop off in the wrong direction.* He stood face-to-face with the men. Uncle Pete, Pedro, and Bob were just coming out of the barn.

"Hey, there, Roady!" Uncle Pete called. "Welcome home. We heard the news from Francis in the barn. You found Heather's sister? Don't that beat all. In the mountains—and a whiteout, ta boot."

Pedro's dark eyes searched his face as the group approached the porch. Roady raised a hand, and everyone's excited chatter ceased.

"I just wanna say, yes, I did find Miss Stanford. She's as well as can be expected after going through such an ordeal and riding so many miles bareback on a mule. She's tired and hungry. It's been a long three days."

The men's eyes widened.

He'd done it now. Let the cat out of the bag without even trying.

"Three days?" Smokey drawled, then looked around at the other men as a smile played around his lips.

Fighting the urge to strike back, Roady took a deep breath. Any defensiveness now would only make things worse. "That's right. She was already at the cabin when I showed up. But like I said, I'm tired and turning in."

He pivoted on his heel and made for the bunkhouse door. He had to wait for Lucky to step aside before he could enter. Everyone filed in behind him like mice following the Pied Piper.

Lucky went to the stove at the far end of the room. "I have a pot of stew if anyone's interested. Just set yourselves at the table, and I'll dish ya up a bowl."

The sound of boots scuffling on the scarred wooden floor prevailed as all the men rushed to the table.

"Thought as much," Lucky said. "Make room for Roady. He has the most need here."

The men scooted around and Roady sat, still feeling defensive and sore. He shouldn't; these were his friends. They all wanted the best for each other. Even the new man, Shadrack Petty, or Shad, as he liked to be called.

Lucky set out several baskets of bread. Some men grabbed for that, or picked up their spoons in anticipation. The cook returned to the stove and with double thick potholders, grasped the wire pot handle and took the stew to the table, where he ladled each man a scoop. When he got to Roady, he doubled the amount.

Roady looked up, and his old friend winked.

Lucky shrugged. "I missed ya, boy. I'm glad that bear didn't eat ya."

A few snickers were followed by the sound of eating, spoons hitting bowls, noises of approval, and then a loud burp. Everyone laughed.

"You know I don't abide bad manners," Lucky barked from the stove. "Whichever one of you polecats is responsible, excuse yerself."

The room was silent, and every man kept his eyes on his bowl.

Roady sighed. He missed the quiet cabin, the warm fire amidst a snowstorm, and Sally, more than he'd like to admit. If he were honest with himself, he missed Sally most of all. He lifted his gaze. The worn-out ranch hands' questions had been diverted by the food. What was Sally doing now? Their checkers game popped into his head at the same time he spooned in a potato, chewing by habit. *Sally Stanford.* Such a pretty name.

"That tater funny?"

What? He looked up. Lucky was watching his every move.

"You was smilin' as you ate that tater." Lucky came closer with a grin of triumph on his mouth. "You were thinkin' on her. Don't try and hide the fact. I caught you red-handed."

"She sure is pretty. I got to hold her when Roady had to dismount," Francis said, coming through the door. He took a seat and grabbed a slice of bread, then spread a glob of butter across the top. He stuffed the whole thing into his mouth, chewed twice, and swallowed. He wiped his mouth with his shirtsleeve. "Sort of looks like Heather."

Shad Petty's eyes lit up. "I think Heather Klinkner is as pretty as a daisy. I might like to see her younger sister."

The new man from Wyoming was somewhere in his twenties, and Roady figured he had a good two or three years on Shad. He was tall and lean with sandy brown hair hung over his forehead in need of a cut, and hadn't said much about his past, but saddle bums seldom did. They came in a mystery and left the same. He was good with the horses and cattle. Roady had no complaints with his work whatsoever.

"Let's all show Heather a little respect," Lucky barked, setting a full bowl of stew in front of Francis. "And Hayden. He wouldn't like his wife bein' the topic of bunkhouse conversation—and neither do I." He glanced around with a sharp stare.

Francis reached for another piece of bread. "Morgan wouldn't like it neither," he said under his breath.

First to finish, Roady stood, took his bowl and eating utensils to the sink, scraped off any remaining food clinging to the plate into the trash bucket, then set them into the wash basin. "That was mighty tasty, Lucky." Satisfied, he rubbed his belly. "Thanks for thinking ahead and having it ready. I was about to roust about in your kitchen, and I know how much you like that."

Lucky followed him to his bunk, where Francis had put his pack and two rifles. "You walk light and you can get through this without too much damage," the older man said softly.

Roady's hands stopped the process of unbuttoning his shirt. He looked up. "Damage?"

"You know what I'm talkin' about. Don't get defensive and don't go to fists. They're gonna be curious. It's human nature."

They stared at each other for a good five seconds.

Lucky winked. "Now, get some shut-eye. Mornin'll be here before you know it. 'Bout here now."

Chapter Twenty-Four

Sally worked the back of her hair with frustration as she gazed at herself in the mirror. She wanted the French knot to be elegant, but her still-damp tresses were not cooperating. She combed the back again and picked up a pin from the top of the dresser. Mrs. McCutcheon had obviously come into her bedroom while she'd been bathing downstairs and provided her with everything she needed for her morning toilette. The woman had also supplied a clean skirt, shirtwaist, and underthings, all that fit her well enough.

A wan smile curled her lips, and she pressed a loving touch to her belly. *It'll be fine, my sweetling. I love you. You're all I'll ever need.* She believed that with all her heart. This baby might have been conceived in a violent act against her, but that couldn't quell the love she felt for her child.

She thought of little Frankie and how Aunt Tillie doted on his every whim, always ready to cradle him in her arms at his first whimper. Her family didn't hold to the popular thought that constant attention and coddling spoiled a child, and she was glad.

Her future might not have a prince in store, or a true love, but she'd make it work. She wasn't the first unwed mother in the history of the world, and she wouldn't be the last. Heather wouldn't abandon her, and neither would Morgan. But what about the other citizens of Y Knot?

A knock jarred her out of her thoughts.

"Miss Stanford, breakfast will be served in five minutes," the maid said in her soft, heavily accented voice.

"Thank you, Esperanza. I'm just about finished with my hair and will be down directly."

"*Sí*, you're welcome, *jovencita*."

Sally gathered herself, now invigorated to see more of the West, meet more of this family, and get on with her life. Her *new* life. One she would take control of and never look back.

Her spirit fortified, she clicked her bedroom door closed behind her, admiring the green and gold runner as she progressed down the hall, then halted to take in the view once she came out on the second-story landing.

Again the beauty struck her. The large living room with the enormous front window. The massive stone fireplace, the lively, crackling flame a welcoming friend. The breathtaking antler chandelier that drew her gaze like a magnet. How lovely it would be with all the candles burning. Her tummy did a nervous little somersault as she descended and neared the dining room. Three persons sat at the table conversing over cups of coffee. They stopped talking and looked up.

Mrs. McCutcheon caught her eye as she approached and smiled. Two men stood. The older man at the head of the table must be Flood McCutcheon, the owner of the ranch that Roady had spoken of in the cabin. The other must be one of the sons. He was tall, dark haired, and very good looking. His intense green-eyed regard made her swallow. Her gaze skittered away from him, then she risked another peek, once, twice. Almost to the table, she put a smile on her face, belying the nervous butterflies fluttering around inside her.

"Miss Stanford, I'm pleased to see some rest on your face."

Shocked, her gaze flew back to the stranger.

Roady! She'd know that slow, deep-toned voice anywhere. It was the same one that had talked her out of her fear in the cabin. The one that made her giggle over checkers when her whole world was spinning out of control. The one that encouraged her on the painstaking ride down the mountain, through freezing, knee-deep snow.

He'd bathed, shaved, and no longer looked like an untamed mountain man. Embarrassment flushed through her at not recognizing him sooner. A small breath escaped her mouth as she tried to calm her pounding heart.

Say something!

"I'm very rested, Mr. Guthrie, all thanks to you. I don't know what I would have done if you hadn't shown up when you did." As she approached, Roady hurried around the table and pulled out her chair. Before she sat, they had a moment face-to-face, where she recognized the look of caring in his eyes.

He went back to his seat, which was across the table from her, and reseated himself.

"This is Mr. McCutcheon, Miss Stanford," Mrs. McCutcheon said with a pleasant smile.

The older gentleman, nicely dressed in clean cowboy-styled clothes, set his coffee cup back in its saucer. "I'm pleased to make your acquaintance, Miss Stanford. Welcome to the Heart of the Mountains."

"I'm happy to meet you, Mr. McCutcheon. Thank you for your hospitality." She chanced a quick glance at Roady across the table. He nodded subtly, which bolstered her resolve. Goodness, his stare was intense.

Esperanza came into the room with two plates. She set the first in front of Sally and the other in front of Mrs. McCutcheon. As hungry as she was, the savory scent of the sausage almost made her look away as her stomach squeezed painfully. She reached for her water glass and took a sip.

"You're welcome to stay as long as you like," Mr. McCutcheon replied. "You can't know how relieved we were when you turned up here. A Montana snowstorm is nothing to shake a stick at."

Roady nodded. "And it was a doozy."

Corralling her wits, Sally replied, "Thank you for these clothes, Mrs. McCutcheon." She fingered the soft fabric of the sleeve of her cerulean shirtwaist. "They fit quite nicely. When I regain my trunk from the Wells Fargo office in Y Knot, I'll have these sent back to you."

"My pleasure, dear. And I believe your trunk has already been sent to your sister's home for safekeeping until you were found."

Sally knew she meant *if* she were found. Things could have ended so differently. She regretted all the worry and hardship she'd caused her family and the people of Y Knot. "Thank you so much. And please call me Sally." She glanced across the table to Roady, and his earnest eyes. She hadn't noticed before how they twinkled in the morning light. "That goes for you as well, Mr. Guthrie." His eyes crinkled at the corners. He wouldn't give away that they were already on a first-name basis.

Straight white teeth appeared when a wide smile blossomed on his face. "I'd be honored to, Sally. But in return, you need to call me Roady. Under the circumstances—"

"That's all fine now," Mrs. McCutcheon said quickly, cutting Roady off. Mr. McCutcheon lifted an eyebrow. "We should eat before the food gets cold."

Esperanza served the two men, and Mr. McCutcheon offered a brief but heartfelt blessing. They dug into their plates.

A knock sounded. Mr. McCutcheon wiped his mouth with his napkin and went to the door.

Chapter Twenty-Five

Roady stood when Heather Klinkner rushed into the dining room. Heather's husband, Hayden, and her brother Morgan were not far behind. Sally practically vaulted into her sister's arms.

"Oh, Sally. Thank God you're safe!" Heather said. "Why didn't you let us know you were coming? Morgan would have met you in Waterloo and fetched you back himself. You've scared ten years off of our lives." They rocked back and forth. "I'm so happy you're here now, safe and sound. I've missed you, sweetie, I've missed you so much. How long are you planning to stay?"

"I haven't decided yet," Sally responded. "I didn't mean to cause such trouble. I'm sorry, Sissy. I'm so very sorry for *everything.*"

Everything? Roady cocked his head. *What's she talking about? She didn't cause the stage accident—or the storm.* He ached to circle the table and take her into his arms himself, to soothe the crease of tension from her brow. Unable to fall asleep last night, he'd worried for hours whether she was frightened in the unfamiliar room.

The two sisters drew apart. Heather gently smoothed a few loose tendrils away from Sally's watery eyes. "No more tears."

Sally's brow furrowed. She slipped into Morgan's waiting arms, all but disappearing in his large embrace.

"Esperanza, please bring out three more coffee cups," Mrs. McCutcheon called, then gestured to the empty chairs. "Have you eaten? You're welcome to join us for breakfast."

"We're sorry to barge in on you like this, but Heather wouldn't wait one more minute," Hayden said. "I didn't think you would object to such an early visit considering the circumstances. And we've eaten, thank you."

Heather sat in the chair Hayden pulled out for her. "Please, go ahead and eat before everything gets cold." She was all smiles now that she'd seen that her baby sister was indeed in one piece and healthy.

Morgan glanced at him, then nodded. "We don't know how to thank you for taking such good care of Sally."

"My pleasure." And it had been. "If I had a sister lost in the woods, I'd expect the same from you. I was happy to oblige." *He's sure taking it in stride for a man whose sister has just spent three unchaperoned days alone in a mountain cabin with a man she didn't know.*

Morgan knew he'd never take advantage of Sally, even if she wasn't his sister. A woman was to be respected. He tried to pull his gaze away from Sally, once again seated in front of her breakfast, but his heart was having none of it. And love…

Love! What was he thinking? He might admire Sally to the moon and back, but that didn't mean he was in love with her. And even if he was, he reminded himself, she was educated, refined, a city girl. She'd worked as a columnist, or reporter, or whatever she'd called it, for a newspaper in St. Louis. That was pretty big stuff. She wasn't planning on staying around for more than a few months. Sally Stanford was as far from him as Paris was from Montana.

"Roady?"

He snapped his thoughts back to the conversation at hand. "Sorry. I missed that."

He might have missed it, but Morgan's expression said he hadn't missed the fact that Roady was daydreaming. It wouldn't be too hard to guess at what. He tensed up, all eyes on him.

"I asked how you happened to end up at the same place in the mountains." Hayden dropped a sugar cube into his coffee cup, mild curiosity in his gaze.

"The weather turned bad so I started down from the high country, not wanting to get caught up there. Once the passes close, ah, well, you know all that. Anyway, the snow came on fast. I wasn't quite ready to cut short my time and head back to the ranch, so instead I struck out for the hunting cabin, planning to wait out the worst of it." He fingered the handle to his coffee cup, feeling Sally's gaze on him. "Sally was already there, having stumbled upon it by chance in a full-blown whiteout."

"We owe you a debt, Roady," Morgan said, setting his cup in the saucer and giving him a direct look. "I hear you were hunting Behemoth again. Any sign of him?"

"None. But I'll keep at it. If that bear is still alive, I'll find him someday."

Sally's warm gaze had his heart pumping. She took a tiny bite of her potatoes and chewed. It wasn't but a second before her eyes grew round, and she stood.

"Sally?" He stood too, as everyone else in the room turned to watch Sally fleeing toward the kitchen, her hand over her mouth. Heather glanced around the table with a look of confusion and surprise, then dashed after her. Mrs. McCutcheon followed.

Roady took a step in that direction, but stopped.

It might seem odd if he followed the women. Was she coming down with the influenza after spending time in her damp clothes? That was certainly possible. The thought petrified him. People died from the malady all the time.

Chapter Twenty-Six

Luke strode down the Waterloo boardwalk, thankful they'd be heading back to Y Knot tomorrow. He'd checked on the mares corralled out behind the livery, the melting snow making the footing soft. Mud was everywhere. They'd cut out in the morning, and be home by about five or six in the evening. It couldn't come soon enough for him.

He glanced at the blue sky devoid of clouds. The storm had passed quickly. For now, he'd shop for the family, then meet Mark and Matt at Stan Locke's gun shop where he'd pick up a Christmas gift for Colton.

Smack!

Something hard hit Luke in the back of the head, making him blink and his shoulders rock forward. A bolt of pain flashed in his head and spread down the back of his neck.

What the blazes?

He whipped off his hat. A large brown blob of mud still stuck to the backside of the new tan Stetson he'd just procured this morning at the haberdashery. Irritation rippled through him as he scraped off the debris with his fingers and flung it into the street.

He searched the crowd for the culprit, ignoring the chuckles directed his way. One woman hid her smile behind her hand as her small son pointed. The train had arrived ten minutes ago, and sightseers were plentiful. People milled in and out of the buildings. Nothing looked unusual. He wondered who in the world would target him.

Turning on his heel, he began his way back the way he'd come, toward the livery, unwilling to just let things be. Someone needed a lesson in polite behavior. He'd paid good money for this hat and he wasn't ready to forgive and forget just yet.

Gabby stood across the street in front of the Willow Tree Restaurant, dressed for work. He waited for three riders to pass, and then a wagon, before stomping in her direction. "Did you see what happened?"

"Sort of."

"Someone thinks slinging mud is funny." His gaze roamed the crowd around him. "I don't agree. Especially when my new Stetson is the target."

She took a closer look at the hat in his hands and wrinkled her nose. "Did you see anything?"

"No." The way her gaze cut away from his made him suspicious. "You wouldn't happen to know the culprit, would you, Gabby?"

Her lips twitched in amusement. "I just might, but I can't be sure. I didn't actually see—"

"Spit it out," he responded irritably. "I've got things to do, but not before I'm reimbursed for my property. Mark and Matt are waiting on me as well. I don't have time for this tomfoolery."

"My best guess is it was Hickory."

"Hickory?" Luke dug deep for some patience. "He got a last name?"

"Nope. Lives behind the China Doll establishment next door. He's to blame for most of the mischief that happens around here. At least, people seem to think so."

That was all Luke needed to hear. "Thanks." He strode toward the alley. It wasn't right to destroy someone's property just for sport. This Hickory was going to pay up. Luke liked this hat, and now he'd have to have it cleaned before departing tomorrow. He rounded the corner of the China Doll and pulled up short. There wasn't a house. There wasn't anything that he could see. Was Gabby getting in on the fun too?

The back door to the China Doll opened and a man stepped out of the building. He descended three rickety stairs and dumped a bucket of liquid in a ditch running alongside the building. He eyed Luke suspiciously, and then hurried back inside. It was then that Luke saw a row of boards leaning up against the brick foundation. Could that be the place he was looking for?

He walked up quietly, leaned over, and stuck his head inside. In a snap, he grasped the skinny arm of a boy and hauled him outside into the sunlight. About ten years old, the boy stank to high heaven. His raggedy clothes were covered in dirt, and his flaxen hair, if you could call it that, flowed all the way to the middle of his back, matted and snarled in fist-sized knots.

"You Hickory?" Luke growled, still thinking about the dark spot on the back of his new Stetson. He stayed the temptation to pull away from the odor.

The little urchin's eyes widened in fear, then narrowed instantly. He sealed his lips tight.

"I asked you a question."

The boy nodded.

"Did you throw mud at me a minute ago and hit my new hat?"

Hickory's chin came up in defiance and he tried to pull away, reminding Luke of Colton on the cattle drive all those years ago when he'd first met Faith. Her adopted son had been a handful who needed a firm hand from someone unafraid to give it.

Luke grasped Hickory's hands and turned them over, seeing the telltale sign of dried mud. Just because this child was poor didn't give him the right to destroy any darn thing he pleased. If he didn't learn some lessons now, he might end up dead before his time.

"Say it," Luke said firmly. "You threw mud and hit my hat. Say it or you'll get a whupping you'll not forget." He didn't intend to do any such thing, but he had to get the boy to admit his wrongdoing so he could give him a good talking-to, as well as a chance to make things right. "Don't test my patience, boy."

"I did it," the boy spat out. His eyes fairly crackled with animosity.

Luke loosened his grip, but didn't let go. "Good. I'm glad you're smart enough to know I mean what I say. *Why* did you do it?"

Hickory wrenched and twisted so hard Luke had a tough time hanging on. The boy lashed out, catching Luke off guard. His boot connected with Luke's shin. Letting go a painful curse, Luke pulled him up close to his body, where the boy didn't have room to sneeze, let alone kick.

He mentally counted to ten and took a calming breath. "You're making things worse for yourself. I asked you why you singled me out?" Luke glared his most frightening stare, the one that could make men run, but only made Faith laugh.

"I've *never* done one little thing to you. I've never even seen you before."

"'Cause I'm mad!"

"Mad? At what?" he asked, but Hickory merely glowered. "You're testing my good nature, boy."

The child's nostrils flared.

"At me?"

Hickory's gaze dropped to the ground, and his breath whooshed out in a body-racking shudder. "No. I'm mad at the world."

Luke's anger evaporated in a single breath. Mad at the world? Yeah, he could understand that. Maybe the kid even had a right to his feelings, living outside all by himself like an animal. Ranchers took better care of their stock.

Suddenly the child's anger returned. "Let me go!"

"Not on your life. You owe me. Where are your parents? I want to speak with them."

Hickory laughed. "You're talkin' to 'em. I'm my own parents! You'll have ta take it up with me!"

At his smart reply, Luke glared until the smile on Hickory's face faded away. No parents. Luke should have realized that when he'd spotted the few boards that the boy called home.

"Fine. This hat cost me five dollars, and now you're going to have to work that off before I leave in the morning. We'll begin right now with your first chore. I'm walking you straight to the bathhouse. You'll work off two dollars by taking a bath and washing your hair."

Hickory's eyes grew larger than the barn owl's that lived at the ranch. "No!"

"Yes."

"I ain't takin' no bath! You can't make me."

"I can and I will." His gaze hardened. "Like I said, you owe me. Or would you rather I take this up with the sheriff?" Luke started for the street with the boy in tow, but Hickory dug his heels into the mud mixed with the melting snow in an effort to stop their progress.

At the end of the alley, Luke stopped and got as close as he could without gagging and spoke softly. "We're going out on the boardwalk. If you walk along nicely with me, no one will notice I'm dragging you against your will. If you make a scene, it will only reflect on you."

"Mister, if you let me go I'll walk along with ya—nicely. I promise. I don't want ya holdin' my arm like I'm some baby."

"You think I was born yesterday?"

Hickory's face turned red and he jerked one more time, trying unsuccessfully to get away. "Pretty much, you big, stupid cowboy! You don't know nothin'!"

"That may be true on some accounts, but I do know how to get back what's owed to me. Now, let's go!"

With a jerk, they went out onto the boardwalk in a full struggle. People stopped and pointed. Hickory was like a feral tomcat, clawing and kicking for all he was worth. From the corner of his eye, Luke caught Matt and Mark watching from across the street. Their mouths hung open like the door of the barn.

Luke didn't care. It was either Hickory or him, and he wasn't going to lose out now. The bathhouse was across the next street. Dragging the stinky brat was worse than trying to go six seconds on a broomtail mustang. Men cleared the way so they could get through without knocking into anyone. Women covered their mouths with their hankies.

"That's enough!" Luke barked. They halted in front of the bathhouse. The boy had worked up a sweat, making Luke's breathing problem all the worse. He called inside the door for the operator to come outside.

A fat bald man appeared. His eyes went wide when he saw Hickory. "Oh no. You ain't bringing him in here."

"Yes, I am. Go get a tub ready, and make it good and hot."

"Let's see yer money."

Damn. He was tired of Waterloo. His return to Y Knot couldn't happen fast enough. He pulled out two bits and tossed it to the worker.

"Soap's extra."

Holding back a curse, Luke fished in his pocket. "How much?"

"Nickel."

"Fine, but make it enough to get him clean."

Luke fished out a dime, and tossed it over. "Make it fast and you can keep the change."

The man's face lit with pleasure. "Yes, sir. Comin' right up."

He and Hickory stood there in front of the door, waiting. Luke didn't want to go inside before he could get the boy into the water; being in the close confines would make his smell insufferable.

A gang of boys across the street laughed and pointed while pinching their noses closed. "Hey, Hick! You're stinking up the town."

"Shut your mouths 'fore I come shut 'em for you!" Hickory hollered back. "I'll whip the lot of you with one hand tied behind my back till you all cry like a baby!"

"Ha-ha, I don't think so. That bloke has a hold on you good and tight. Looks like you done crossed one fella too many," the tallest boy shouted. "He gonna give you a baffie like you were some baby? Maybe he thinks he's your mommy."

The gang of boys laughed with gusto and pointed all the more.

Luke felt a shiver run through Hickory's arm as the boy's bravado waned. He didn't have an easy go of things here in Waterloo, that was plain to see.

Luke turned on the bullies. "Which one of you wants to be next? I have a whole handful of change I'm dying to throw away. The next one to open his mouth will be in a tub before he can say, 'Not me'!"

Chapter Twenty-Seven

Luke paced back and forth across the water-stained floor of the bathhouse. The sad fact was a good number of children grew up homeless, he repeated to himself, realizing it had grown very quiet behind the door where Hickory bathed. Just because the kid reminded him of Colton didn't mean Luke was responsible for his welfare. If he set out to help each and every orphan living on the streets, he wouldn't have time for ranching, or for his own family.

Feeling uncharitable, he stopped in front of door number one and pressed his ear to the cool wood. His eyes narrowed at the lack of sound. "Hickory?"

"Yeah?"

"Don't forget to scrub behind your ears." There was enough dirt caked there to plant a garden.

"I won't."

"And wash your hair three times." Disgruntled grumblings came from inside, but couldn't make out the boy's words. "Hickory?"

"I know!"

The bald man was back, finished with filling the tub of room number two for a cowboy who'd entered right after Hickory closed Luke out with a frosty glare and slam of the door. The new customer had paid the operator, saying he'd be back in five minutes when the tub was filled, and left.

Luke met the worker in the middle of the room. "How well do you know this kid?" he asked, keeping his voice low. He hooked his thumb over his shoulder toward the room Hickory occupied.

"Everyone knows Hickory," the man replied. "Been livin' on the streets for about three years now. If I remember correctly, he come west with his family or somethin'. Leastways, that's what he claims. They died somewhere somehow, then he bummed a ride with a wagon to get here. Those fellas dropped him off and kept goin'. Waterloo was as far as he got."

The boy was pretty darn young now. How had he managed all those winters outside? "He must have been just a small tyke. I can't imagine he's been on the streets for that long."

The fellow nodded. "Don't let him fool ya. He can cause more damage than three boys put together. He's tough as nails—and cagey like a mountain cat. He ain't welcome much anywhere. People tried to help along the way, but he always ends up runnin' away."

A strange *thump, click, thump, click* sounded just outside, making Luke pivot to the entryway. Was a herd of goats on their way inside?

A wiry old woman charged through the door and halted when she saw him. She took several large breaths, and then rested both her palms heavily on her ivory cane handle. Her face was ruby red, so Luke prepared himself to catch her in case she fainted. Her animosity toward him radiated about the room.

"What have you done with Hickory?" she cried, looking behind the operator's desk and peeking into an alcove. She turned to face Luke. Angry sparks fairly flew from her eyes. "I was all the way down the street when I witnessed your assault on the poor child!" She turned back to the owner. "Mr. Dungeness, where is he?"

Swiveling back to Luke, she pinned him with her gaze. "What have you done to him?"

The entryway darkened again. When Matt and Mark entered, Luke felt a moment of relief for the backup.

Her eyebrow arched. "My patience has almost run out, Mr. Cowboy."

Luke hooked his thumb over his shoulder. "He's in there, ma'am, taking a much-needed bath. And my name is Luke McCutcheon. My brothers and I reside over in Y Knot."

She calmed and the angry scowl melted off her face. Maybe she'd heard their name before. Using her cane, she went to the door and knocked. "Hickory?"

"Yes'm?"

"Are you all right? Did this man hurt you?"

The weight of the old woman's stare still had Luke on edge. A prolonged moment of silence passed. That boy knew exactly what he was doing. Finally he said, "I'm fine, Mrs. Margaret. No one hurt me."

She blinked several times and then pulled a blue-and-white tatted handkerchief from her sleeve and pressed it to her forehead, and again to her lips. "Well, I'm very relieved to hear you say that, Hickory. Take your time…and don't forget to scrub behind your ears."

When Luke chuckled, she swung back toward him with a scowl, making it plain that he wasn't off the hook just yet.

"He's just a boy. You needn't have handled him so roughly."

"That boy had me jumping through hoops to stay away from his feet and nails. It's him you should be scolding, not me."

Luke couldn't believe his eyes when her lips wobbled and a small smile appeared. "Maybe you're correct," she said. "Hickory *can* get carried away. I just can't believe you actually got him into a bathtub. He hates that worse than eating green beans."

She studied his silent brothers for a moment, then said, "My name is Mary Margaret."

"Ma'am," Mark responded.

She looked between them again as if taking their measure. "You're all married, with homes over in Y Knot?"

"Oh yes," Matt said. "With children too."

Luke tried to send Matt a silent message, but it was too late. The old woman's eyes practically lit up the room. Luke stepped forward. "Ma'am, I've learned that this boy, Hickory, lives on the street behind the China Doll all by himself. Doesn't Waterloo have an orphanage?"

"The sad fact of it is, young man, Waterloo does not, but it's in great need of one. The citizens feel it more important to have four saloons, two card rooms, and two houses of ill repute. I've voiced the need for one for a good ten years, but each election the measure gets voted down." She shook her head, and Luke could see her sincerity to do good. "But even if it did boast a home for orphaned children, they would not be able to keep Hickory there even if they locked him away. He's very smart and resourceful. I've invited him to live with me, where he could have a bedroom of his own with clean sheets every week."

She shook her head sadly, and the operator of the bathhouse came closer, wanting to hear what happened. "He lasted one night. Actually, not even a full night. I worry about him sleeping alone in that alley day after day, month after month. He's vulnerable to many ill fates that could befall him." She pressed her hanky to one eye.

Luke dropped his gaze to the floor. Lucky and the bunkhouse had proved to be a refuge for Francis when Flood had brought him home as a young orphan. Look how well that had turned out. Francis was one of the family now. Hickory was awfully young, though, to be living in a bunkhouse full of men. He'd need to live with one of the brothers.

"Think about it," she went on. "Freezing in the winter and broiling in the summer. Scrounging for food. Going to bed with an empty stomach when there was none to be found in the garbage. It's enough to break your heart."

"Just what are you suggesting, Mrs. Margaret? I think you have an ulterior motive to your lengthy oration."

She pulled up, affronted. "I should say not, Mr. McCutcheon, but I can see from the look of you three that you come from good stock—and are affluent."

"You can tell that how, ma'am?" Mark asked, his head tipped in curiosity.

"In the way you dress, and the way you speak. In addition, the fact that you saw Hickory's need of a bath, and then paid so he could have just that. I'm sure that giving him a safe place to sleep and food to eat would be easy for any one of you."

The three of them just stood there staring at her, surprised at her forthrightness.

Luke folded his arms and leaned against the wall. The stove heating the large pots of water had the establishment toasty warm. Or maybe it was the life-changing decision he was actually considering. "And an education too, ma'am?"

"Why, of course." She blinked in surprise. "Everyone needs to know how to read, write, and do arithmetic."

The door to bathing room number one opened. Hickory stood under the door frame, redressed in his dirty rags. He had to tip his head back to see all the way up into Luke's face. The boy had removed most of the tangles from his lengthy hair with the comb provided inside. Now clean, he looked much smaller, younger, and uncertain of where he stood. At closer scrutiny, his scrawny arms looked like branches of a tree. Luke was amazed he'd been so strong. Everything the woman had said was true. The Heart of the Mountains could easily provide for the scamp.

"Hickory, Mrs. Margaret here seems to think you'd do well working on a cattle ranch," Luke said, watching his face closely. "How would you feel about that? Moving to Y Knot and living with us?" He pointed to Matt and Mark with his mud-spattered hat.

Surprise registered. The boy's vivid blue eyes quickly searched out the old woman. The nonverbal interplay, a dance between the boy and his benefactor, made Luke's heart constrict. The old woman's brow arched with possibility; his crunched down in worry. When she gave an almost imperceptible nod of encouragement, he took a tiny step back.

When Hickory sucked his bottom lip between his teeth and began to chew, Luke was afraid he might draw blood, so he hunkered down to his level. "Before you say anything, let me first tell you a little more about the offer, so you can make a knowledgeable decision. You could pick between living with me and my family, or the ranch's bunkhouse with the other ranch hands. They're a nice lot. Mostly older fellas, like myself, but one is not yet twenty."

Luke looked up at his brothers waiting patiently, then fixed his gaze back on the boy's face. "Between the three of us, we have three boys and four girls. Age wise, you'd be somewhere in the middle. We live in separate houses on a large home ranch. The children do their book learning at home until they're old enough to ride into town for school. They do chores, talk respectfully, go to church on Sunday, and you would too. If you lived in the bunkhouse, you'd get paid for the work you do. There's no lying or stealing, or pelting people with mud. We have rules we live by. And that makes things good for everyone—including you."

The boy's stoic face gave nothing away. Even though Hickory had bathed himself clean, the lingering reek of his clothes was off-putting.

Mrs. Margaret came forward, compassion misting over her sunken eyes. She cupped his cheek in her wrinkled hand. "I think you should go, Hickory. As much as I'll miss you, the McCutcheons are fine men. They have a good reputation. Over the years, I've heard many good stories about them and their ranch." Her hand left his cheek and strayed to his forehead, where she pushed back his still-damp hair. "I believe this is one of those defining moments in your life that will not happen twice. The McCutcheons are offering you something very valuable. I know it may be a bit scary now, but you'll get used to it just fine. You're not a little boy any longer. You have to plan a future for yourself that is more than living on the streets."

Luke stood. Perhaps the boy wouldn't come along. Surprised at the disappointment he felt, he placed his hand on Hickory's small shoulder. "Well, Hickory, what do you say?"

Hickory's eyes narrowed. "Am I still in hock fer three dollars?"

"You better believe it. A man always takes responsibility for his actions, as well as pays his debts. You owe me that whether you come along with us or not."

Mrs. Margaret's head jerked up. "What's this about owing—"

Luke stopped her with a look. "It's between me and the boy."

Hickory's bravado wavered. "I need some time to ponder."

"That's fair enough. Meet me in front of the Oyster Hotel today around four, and I'll give you another chance to work off the rest of what you owe me. I have some parcels to pick up that I've been purchasing around town for my family. You can help me take them to the stage office to be packaged for the next stage bound for Y Knot." He looked at his brothers, who both nodded. "Then if you've decided to stay here, you won't be beholden to me. If you decide to come along, we're leaving at four o'clock tomorrow morning. You'll ride with me."

The old woman's lips wobbled. "My, that's early." She drew the child into a long hug, then stepped back. "If I don't get a chance to see you before you leave, Hickory, I want you to remember to say your prayers every night—no matter how sleepy you are. I want you to spend a little time each day thinking about heaven, and the wonders that await all of us there when our journey on earth is through, because that's something we all should do. And your parents, as well. They're still alive as much as they ever were. They love you and are watching over you. Do you promise me you'll do that?"

Hickory took a large swallow and then nodded.

"Where is he!" A commotion sounded outside. "Hickory! You've gone too far this time, boy! When I get my hands on you—"

"Oh my, that's Deputy Anderson," Mrs. Margaret said, her face blanching. "What mischief have you done now, dear?"

"I gotta go," Hickory said, ducking under Luke's arm without giving an answer. He made for the back door. "I'll see you later!"

"Four o'clock," Luke called to the boy's retreating back. The door slammed and the sound of boots tromping down the back steps made Luke smile.

Matt and Mark closed the circle. "He's the spitting image of Colton a few years ago," Matt said. "But with long hair."

"Yeah, that's what I thought as well," Luke replied. "But Colton had Faith to bathe him now and again. I wonder what she'll think when she sees Hickory?"

Mark removed his hat and fingered the crown. "We'll know about six o'clock tomorrow evening."

Matt nodded. "That's *if* the little outlaw decides to come along. If I had to guess one way or the other, I'd say he's staying here."

The cowboy who'd ordered up the hot water ambled in. He pulled up short when he came face-to-face with a crowd in the bathhouse, a place that was usually pretty quiet. Confusion crossed his face when he saw the woman, and a blush crept up his neck. He all but jumped out of his boots a second later when the deputy stuck his head inside, his angry face resembling a ripe Jonathan red apple.

"Have any of you seen Hickory?" he barked, looking around the room. "That darn boy tests my patience every moment I'm alive!"

Mrs. Margaret's eyes went wide in innocence. "I see him every day, Deputy. Why do you ask?"

Why the sneaky old lady. Luke cut his gaze to his brothers, who both shrugged and kept their mouths shut.

"Trouble at the undertakers 'bout an hour ago. They was takin' the postmortem pictures of the Browns' little girl, had her sitting all pretty in her—" He snapped his mouth closed, exasperated. "Well, someone sneaked in and stole several of their belongin's while they was busy posin' and smilin'. It's darn shameful! No one else would do such a thing except that filthy little scoundrel."

Her brows rose in censure. "Deputy, aren't you being a mite harsh? You seem to have a problem with your anger. If I were you, I'd..."

Luke touched his forehead in a mock salute, then pressed past the speechless cowboy who'd just wanted a bath. Luke grabbed Mark and Matt's arms, bringing them along toward the door. The three exited past the deputy and Mrs. Margaret, sure the cagey widow would keep Deputy Anderson occupied for a good long time.

Chapter Twenty-Eight

Snuggled next to her sister on the front seat of Hayden and Heather's surrey, Sally knew she should feel relieved. She'd made it. After several harrowing days, she would finally arrive in Y Knot in the next few minutes. Morgan rode his horse alongside the conveyance. She glanced over at him and he smiled, but he'd been close-lipped much of the way. Why?

The image of Roady standing tall beside Mr. and Mrs. McCutcheon as they all waved good-bye popped into her mind. He was handsome, to say the least.

"That's the Biscuit Barrel," Heather said, then pointed to a white clapboard building on the corner, just as they entered Y Knot proper. The windows of the eatery were trimmed in blue, a bright rectangular banner with the name embroidered on it extended a couple of feet from a porch post on a wooden dowel, adding a happy feel to the place.

"Hayden and I go about once a week for pie." She laughed and pulled Sally closer with the arm she had around her shoulders. "Chance and Evie meet us there on Wednesdays if Chance can get away from the ranch. And if he can't, we still go. Living in town does have its advantages."

Heather's face glowed with happiness. "Now you can come along also, Sally. When I heard what you'd done, and that you were lost in the snowstorm, I was beside myself. I've never prayed so hard in all my life." She squeezed her husband's arm. "I think I'm going to cry."

"No tears," Hayden said in his deep voice, and then chuckled.

Hayden was everything that Heather had claimed in her letters home. Handsome, kind, funny, and attentive to Heather's every move. Mother would be very pleased if she could see the two of them together.

"Y Knot's charming," Sally replied, trying to keep her thoughts centered on her sister's excitement, and the new town that would be her home. "The lack of tall buildings lets in the sun, and the air smells nice." She wanted to get past the sentimentality. If Heather knew the real reason she was here, she'd be crying for a different reason. "Melba made me promise to tell you that she's coming out next year. She's determined to come west."

Heather sucked in a breath. "How is she?"

"Getting stronger every day. It's a miracle."

Hayden slowed the horses and pointed. At first, Sally thought he was showing her a group of women strolling down the walkway, until she read the sign of the building they were walking past.

She sucked in a large breath. "Stanford's Fittings. Oh, Morgan, it's beautiful. Can we stop so I can take a tour?"

A thrill ran up Sally's spine. Morgan had been fantasizing of owning his own furniture shop for as long as she could remember. When he was a boy he'd spend hours at the neighborhood junkyard hunting for two-legged stools, broken mirrors, and anything else he could find. He'd cart his treasures home to their smithy, to repair and sell. Nothing was beyond his talent, and he actually made some money. She was happy for him.

"My thimble-sized shop is hardly beautiful, Sally," he replied. He tried to keep a straight face, but that was impossible. Soon, a handsome smile stretched from ear to ear as he sat a little taller in his saddle. "But it *is* a dream recognized. And I actually have an order from someone I don't know."

She gave him a funny look.

"Hayden here has kept me plenty busy making things for the home he and Heather plan to build come spring. And I'm building a living quarters upstairs. Until then, I'm living at the boardinghouse in town."

"It all sounds very well planned out." She leaned into Heather's shoulder, thankful things had turned out so well for her sister's mail-order marriage, and now for her brother as well.

"What do you say to stopping?" Heather asked as she looked around.

"Sally's been through a lot," Morgan said protectively. "Her getting sick at the McCutcheons' has me worried. Seeing the shop can wait until she's rested. I'm not convinced she's not coming down with something." He actually rode closer to the side of the surrey and reached out to feel her forehead.

Sally arched her brow. "I'm fine, silly brother. You needn't worry about me."

At least, not for a few weeks when you learn the truth. Your thoughts will be a whole lot different then.

He tipped his head. "You tossed up your breakfast."

"I'm okay," she said with conviction, wanting to put the subject to bed. She couldn't look him in the eye. "Tell me more about the town."

Heather brightened. "Well, that's Dr. Handerhoosen's next to Morgan's. And Lichtenstein's Provisions next to that. That's where you'll collect your mail." A white-haired man in a brown apron was sweeping the porch. He lifted a hand and smiled as they approached.

"That's Mr. Simpson. You'll get to know his forgetful ways. But he's an angel. Mr. Lichtenstein, the proprietor, just got in the most wonderful supply of nutcrackers, shipped all the way from Germany. They'll remind you of the store in Germantown Mother used to take us to each year in December."

"I remember those," Sally said excitedly. "Mother would line us up shortest to tallest. We were to keep our hands in our pockets and our voices down. Mrs. Hahn would take the nutcrackers down one by one, and tell us a little story about each one." She gave a heartfelt sigh. "Those were the good old days, all right."

Heather nodded. "They *were* the best of times. I never realized we were so poor because Mother made us feel rich with love, knowledge, and understanding. If we went a little hungry at bedtime, she'd tell us it was God's way of reminding us there were children everywhere who had less than we did—who were hungry as well. And to be thankful for what we had."

"I remember that," Morgan said in a hushed tone.

"Enough," Heather said. She gestured to another building on the opposite side of the street. "Some memories are a little sad. That's Lou and Drit's boardinghouse. That's where I lived before Hayden came to his senses and proposed—and where Morgan lives now."

Hayden nodded. "That's right, Sally. She had all the men of Y Knot in a stir."

"And Mr. Guthrie as well?"

"You betcha," Hayden said with a laugh. "Especially Roady."

"That was only to make you jealous, Hayden," Heather corrected. "He didn't have feelings for me."

"Think what you will. When you said yes to me, what else could he say to save face? I can assure you that if you'd picked him, you'd be the wife of a ranch hand right now."

Sally straightened. "Roady saved my life."

"I didn't mean anything bad by that, Sally." Hayden looked across Heather to catch her eye. "Roady's one of the nicest men I know. He's a good friend. But he is a ranch hand, after all."

"That little man is Mr. Tracy." Heather pointed out a very short fellow going into the telegraph office.

Hayden's statement had derailed Sally's attention. Roady himself had said he'd stepped out with Heather, and tried for her hand. Hayden hadn't meant any disrespect, she was sure, but the way the statement came out just didn't sit right.

"Look back over there, Sally, across the street. That tall building is the Cattlemen's Hotel. For such a small town, it's actually quite a nice establishment. They have wonderful rooms and a fine restaurant. Don't look, but across from it is the Hitching Post Saloon. Stay away from that and keep to the opposite side of the street."

"They have saloons and gambling houses in St. Louis, Heather," Sally said. "You're treating me like a baby."

"Well, you *are* practically a baby. And I'm responsible for you now. You don't have Mother here to look after you, so I will. Even out west we have to observe the rules of propriety, be a lady of good standing. Show others we come from a respectable line of people. Most women walk on the opposite side of the street from the saloon."

She leaned in closer so only Sally could hear her next statement. "But I have to say, I've run into the saloon girl, Fancy Aubrey, and think she's a very nice woman—and beautiful as well. I wish things were different. I feel sorry for her, not having any women friends to talk with. Evie introduced us. She and Evie arrived on the same stage and became friends." She leaned away again and said for everyone's ears, "I just can't wait to introduce you to Evie and Kathryn. You remember me talking about the other mail-order brides?"

"Of course."

"And Evie is expecting. It's just too wonderful to contemplate. Everyone's very excited for her baby."

A stone dropped in Sally's stomach. She thought of her little one. People would feel very differently about her child. It would be scorned. When decent women saw her coming, they'd hurry to the opposite side of the street.

Heather patted her leg. "You've arrived at the perfect time. Next Saturday is the harvest social. All the young men will be there. What better way to introduce you to the community? And who knows, if you meet that right someone, perhaps you'll end up staying in Y Knot. Nothing would make me happier. As it is, I don't think I'm going to let you go home."

Sally's smile felt as if it would crack off her face.

Heather pointed. "Oh, and look back to the other side again, that's Berta May's sewing shop. I worked there as well, before—"

"Before I wised up." Hayden shook his head, then snapped the reins over the horses' backs. The animals picked up their pace. "Will I never live down my errant ways?"

Heather hugged his arm again, something she seemed fond of doing. "I don't think so."

He sighed and looked at Sally, his expression asking for understanding. "A man can only take so much."

Sally looked away, pretending to be curious in the storefronts and townspeople. Her pregnancy would not only affect her siblings, but Hayden's good name as well. Why on earth had she believed that once she got to Y Knot, all her problems would melt away like snow? Now here, she felt as if they'd grown into an insurmountable mountain of deceit and lies, which would shatter more lives than she cared to think about.

Even though the time was fast approaching when her pregnancy would start to show—and all choices would be taken from her—she still had no idea what her next step should be.

Chapter Twenty-Nine

The McCutcheons rode into Y Knot around five o'clock Tuesday afternoon. Luke and each of his brothers ponied two mares by their side. Hickory had shown up at two minutes before four that morning, a small cloth bag in his hand. Luke had handed him some new clothes he'd purchased after their encounter on Monday, telling him to change and throw the others out. As charitable as it sounded, the long ride home would be more pleasant without having to breathe through his mouth the entire trip. Since then, the boy had straddled Luke's horse behind the saddle, his hands clutched tight to the cantle.

They reined up in front of the sheriff's office, and Brandon Crawford stepped out.

"Boys, it's darn good to see you. I was just getting ready to send up a red flag," he joked. Luke didn't miss his surprise when he spotted Hickory.

"Greetings, brother-in-law," Matt said to Brandon. "Where's our sister?" He stretched in the saddle as if trying to see into the jailhouse.

"You won't find her in there, Matthew." Brandon hooked his thumb toward their small house behind the sheriff's office. "She's home cooking supper, where every good wife should be."

Luke laughed. "You better not let her hear you say that. I can't imagine what she'd be cooking, having done very little herself growing up."

"I don't ask. I just eat and sing her praises," Brandon responded. "As long as it's hot and a lot, I'm happy. Besides, she's getting better every day." He patted his stomach. "I'm not wastin' away, as you can tell, but I do look forward to our outings to the Biscuit Barrel."

Brandon stepped off the boardwalk and strolled around, looking at the mares. He stopped by Luke's side. "Who do we have here?"

Luke glanced back at Hickory, and wasn't surprised to see how the boy's eyes were fixed on Brandon's badge. "Our new ranch hand, as soon as we get him mounted. Hickory, this is Brandon Crawford, the sheriff of Y Knot, and our new brother-in-law." Luke smiled. "It's nice to finally be able to say that. Brandon, this is Hickory, a fella we met in Waterloo looking for work. Being one hand short at the ranch, we were happy to oblige."

On the long ride home, Hickory had informed Luke and his brothers he wasn't taking any charity—well, his actual words were *no* charity, but Luke hadn't corrected him like he would have Colton. There would be time for that later. The boy told them he preferred living in the bunkhouse and working off his board and keep, as well as the cost of the new clothes and boots Luke had given him. Luke admired his decision.

"I'm happy to make your acquaintance, Hickory. Welcome to Y Knot," Brandon said without missing a beat. He held his hand out until the boy finally took it, and they shook hands. "You be sure to say hello to Lucky, Francis, and the rest of the fellas. They're a good lot."

Luke felt the boy nod and then let go a deep sigh, as if he'd been holding his breath. It must be a scary feeling, changing his whole life like he was doing, and trusting people he hardly knew.

Brandon stepped back to the boardwalk and looked at Mark. "Amy had a visitor while you were away."

Mark's face darkened. "Who? I can tell you didn't approve."

Brandon nodded. "You know me pretty well." He went over to Luke's horse and held out his hand to the boy and helped him down, then pulled a nickel from his pocket. "Why don't you run on over to the mercantile. Mr. Lichtenstein just got in some grape-flavored sourballs. They're mighty tasty."

Hickory looked at Luke. When he nodded, the boy took off running.

"Amy's brother," Brandon continued once Hickory was out of hearing range. "Cade Morrow. He showed up the day of the big snowstorm. I don't trust any man who doesn't look me in the eye. I was relieved when Flood and Claire insisted all the girls and children stay with them until the weather passed. Morrow remained at your house—alone."

"Hmm," Mark replied, glancing at Luke and Matt. "I wonder if it was just a social call. Amy never speaks about him, or her younger brother."

Frowning, Brandon said, "I'll confess right now, I didn't like him. I did some digging the next day. Sent some telegrams. As far as I know, he's not wanted by the law. Still, I'm not convinced one way or the other about him. When Amy returned to the house on Sunday afternoon, he was gone. I've ridden out your way a time or two, keeping watch."

"I appreciate that," Mark offered.

"He showed up in town last night. Spent some time in the saloon, then had a quiet supper at the Biscuit Barrel. Maybe I was wrong about him." He shrugged.

"I look forward to meeting him," Mark said.

Brandon crossed his arms, getting comfortable. "What kept you three from coming back to aid the search party? Thought you'd be the first ones here."

Luke didn't like the sound of that.

"We didn't hear anything about a search, just the stage breaking down," Matt said. "And that you had it covered. We were on our way out to help until we were called off."

Brandon's brows drew together. "I didn't think you knew. We had almost every man in Y Knot scouring the countryside for a young woman."

Alarmed, Luke leaned forward in the saddle. "What are you talking about? We understood the stage went off the road and you had two buckboards en route to collect the passengers. That everything was under control." Luke looked angrily between his brothers, and then back at Brandon. "You telling us there's more to the story than that?"

"You better believe it!" Brandon pushed his hat up. "A whole lot more. With the snow coming on, the shotgun messenger, who'd been hurt, let a girl take one of the mules and ride for help in Y Knot. They had a sick woman, an old woman, and a little boy. The young woman he sent just happened to be Sally Stanford, Heather Klinkner's younger sister."

"What!" the three barked in surprise.

"That's right. But she got lost and never made it to Y Knot. With the snow dumping like it was, every minute counted."

"What happened? Did you find her?" Mark's voice was laced with tension.

"Nope, we didn't. But somehow she made it to the hunting cabin, exactly where Guthrie was headed because of the storm. They stayed a few days until the weather let up and they could safely make it down the mountain."

Jack Jones walked out of the sheriff's office, a cup of coffee in hand. One side of his shirttail hung out of his britches, and he looked as if he'd just woken up. He smiled and nodded to each McCutcheon. "Boys," he said lazily. "You have a good trip?"

Luke's eyes narrowed. He couldn't believe how such an important dispatch had gotten so contrived. He and his brothers would have left the mares in Waterloo and beat it back to Y Knot if they'd known someone was in danger, especially a young woman. Anger rippled through him.

"How is it the sheriff of Waterloo told us about the stagecoach, and that help was on the way from Y Knot—but *failed* to tell us about a missing girl lost and in danger of freezing?" he asked, his voice heavy in condemnation. "He called everyone off on his end and never said anything about it."

Brandon glared at Jack. "Who told him *that?*"

Jack took a slow step back, almost tripping over the jail's threshold.

Teeth clenched, Brandon stepped toward him. "Spit it out, Jones. Your guilty face says it all."

"I d-didn't hear all the specifics, I guess. It was cold, and if you recall, I was comin' down with this horrible cough—that I *still* have." He coughed a few times to make his point. "It all turned out fine."

"Didn't hear the specifics?" Brandon spoke in a low, dangerous voice. "I called everyone around and assigned duties." He shook his head in disgust. In a swift move, Brandon had Jack by the shirt collar and pushed him up against the brick wall.

Jack's eyes widened. "Once I realized my mistake, I intended ta send another telegram to Waterloo, tell the sheriff, but then word came that the girl had been found and was safe at the McCutcheons'."

"You've screwed up one too many times. You're fired." Brandon unfastened the star on Jack's shirt and slipped it into his pocket.

Jack glowered at Brandon and then retreated into the jail.

"Collect your things and get out," Brandon called. "Laziness is one thing, incompetence is another. I can't look the other way this time. A life was involved. I don't want to see your face for a good long while, Jack. You understand? If I do, I may not be able to hold back my anger like I'm doing now. You hear?"

"Yeah, I hear ya. I'm goin', I'm goin'."

Chapter Thirty

Hickory fingered the nickel in his pocket as he eyeballed the row of candy jars along the wall behind the cash register. There were red candies, blue candies, and even yellow. At the end was a full jar of purple.

Must be the grape-flavored the sheriff was talking about.

He smacked his mouth as if he could almost taste the treats already. His eyes strayed to the left of the confections to a bottle of perfume, and several china teacups with itty-bitty handles the kind only womenfolk liked.

At the moment, he was the only one in the front of the store, but voices coming from the back let him know he wasn't alone. His palms itched as he looked at all the fine things on display. A glass case filled with pocketknives, all shapes and sizes, was right under his nose. Several were even out on the counter as if someone had been trying them. Stuffing his hands into his pockets, he diverted his attention to a side shelf where carved men about a half foot tall stood in a row. Brightly painted, they had tall hats, swords, black boots, and white beards. Some looked quite cross. Were they toys? Hickory couldn't imagine who'd want one. But the watches—*gosh*—that was another story. There must be fifteen, if there was one.

This store had everything! A real treasure trove. He could have several items inside his shirt in moments, before anyone was the wiser. Thoughts of Luke McCutcheon outside, as well as the sheriff with the piercing eyes, made him think twice. He didn't want to mess things up quite so fast.

"Thanks, Mr. Simpson. This'll do me fine."

Two men came out of the back room. One was as old as the hills, and clomped along as if his boots were made of fifty-pound irons. The other, a drifter sort, was acting all proper, but Hickory didn't miss his shifty eyes taking in just about every detail of the place.

The old man's brows shot to the rafters when he noticed Hickory standing in front of the counter. Hickory pulled out his nickel in plain sight so the man would see he was a paying customer, and wouldn't run him off.

"Son, I didn't hear ya come in. Give me a moment ta ring this gentleman up, then I'll be right with ya."

Hickory offered his best smile.

The clerk set two cans of beans on the counter. The other man walked over to the store-made shirts and pulled one out, held it up to himself, then added it to his things on the wooden countertop.

As the old man was busy writing up the order, his customer palmed the shiny pocketknife next to his hand. The thief must have felt Hickory's gaze, because he peered over his shoulder and narrowed his eyes.

Hickory swallowed, then glanced back at the candy as fast as he could.

Finished, the clerk stuck his pencil behind one of his ears. "That'll be two dollars and fifty-five cents."

The man, still concealing the knife in his hand, reached into his pocket as easy as pie and brought out some money, leaving the stolen object behind. He placed a handful of coins on the counter and started sorting through. He looked up. "I only got one dollar and eighty-six cents."

Hickory couldn't see his face, but by his tone he'd bet the bum was giving the poor old clerk his best hangdog, down-on-his-luck look.

The old man's smile died.

Don't fall for it!

The clerk rubbed his chin thoughtfully. "I'm sorry, but this ain't my store to extend ya any credit. If you'd like, jist put back the shirt and come back when ya have the money."

The crook scuffed his dirty boots, and Hickory hid his smile.

"Actually, I just remembered…" The man reached into his other pocket and pulled out some more money. When he opened his palm, a pretty thingamabob rolled off onto the counter. He snatched it up, but not before Hickory saw a pink stone in the center. It almost looked like a flower. A real prize, in his opinion.

Hickory scratched his head and glued his gaze on the floorboards when the man once again looked his way.

A bright smile broke out on the clerk's face. "There ya go. That'll do ya." The exchange was finished and the man went for the door.

"Now, son, what would ya like? I seen ya lookin' at the candy."

"Yes, sir," Hickory said enthusiastically and stood straight as an arrow. "I'd like a full nickel's worth of the grape—*please*." He glanced over his shoulder to see which direction the man with the pinched knife had gone.

Hurry. Hurry. Hurry.

After what felt like an eternity, the clerk handed him a small white bag and took his nickel. "Here you are. One nickel's worth." He winked. "Don't eat it all at once."

Hickory turned.

"I forgot to ask you if—" The other customer had returned. His sentence was cut off when Hickory ran into his middle for all he was worth. His breath whooshed out, and he gripped Hickory's shoulders to keep himself from falling. "Watch it, kid!"

Hickory struggled out of his grasp. "I'm sorry, mister. I'm in a hurry and didn't see ya." He stepped away, warm satisfaction moving through his veins. Hickory glanced back at the surprised store clerk. "Thank you!" he shouted and ran out the door.

Chapter Thirty-One

Amy and her sisters-in-law had waited at the main ranch house since that morning. Mark, Matt, and Luke were due back anytime, and excitement was at fever pitch. With Mark home, it would be such a relief to tell him about her brother. His visit still puzzled her. Holding Cinder, she watched from the side of the ranch yard still dotted here and there with patches of snow, a fierce game of horseshoes between Francis and Lucky. Billy, Colton, Adam, and Dawn, bundled in coats, waited impatiently for their turn.

Lucky took two large steps and let his horseshoe fly. It sailed through the air and hit the spike with a loud clang and circled around, a dead ringer.

Francis looked on in dismay.

"That does it. I win again, you young whippersnapper," Lucky said with a laugh. "Three games in a row. Maybe now you'll keep that trap of yours closed about how good you are tossin' the iron."

Lucky was only kidding. Everyone knew he was very fond of Francis. The cook closed the distance between them and slapped Francis on the back.

"Don't be too hard on him, Lucky," Shad Petty said, coming out of the bunkhouse just in time to see the big win.

"He's young. He'll get better with time. Isn't that right, Francis?"

Francis grumbled something and handed his horseshoes to Colton as Billy ran down to Lucky's end of the pit.

At the sound of approaching horses, Amy turned in the direction of the road and put her hand over her eyes to block the descending sun. "The men are home! Adam, run inside and tell your mama and the rest. They'll want to be here when they ride in."

Adam, now as tall as Colton, dashed away.

Amy thrilled at the sight of her husband, who rode in first looking saddle weary and ready to be home.

The ranch house door flew open and the whole family hurried out into the yard. Shad and the rest of the men spilling from the bunkhouse gathered the stock and led them away.

"I missed you, sweetheart," Mark said, pulling Amy close. Before she could reply, he kissed her, making everything right. He placed a kiss on Cinder's head when she reached for him, then took the child and held her close. "It's good to be home. The next time I go to Waterloo, the whole family goes with me." He ran his hand affectionately down Amy's arm, and then settled it on her growing tummy. "How're you feeling?"

She laughed as she gazed into his eyes. "Fine, now that you're home. We missed you."

"Who's that?" Colton's loud voice rippled across the yard. Matt was already at Rachel's side and took little Beth from her arms, surrounded by Claire, Flood, and Faith. The children were everywhere.

Amy didn't know who Colton was talking about until he pointed to Luke who was the last to ride in. A boy with hair as long as an Indian's sat behind his saddle,

Luke waved and smiled. "Give me a second to say hello to Faith and the young'uns, Colton, and then I'll introduce everyone." He dismounted and reached up to give the boy a hand down, but the newcomer was too fast. He grasped the saddle horn and swung to the ground.

After all the greetings, the family gathered closer. The boy stood at Luke's side, where her brother-in-law had his hand protectively on his shoulder.

"Everyone, this is Hickory. He's from Waterloo, and we've hired him on as a ranch hand. He'll be living in the bunkhouse with Francis and the rest of the men."

Lucky inched in through the family gathered around. "Ain't he a mite young, Luke? I mean, I ain't no babysitter."

Hickory stiffened. "And I ain't no baby."

"He'll behave, Lucky," Luke assured him. "He knows the rules and he gave me his word. Congenial is his middle name."

Chapter Thirty-Two

On Saturday night, twelve days since Roady had waved good-bye to Sally at the McCutcheon ranch, he rode into Y Knot on Fiddlin' Dee alongside Shad Petty and Pedro. The three ranch hands—bathed, shaved, and wearing their best—dismounted at one of the few available spots on Main Street, two blocks from Lichtenstein's, where the harvest social was in full swing. They pushed their mounts between several other horses and tied them to the hitching rail.

"Looks like a full house," Shad said.

All three gazed at the lantern light blazing from the mercantile windows down the street. Amid laughter, people bundled in coats and gloves milled out on the boardwalk and into the barricaded street. A handful of sawhorse tables with benches were set about, each topped with a lantern that glowed in the darkened street for those brave enough to sit outside and admire the star-filled sky. Several strings of Chinese lanterns stretched the expanse of road, giving the area a romantic feel.

Shad rubbed his palms together and then slid them down his pants.

Pedro nodded.

Feeling nervous, Roady silently cursed himself for deciding to come at all. "It's usually chock-full since it's the last big shindig before winter sets in."

He'd thought about Sally every night in his bunk, and tried to keep her from his mind during the days with his work. He'd forced himself to stay away from Y Knot, and especially the Klinkner mill where she lived. Now that there was a very distinct possibility of seeing her, it felt like a cornfield had sprouted in his belly.

They progressed down the boardwalk, passing handholding sweethearts and a few old duffers.

"There's Francis." He pointed to the tall, slender shadow in a group of young fellows standing in the middle of the street, all most likely too shy to go inside and talk to the girls.

"How can you tell it's Francis?" Shad asked, his normally friendly tone amazed. "It's too dark to see his face. They all look the same to me."

Pedro chuckled. "His bent-up hat."

They all laughed, and it felt good. Roady hoped it covered his growing nerves.

"Well, let's get on down there." Shad's eyes were wide with anticipation. The new hand was taller than Roady by an inch or two, and had the wide shoulders to match. To his credit, he turned more than a few feminine heads.

When they were within a block of the mercantile, music started up, and the sound of boot heels and smooth leather on the mercantile floor wafted out into the street. Pulling open the fogged glass doors, Roady and the other ranch hands carefully shouldered their way inside, removed their hats, and stopped to take in the gaiety.

The front half of the store had been stripped of merchandise and shelves, which had been moved to the back.

The dance floor was alive with ruby-faced townsfolk, dancing and stomping around to the music of the Twilight Singers, who'd come over from Pine Grove. The customary black vests of the four men and one woman had been replaced with garments of gold and green to signify the harvest. The woman fiddled away, and two of the men accompanied on guitars. Casper Slack, Y Knot's mule-riding mandolin player, was slouched against the wall, his eyes glued to the group, the fingers of his empty hands moving as if he were playing. His enormous smile was proof he didn't mind at all that someone else had the limelight for a few hours.

"Looks dangerous to me," Roady said with a smile as relief flooded through him. Sally wasn't on the dance floor. "Come on, let's hang these hats."

After a challenging moment, they found spots on the hat rack.

Roady let his two friends precede him into the multitude of finely dressed cowboys, distinguished businessmen, and young ladies clad in fancy gowns. There were singles, married couples, and children galore. On the outskirts of the dancers, Lenore Saffelberg, the waitress from Cattlemen's restaurant, was in conversation with Lou, owner of the boardinghouse. Used to seeing the spinster in her black skirt and white apron, the colorful dress Lenore wore made him do an obvious double-take that she'd seen. Embarrassed, he nodded politely when he passed, ignoring her palpable look of interest.

"Roady, good to see you," Tobit Preece, a local farmer, said when they came face-to-face.

Jostled from behind, Roady turned. He caught the apologetic look of Berta Mae as she walked by, her head close to some woman he didn't know.

"Hazardous in here," he joked after he turned back to Tobit and moved a few inches closer.

Tobit's new mail-order bride from Boston held his arm, looking as elegant as ever. Kathryn Preece's dress was one of the finest Roady had ever seen. The material was shiny, but looked crackly and stiff. Lengths of maroon fabric cascaded down in waves, almost giving the garment motion.

"Tobit. Mrs. Preece," Roady said. "Looks like everyone has turned out tonight, eager for some entertainment."

"Yes, Mr. Guthrie," Kathryn replied with a saucy tip of her head. "An evening of fun before winter sets in. Tobit has warned me about the many cold months ahead, and the abundance of snow. He forgets I grew up in Boston, where we have harsh winters as well." She glanced affectionately at her husband.

Tobit patted her hand. "But you had a mansion and servants to do all the work. Boston and Montana are as different as milk is to vinegar."

"Anyplace is sweet with you," she replied, her cheeks deepening in color as she tried to hide her telling smile. Whatever Tobit was doing, he was doing it right.

Roady glanced around. "Isaiah here?"

"Couldn't keep him away." Tobit nodded to the far wall.

Through the people, Roady caught a glimpse of Tobit's wrinkled grandfather jabbering away to Mr. Herrick, owner of Y Knot's leather shop. Seemed nobody wanted to miss Mr. Lichtenstein's party. He spotted Luke, Matt, and Mark on the other side of the room, as well as their wives.

Roady's gaze shifted to the left. When he saw Sally, his heart gave a jerk. She and Heather were surrounded by a handful of eligible men, all interested in the new girl in town.

Shad hadn't wasted a moment, for he stood across the circle, smiling like a fool.

Before Roady had a chance to react, he heard his name called over the music. He turned and smiled, truly happy to see an old friend. "Judge Wesley, good to see you!"

Judge Harrison Wesley, one of the circuit judges for the Montana Territory, reached out a hand. He wore his usual black woolen vest, string tie, and double six-shooters tied to his legs. Always said he didn't want to get caught unawares by a disgruntled relative of someone he hanged. He was clean-shaven and tidy.

"Guthrie, it's been too long."

"That it has, Judge. I didn't know you were in town. Does Brandon have someone locked up who needs judgin'?"

"No. Just on my way north and thought I'd stop over in Y Knot. I don't pass up a chance to stay at Cattlemen's, if I can help it. Gives me a chance to catch up with Crawford. I spent the afternoon at his office, talking business."

Roady laughed. "And playing checkers?"

"Maybe a little of that too."

"Then you heard he fired Jack Jones."

The judge nodded. "I'm amazed Jack lasted this long. Proves Brandon's willing to take up the slack. I plan to tell my son, Justin, about the opening. I can't seem to talk him out of following in my footsteps."

"Might be a good place for him to start," Roady replied.

Harrison's expression was resolute. "You may be right. I didn't know there was a shindig tonight," he said, looking around. "I couldn't have planned it better if I'd tried."

Roady again scanned the crowd to check on Sally. Charity and Brandon had joined the McCutcheon group, as well as Flood and Claire. "How long will you be in town?"

"I ride out on Tuesday."

Roady grew serious. "I'm real sorry about your wife. My condolences."

A dark look passed behind the judge's eyes. "I appreciate that. At least she's no longer in pain. That gives me a bit of comfort."

"How's your little girl?"

"As good as can be expected for a five-year-old who's lost her mother. When I'm gone, Agnes's sister watches Carlie for me."

They clasped hands again and a silent connection passed between them. "I'll be sure and come into town before Tuesday so I can best you a few times at the board."

Judge Wesley nodded. "I look forward to it."

Like a bear drawn to honey, Roady ambled closer to Sally's circle of admirers. Sally's pretty yellow dress fit her perfectly, and was a far cry from the men's denims she'd worn in the cabin. Her cheeks were an attractive pink, either colored by the warm temperature in the room, or by something Trent Herrick had just said. Trent, the son of the leather shop owner, had just returned to Y Knot a week ago, and Roady had yet to catch up with him. Two others were brothers from Grassy Gulch he'd yet to meet, and a nephew of Mr. Tracy, the telegraph operator, but he was on the short side, making it difficult to hook her attention.

Heather caught Roady's eye. "Good evening," she said, waving him over. "We expected to see you around town this week. You must be busy out at the ranch."

He nodded, then glanced toward Sally, giving his best nonchalant smile. He couldn't help but notice how her lashes lowered, and the pleased look he knew so well from their time in the cabin. He'd missed her, and that was a fact. She was a prize to be won.

Trent gazed at Sally appreciatively, and Shad seemed smitten speechless. The two unknown brothers pushed out their chests, cocksure of themselves. He wondered which one Sally would choose.

Chapter Thirty-Three

Sally's face heated painfully as she smiled back at Roady. The minute she, Heather, and Hayden had arrived at the mercantile, she'd secretly observed the crowd for his arrival. After forty-five minutes, her hope had begun to fade.

For the past twelve days she'd struggled with her options. Every time she decided it was best to tell Heather the truth, her insides froze up. Her sister had married into a beautiful family with wonderful in-laws...the perfect life. How could she spoil such a fairy tale for her—not to mention what her news would do to Morgan? Laying her problems in her siblings' laps was the very last thing she wanted to do.

There was one other way. And he was standing before her right now. Last night, from midnight on, she'd tossed and turned until she'd come to a firm decision. She wouldn't turn back now just because her stomach felt as if a billion red ants had set up house. She blinked once, taking in his dear face, more handsome than she remembered.

Roady shifted his weight. "As they say, a cowboy's work is never done."

Heather laughed, but the coal in Sally's stomach fanned hot. She forced a smile, and the other men groaned at the silly joke.

"I think it's a woman's work that's never done, Roady," Heather teased back. "Surely, you've heard that before."

He chuckled. "Now that you mention it, I guess—"

"Roady?" Trent Herrick said, interrupting the flow of conversation. He stuck out his hand and Roady grasped it. The thirtyish man had stayed by Sally's side once they'd been introduced, trying to get her attention.

"Sure is, Trent. It's good to see you back home in Y Knot. I've been meaning to come by and say hello, but—"

"The ranch work, yeah, I know. Until I find other work, I'm helping Pa out in the leather shop. Come by for a cup of coffee and sit a spell. It's been years."

The men's conversation offered Sally the opportunity to look at Roady—*really* look—when he wasn't looking at her. His hair appeared trimmed, and his pressed green shirt brought out the depth in his eyes. His strong, square jaw brought a flutter to her tummy, as did his expressive dark brows. A small hitch disturbed her breath when she thought back to the time spent in the mountain cabin alone, just the two of them, surrounded by snow.

The tall, good-looking cowboy named Shad Petty leaned into the circle and handed her a cup of punch. "You looked a mite thirsty, Miss Stanford. I'd be pleased if you'd give me the next dance." He smiled shyly. "After you finish your cup of punch, of course."

Sally took a small sip, wetting her throat. When her eyes met Roady's over the rim, she flashed back to their ride down the mountain with her arms snugly round him and her head on his chest.

"Miss?"

"Sally?" Heather whispered, nudging Sally with her shoulder.

She had to give the cowboy credit. He'd been the only one in the group to muster the courage to ask her for a dance. It would seem strange if she turned him down now.

"It would be my pleasure, Mr. Petty."

His eyes brightened.

She took another sip from the dainty pink glass and handed it to her sister. "Would you mind holding this for me?"

"Of course not. Go and have fun."

Mr. Petty tucked Sally's hand into the crook of his arm and led the way to the front of the store, where the previous dance had just ended. Taking her out to the middle as a waltz began, she reached to his shoulder with her left hand and placed her right into his waiting palm. Hesitantly at first, and more confidently as they warmed up, they followed the circle of dancers, a respectable distance separating her from his tall form.

"This is nice," he said, looking down into her eyes. "Thank you for accepting my invitation."

She smiled. There was just enough light in the room that she could see the blueness of his irises. "You're welcome. Thank you for asking."

His hand tightened slightly. "How do you like Y Knot? I hope it's not too remote for your taste."

"I like it very much."

He glanced away for a few seconds, and then back into her face. "You seen any of the sights?"

"I have. Heather, Hayden, and Morgan have kept me busy all week."

A few more moments passed, but this time Sally felt the strain. It wasn't that she didn't like Shad Petty, it was just she had important things on her mind. Unfortunately, getting to know him—or any of the young men of Y Knot—wasn't on that list. However, if she didn't cooperate and look like she was having fun, maybe flirt just a little, her sister would want to know what was what.

"That's good to hear. Like what?"

"Oh, let's see," she replied with a smile. "I've had tea at the Biscuit Barrel. Spent a few minutes at the fossil outcropping above town. We would have stayed longer, but a cold wind whipped up out of nowhere." She looked away, thinking. "We also took a walk on the land where she and Hayden will someday build a home."

The song ended. She and Shad stood in awkward silence. She glanced over her shoulder, looking for Roady.

"I can see you're anxious to get back to your sister, Miss Stanford. Thank you. I enjoyed our dance."

"I did as well, Mr. Petty. Thank you."

When they got back to the circle, Roady was gone. Alarm gripped her, and she hastily searched the crowd.

Heather leaned close. "He's over at the dessert table. If you hurry, you can catch him."

How had Heather known? Sally hadn't let on about her plan. All Sally knew after spending almost a week at the Klinkners', and meeting all of Heather and Morgan's friends, was she couldn't bring this shame down on their heads. After all, they hadn't invited her here; she'd come on her own. There was only one way that she could think of that might fix things. A solution that might lessen the tarnish she would inflict on the Stanford name. She owed it to her family to try—and time was of the essence.

She gathered the hem of her dress, looking around the circle of hopeful faces. "Will you gentlemen excuse me, please?"

"Me, as well," Heather added. "It's time I found my husband and claim a dance. The evening is half over, and I've yet to get on that dance floor."

Sally made her way to the dessert table where Roady was eating a cookie. She fortified her resolve and took a deep breath.

When he saw her, his eyes widened in surprise. "Sally, you look mighty pretty tonight."

"A bit more feminine than the pants you've seen me in."

"I liked those too."

My, Roady seems different.

"Has your dance ended so soon?"

"Yes. I'm a bit hungry and thought to come try this fudge I've been admiring all night." She reached for the chocolate and picked up a cube-sized piece.

Roady nodded. "Looks good."

He kept glancing around. Was he nervous? She nibbled off a corner. His smile was so charming, she couldn't help but respond warmly. Something about him made her feel safe and protected. They were alone at the table, but that could change at any moment, so she pressed on.

"Roady, I was wondering if I could have a moment of your time. I have something I'd like to discuss with you."

Again, surprise flitted over his face. "Of course. Go on."

"It's of a delicate nature. Do you think we might walk out into the street for a moment? Where we won't be interrupted."

Leaving the cookie behind, he turned and placed his hand on the small of her back. "Let's get our coats and take a short stroll, all within the lamplight, of course. We don't want to start any talk, or damage your reputation."

She swallowed nervously. "No, we wouldn't want to do that."

Finally bundled and with a secure hold of his arm, she walked with him slowly past the doctor's office and stopped in front of Morgan's shop.

Roady looked around. "How's this?"

His deep voice sent shivers down her spine. Or was that her fear at bringing up the subject at hand?

She glanced around too. "Perfect." Turning, she looked up into his eyes. His earnestness brought a lump to her throat.

"Yes? If you don't spit it out soon, we'll both turn into snowmen."

She tried to laugh, then rubbed her gloved hands together. "Roady?"

This was the most difficult conversation she'd ever had. The moment he understood her meaning, he'd think the worst of her. And why shouldn't he? She felt each and every spot where his warm gaze touched her face.

"Sally?"

Unsure now, she dropped her gaze, staring straight ahead at the button on his coat. What had she been thinking? She couldn't draw him into her troubles. They'd just met.

"Sally?"

Fear rippled slowly in her belly. She was out of options, and out of time.

"Roady, I'm in trouble."

Chapter Thirty-Four

Roady picked up her hands. "Trouble?" What kind of trouble could Sally have? Although she barely came to his chin and a strong gust of wind just might blow her away, a deep determination burned in her eyes. "With money?"

She shook her head.

"The law? Brandon Crawford is a good friend of mine. He'll be able to help. He's a—"

She shook her head again, cutting off his thoughts. If it wasn't money or a problem with the law, then what? All of a sudden, he felt as if he'd been kicked by a horse.

"Please don't tell me you're dying." The sadness in Harrison Wesley's eyes a few minutes before made him shiver. After losing the love of his life, the judge would never be the same. The way Sally looked tonight, and the way he felt right now, he knew he'd be in the same plight if something were to happen to her. "Tell me it's not that."

"No, Roady, I'm not dying, even though sometimes I wished I would."

The breeze moved a few fine hairs around her face.

"Don't say that!"

"I'm in trouble," she said again softly. "I'm in the family way." Her lips trembled as she gazed into his eyes.

Surprised, he took a small step back, letting the words sink in. Had he heard her correctly? Family way? *Family way!* She was having a baby. Running from a history in St. Louis that hadn't turned out well.

"Do you understand what I'm saying?"

Emotions crossed her face so fast, he didn't know which to address first. "I do. I know what that means." *Stupid. Of course you know. Get your wits about you.* "That's why Heather and Morgan didn't know about your plans to come to Y Knot."

She nodded. "That's right. I didn't know what else to do, so I ran away. My mother and my family know I came here, of course, but not the true reason behind my sudden decision."

He rubbed his thumbs across the top of her gloved fingers. Every now and then she'd shiver, and then he'd hear the chatter of her teeth. He glanced around at the shops, all closed for the night. Everyone and his brother were at the social.

"Let's get you out of this cold," he said, unwilling to let her dissuade him. A short walk to Drit and Lou's boardinghouse, which would be unlocked, would give him a moment to gather his thoughts.

"This way." He replaced Sally's hand on his arm and they crossed the street. The boardinghouse sat directly across from the mercantile. He hoped they wouldn't draw any attention, and a quick glance behind relieved his worry. No one was looking their way. Laughter and music hung on the air, but for him, the spirit of the evening had changed. He escorted Sally up the walk and opened the door.

All was quiet. Warmth from the potbellied stove on the far wall of the parlor enveloped them, and the lantern on the table next to the stairs lit the room. When Sally began to unbutton her coat, he stilled her hands. "Keep that on for a while until you warm up. You're cold through and through."

Nodding, Sally sat on the settee without a word, then peeled off her gloves and rubbed her hands together. He knelt, put another log into the stove, and stirred the coals until flames emerged and gathered strength. He set the poker aside and refastened the latch.

Family way? Sally didn't seem like the kind of woman who would...

He'd thought the walk to the boardinghouse would give him time to gather his wits, but he was still as surprised as he'd been when she'd first uttered the words.

He stood and went into Lou's kitchen, remembering the cookie jar. Grasping several cookies, he put them on a plate and returned to the parlor to tackle this problem head-on. He wasn't sure he knew what kind of help Sally wanted, but if he had to guess, she needed a husband, and she needed one fast.

Was Sally actually considering him? If that was the case, could he marry her knowing she loved another man? He wasn't sure. The thought was pure torture. He'd like to get his hands on the scoundrel who'd wooed her just long enough to promise her the moon and then steal her innocence. A man like that wasn't fit to walk the earth. Playing with a girl's affection wasn't amusing in the least.

"Here, eat one of these," he offered softly. "The oatmeal is good for you." *And the baby.*

He slowly lowered himself to her side, but she just looked at the plate in his hand. "Go on. I insist. We aren't going to talk until you eat at least one." He put the plate on her lap.

Still slightly shaking from the cold, Sally picked up a cookie and took a healthy bite. She chewed and repeated the process until the confection was gone.

He reached over and brushed a crumb from her chin.

"Good. Now…" "I—" Their voices mingled as they both spoke at the same time.

"You first," he said. She'd never looked so solemn. But then, this was serious business.

"As you've probably figured out, I need a husband. You're the only one I know who might say yes."

Disappointment dulled his heart. *I'm her only option. I win by default.*

"There's a whole crowd of fellas over in that mercantile that would jump at the chance you're offering me."

"Not after I told them what I just shared with you. And I wouldn't dupe them—or you."

Makes sense. "Does anyone else know about the baby?"

She shook her head.

"Heather or Morgan?"

Again her head moved from side to side. "I don't want the baby to be raised in disgrace. People whispering behind their hands whenever we walk by, wondering who the father is. I want everyone to believe it's yours."

He let that sink in. She was trusting him with the most important secret of her life. "What about him?"

"Him?"

"The baby's father."

Her mouth firmed into a straight line and she gazed across to the window, as if remembering. "He doesn't know." Her voice was brittle, small.

"Would it matter to him if he did?"

She pressed her lips together, again shaking her head. Seemed some things were dumped in one's lap, ready or not.

"Okay, then," he said. "Since you ain't showing any signs yet, if we marry up as soon as possible, most won't think a thing about a baby right away—except that it came a little early. The busybodies will, though. They'll count the months on their fingers and think it happened when we were snowed in at the cabin. Nothing we can do about that. We won't be the only couple on earth that did things out of order."

Roady rubbed his hands together, grateful for the warmth from the fire. It felt good. He hoped she was thawing out. Glancing at Sally, he asked, "Is that what you want?"

A loud burst of laughter from across the street reached the room, and then the music started up again. He could see her heart was breaking in two. "Sally?"

Her crestfallen brow smoothed away. "I think so."

"You gotta *know* so. Once it's done, it's done. I'm a ranch hand, have been all my life, and I'm not ashamed to say it. I have some savings in the bank, enough to buy a little place somewhere—but that's about it. I'll have to figure where we can live until then. At the moment, nothing comes to mind."

He'd dreamed of this day, but not under these circumstances. As much as he wanted to help her, this was his life too. He knew he could love her, and was halfway there already. But would she ever love him? Would the other man's memory be between them forever, her longing for what could have been? If he was to tie the knot, he wanted a real marriage. A home, more children, the whole kit and caboodle.

She nodded. "Yes. I'm sure. And I'll be a good wife to you."

He was taking a chance. But life with Sally—if everything worked out, and that was an awfully big *if*—would be worth it. "When?"

"As soon as possible."

A flutter of excitement warmed his belly. "If you agree, I'll plan on a private service after church tomorrow. I'll have to speak with Morgan beforehand. Does that suit you?"

Her throat worked as she swallowed. "Yes. I'll be ready."

Chapter Thirty-Five

Muffled voices filtered up through Sally's bedroom floor. Norman Klinkner's husky laugh was followed by Ina's softer one—then a few clinks and clanks of pots and pans, typical of a breakfast kitchen on Sunday morning.

Sally slipped on her corset and pantaloons with tired arms. She needed to hurry. Heather would be up at any moment, asking why her eyes were puffy. Going to her washbowl, she splashed her face again, being careful not to muss her French twist.

Today was her wedding day. Where was the joy she should feel? Fear of the unknown made her hands shake. Remembering the card the woman in Waterloo had given her, Sally went to her reticule and opened the soft fabric. She pulled the card out and gazed at the name printed carefully on the front.

Mrs. Mary Margaret, 828 Lindor Street, Waterloo. Below that were two words—*Call anytime.* Not having thought of it before, Sally turned the card over to see more words written in an elegant hand. She read aloud, "This day God gives you strength as your steersman, might to uphold you, wisdom as guide. His eyes are watchful, His ears are listening, His lips are speaking, friend at your side."

Overcome, Sally collapsed to her knees in the middle of the bedroom rug, and felt her eyes fill once again. Her pounding heart was all she could hear. She closed her eyes and her tears ran over, scalding her cheeks. She was tired of her indecision. The unknown. The hurt she thought she would bring to her family.

Lord, what should I do? Return to Waterloo and live with Mary Margaret, who has offered me a place to stay? Heather would never willingly let me go, so I'll have to sneak away like a thief in the night, give up my family, start over completely. I don't want to do that. I love them all so much. But involving Roady ruins his life. What is the right thing to do?

She heard Heather come into the kitchen downstairs, and then more conversation and laughter. Time had run out.

Lord?

She *had* to make a decision—right this second. Which way should she turn? Roady was willing, but would he love her forever, and the baby? There were so many things to consider—so very many.

Lord?

Heather was ascending the stairs.

Lord!

If you follow your heart, you will trust in Me.

The words were as clear as a bell. A shiver ran up her back, and then the clarity she'd been praying for filled her soul. Would the resolution be easy? Not at all. But did she feel confident that she was making the correct decision? Her calming heart told her absolutely *yes*.

A knock sounded. "Hey, sleepyhead, Ina said you haven't taken any breakfast. Do you want me to bring you up a piece of toast to eat while you dress? Hayden is hitching up the surrey, and it'll be time to go in just a few minutes."

"No, thank you, Heather. I'm just about ready." She pulled on her robe and went over and opened the door.

In less than a second, Heather spotted her red, puffy eyes. Her brow wrinkled in concern.

"Can you come in for a moment? There's something I'd like to tell you."

Heather stepped in and shut the door behind her, her eyes wary. "What's wrong? I've felt there's been something troubling you for some time. Tell me this instant."

Sally gathered her courage. She had to make Heather believe her. "I've fallen for Roady," Sally said, not wanting to draw things out. "We're getting married today. After church."

Heather's blank stare almost made Sally smile. "What did you just say?"

"I said, Roady and I are getting married. He's asking Morgan's permission this morning."

Heather dragged Sally over to the bed and pulled her down beside her. She searched Sally's face. "I wondered why you were being so quiet after your walk with him last night. And now that I think about it, all last week." She reached over and tucked a lock of hair that had fallen into Sally's face behind her ear. "Did something happen in that mountain cabin?"

As much as she'd like to share her burden with her dear sister, Sally knew her closest ally now was Roady, and she owed him her total loyalty. If they kept the secret between them, the baby would grow up with the Guthrie name, and no one would be the wiser. That was what she wanted more than anything, what they *both* wanted. His selfless gesture of marrying her was more than anyone should be asked to do.

"Nothing happened. Except that he saved my life. He was kind and considerate, made me laugh when I was scared.

Roady was a gentleman the entire time. How many men would do the same?"

"And now you want to *marry* him?"

"Is that so strange?"

"Well...yes. You've always wanted to be a writer. You've made everyone so proud already working for the newspaper. You've had articles published. You're on your way. I'm just trying to understand your motivation."

"I love Roady. And I can write anywhere. Don't you like it here, Heather? I thought you loved Y Knot, and never wanted to live in a large city again. Morgan as well."

They sat face-to-face. Even though Sally longed to tell her sister the truth, she knew this was best—and right.

"I insist you wait—just a little while. A month or two. Let him court you. Give yourself time to be sure. Your feelings may stem from being thrown together in a perilous situation." She patted Sally's hands, her smile tremulous. "You may change your mind. You don't really know him at all."

Sally was realizing just how well she did know Roady, concerning the important things anyway. He was honorable and steadfast. Although she understood Heather's concern, Sally couldn't stop her budding irritation from getting the best of her.

"You traveled to Y Knot with the intention of marrying Hayden the day you stepped off the stage," she said bluntly. "How is that so different from this?"

Heather blanched at the attack. "We'd exchanged letters."

"Not really. They were written by his mother."

"But I didn't know that. I believed I was writing to him. Sally, be reasonable. Where will you live?"

Agitated, Sally stood. She marched to the window and looked out. "We're not sure just yet, but we'll work it out."

Heather stood too, but remained by the bed. "Please wait until you telegram Mother. Can you at least do that?"

She didn't like being angry with Heather, and in her heart Sally knew she'd do exactly the same thing if the tables were turned. But her life had been derailed against her will, and now she had a chance to make things better. Roady was a good man. He deserved more than he was getting. Having a baby out of wedlock was the road to ruination, especially for the innocent child. He or she would be labeled a bastard, and shunned from society.

She strove to soften her tone. "I'm sorry, Heather. Roady and I are getting married today whether you like it or not."

Chapter Thirty-Six

Roady paced outside Lou and Drit's boardinghouse. He'd tossed and turned most of the night, pondering what he'd say to Morgan when Sally's brother emerged on his way to Sunday service. Roady pulled his watch from his pocket. Only ten minutes before the service would commence. Maybe the social had proven too much for Morgan and he'd decided to sleep in.

Roady rolled his shoulders several times to release his pent-up tension, then took a deep calming breath. He'd dressed in his black vest and red tie. Not that you could tell by the thigh-length leather coat that covered everything except for the bottom of his best pants and his freshly polished boots. He didn't know what Sally expected of him, but he'd made it plenty clear yesterday that he was only a cowboy, and would be until the day that he died. He hoped she understood what that meant.

Edgy, he paused and kicked the gatepost. He had about an hour and ten minutes to call this off if he had a mind to do so.

The door opened and then closed. Roady looked up.

"Morning, Roady," Lou called with Drit close to her side. Both were dressed for Sunday service. "What're you doing standing out here? If it's Morgan you're waiting on, go ahead inside where it's warm. He's moving pretty slow this morning." She looked at her husband and shook her head. "As well as others."

Drit shrugged off his wife's words. "I don't think Morgan was none too pleased at how many times that new fella, Shad Petty, asked June to dance. For one minute I thought they might come to fisticuffs." Drit's brows rose. "Unless it's important, Roady, you may want to wait till he's of better humor."

Lou plopped her hands on her hips. "I say, let Morgan be angry. Poor June's been expecting him to make a move for some time, but he's dragging his feet. Maybe he's not the one for her after all. Maybe it's the new man. He sure has a charming smile."

"You keep your opinions to yerself," Drit scolded. "That's all those young'uns need is others getting involved in their business and telling 'em what to do. It'll work itself out if left alone."

"You're probably right," Lou said, a warm smile aimed at Drit. "Since it's Sunday, I'll agree with you, so we won't have an argument." She nudged Roady. "Go hurry Morgan along. A little church time will do you both some good."

When Roady just stood there like his feet were stuck in a bog, she pulled back and laughed. "What's wrong with you this morning? You're acting strange." She reached out and pulled open his coat, her brow drawn down in confusion. "Pretty fancy. And your face is the color of milk. Is there something you ain't telling us?"

"Nothing," Roady mumbled. He'd better get a move on before they asked him any more personal questions. He nodded and started up the boardinghouse walk right when Morgan came out.

Drit smiled. "Speak of the devil."

Lou smacked her husband on the arm and tugged him along. In a moment, the couple was halfway down the street.

Surprise registered on Morgan's face. "Roady?"

"Morgan."

Morgan looked around as if he was trying to figure out the reason for the early morning visit from his friend. His wavy black hair had grown long since coming to Y Knot, and he had pulled it back in a leather thong.

"You have something on your mind?" Morgan passed him by, his customary limp hardly noticeable anymore. When Roady didn't fall into step, he stopped and turned around. "If you're on your way to church, we should walk and talk at the same time if we don't what to upset Reverend Crittlestick by coming in late. I don't cotton to being at the wrong end with a preacher."

Even in the cool of the morning, Roady's body heat ratcheted up several notches. "I think it best we stay here a minute. What I have to say is a private matter."

That got Morgan's attention. He retraced his steps until they stood face-to-face. "What's on your mind?"

"Sally."

Morgan took a small step back, digesting that. "Oh?"

"I'd like your permission to marry her."

Morgan's mouth fell open, then he clamped it shut. It wasn't a moment before his eyes narrowed. "What are you talking about?"

The way Morgan punctuated each word, Roady knew he'd blindsided the man. If they had some time, he and Sally could ease into this and spare a lot of sore feelings. As it was, he expected more than surprise out of Morgan when understanding set in.

"Exactly what I just said. I'd like your permission to marry your sister. This morning after church."

Morgan's gaze dropped to the ground for all of five seconds, and then he lunged forward and grasped Roady by his coat lapel and pulled him close. Anticipating this response, Roady didn't resist.

"*That's* why Sally's been acting so strange," he said low, almost under his breath. "You dog. You took advantage of a young girl while you were alone in that cabin. Now you want to cover your tracks in case she ends up in trouble." Morgan shoved him away, and his voice turned menacing. "You think you're good enough for my sister? A ranch hand who doesn't even have a home of his own?"

Roady knew Morgan's words stemmed from the surprise he'd been dealt, but that didn't stop the sting they caused. "You didn't have a problem when I was courting Heather." He only brought that up to keep Morgan talking. It would distress Sally further if the two came to blows.

"That was only to make Hayden come to his senses, and you know it. This is my baby sister we're talking about. She's only eighteen."

"Eighteen's plenty grown."

Morgan paced away, then came straight back, getting into his face. "How long you two been talking about marriage?"

"Roady, are you married? I've been telling you all about my family, and you already know Heather and Morgan. Just thought I'd ask."

"No, I'm not married, but I'm not opposed to the binds of matrimony. The opportunity just never presented itself. Guess I'll know when the right gal comes along."

"Since the cabin." Roady lowered his voice, then nodded at Berta May on her way toward the church just as the bells pealed.

Across the street, the door to the mercantile opened, and Mr. Lichtenstein came out and locked it. He placed his keys in his pocket and hurried away.

Surely Sally had already arrived at the church by now, and would wonder where he was. She'd worry that he'd changed his mind. They needed to conclude business here and now, then be on their way.

"So you're admitting to compromising my eighteen-year-old sister when she was alone and frightened?" Morgan clenched both fists. "Frankly, Guthrie, I'm more than shocked, I'm disgusted. I would have expected more from you."

Roady held Morgan's gaze without flinching. Being a ranch hand his entire life, all Roady had of value was his good name and moral code. He straightened and leaned in close to Morgan, their faces almost touching.

"Listen real good, Morgan. Nothing happened between Sally and me at the cabin. Nothing except talk. We got to know each other. Feelings started to grow. Now, are you going to give us your blessing, or am I going to marry your sister while her heart is wounded from you?" He had taken enough guff from Morgan. Sally was waiting. "I don't care how you feel about me. I'm marrying Sally today. In approximately"—he pulled out his pocket watch and took another look at the time—"one hour. You can be there, or not. Doesn't matter to me." He narrowed his eyes. "But it'll matter a *whole* lot to Sally."

Morgan glared back. "Does Heather know?"

"I'd imagine she does by now," he said, done with talking. He turned and walked away.

Chapter Thirty-Seven

Dressed in her best dress and the straw hat her mother had given her, Sally sat nestled in the crowded church pew between Heather and Mrs. Klinkner. Sally hadn't heard a single word that the minister had said. The staccato thumps of her heart had her breath rasping in her ears.

Several minutes after the service had commenced, she'd heard a murmur of voices as latecomers entered the church. Glancing back, she'd seen Roady, flanked by a stormy-faced Morgan.

"You're positively sure?" Heather whispered, jolting Sally out of her thoughts.

Her sister's negative reaction was still fresh in her mind. "Absolutely. I fell for him the moment he lifted me off the floor. He saved me, Heather." She had to make this good, so her sister would believe this was what she wanted.

It is what I want, isn't it? She sneaked a peek over her shoulder to where Roady sat in the last pew. Their eyes met briefly, and something inside Sally ached with anguish.

Mr. Klinkner looked across his wife to see who was whispering. Heather shrugged and looked away. A full moment hadn't elapsed before Heather leaned closer to Sally's shoulder. "Because if something *did* happen, and you're only doing this because you think it's the right thing to do, don't. Your actions aren't anyone's business except your own."

"Don't you like Roady?"

Heather blinked, then her eyes widened in surprise. "Of course I do. Very much. It's just, well, there should be more to a marriage than—"

"What?" Sally asked, feeling defensive again. They'd already been through this. "Passion? Romance? We have all that."

Heather's eyes widened, and Sally felt a jab of guilt for scandalizing her sister. Turning, she realized it wasn't her conscience jabbing her, but Mrs. Klinkner's thumb pressed into her side.

Reverend Crittlestick, whom she'd met the other day in the mercantile, had stopped preaching and stared at them straight-faced. He cleared his throat.

"Sorry," Sally offered, squeezing her sister's hand. And she *was* sorry. Sorry for the anguish her dilemma would have on Heather.

In a haze, the rest of the hour practically melted away. Soon people stood and began filing out the door. She waited with Heather in the pew. When Hayden asked why they weren't leaving, Heather took him aside and whispered into his ear.

Once almost everyone had departed, Roady and Morgan strode to the front where she waited. As difficult as it was, Sally made herself look Roady in the eye. Did he regret his decision? Did he feel trapped? Not knowing what to expect, she was surprised at the resolve she saw there.

He smiled and reached for her hand. "Morning, Sally," he said softly. "Are you ready for our big day?"

She gulped down her nervousness. She glanced at Morgan's stern face and back to Roady's. "I am. Shall we go talk to the reverend?"

Roady nodded. "Wait here a minute," he said to everyone else.

Walking side by side, they proceeded to the back of the church where Reverend Crittlestick stood at the door, shaking hands with the last of his congregation.

"Roady. Miss Stanford," he said robustly. "Something on your mind?"

"Sally and I are aiming to get married," Roady replied, lifting their joined hands. "We'd like you to do the honors."

The minister wrinkled his brow. "I see. This is all very sudden. Didn't you just get to town, Miss Stanford?" He'd lowered his voice and stepped closer, as if the others waiting didn't already know their objective.

Roady squeezed her hand reassuringly. "Yes, it's sudden."

The reverend's eyes held a bit of censure. "When were you thinking?"

Holding his gaze, Roady replied, "Right now."

Astonished, Reverend Crittlestick straightened. "This minute?" His gaze darted back and forth between them and then to Sally's family. "Why don't we put it off a day or two so I can counsel you on the rigors of married life, as well as give Miss Stanford a chance to get to know a few people and the town. There's a possibility she may not cotton to Y Knot after she's been here for a few weeks."

"Y Knot pleases me very much," Sally said. "Heather and Morgan are here. I want to marry Roady with all my heart. If you won't do it today, we'll..." She closed her mouth. She didn't know what they'd do if he refused.

Roady squeezed her hand again and picked up where she left off. "We'll have Brandon Crawford do it. But it means a lot to Sally, and me, to be married in a church."

The reverend didn't look convinced.

"You do remember I found Sally during the big snowstorm, don't you, Reverend? We were snowed in for two and a half days. Had plenty of time to get to know each other—we talked a lot. I can tell you, we're ready."

Sally's cheeks scorched. Roady was holding the reverend's feet to the fire.

"Of course I recall, Roady. And thank God you found her."

"I do thank God, Reverend. I do."

Reverend Crittlestick looked between them one last time, then finally shook his head. "Fine then. Let me get my book."

In the sanctuary of the small blue church, Roady held Sally's ice-cold hands as they stood face-to-face. Heather flanked her right side and Morgan his left. Hayden sat in the front pew, watching.

Reverend Crittlestick cleared his throat and gave each individual a look that spoke to the seriousness of the event about to take place. "Roady and Miss Stanford have asked me to keep this brief. I will honor their wishes. Do you, Sally Stanford, take Roady Guthrie to be your lawfully wedded husband?"

"I do."

Those two small words reminded Roady of the peaceful sound of a mourning dove when the last vestige of the day's light gave way to evening, and there was nothing left to do but watch for the first star.

"Do you, Roady Guthrie, take Sally Stanford to be your lawfully wedded wife?"

"I do." And he did. He'd do anything to make her happy.

"By the powers vested in me by the Montana Territory, I pronounce you husband and wife."

Just like that, it was done. Quicker than saddling a green-broke colt for the first time.

"Roady?" Sally had a funny look on her face.

Morgan nudged him from behind, none too gently. "Reverend Crittlestick said you can kiss the bride."

Roady stepped forward. When he put his arms around Sally, she stiffened and scrunched her eyes closed. A mite embarrassed, he leaned in under the brim of her hat and placed a chaste kiss on her lips. Then he stepped away and smiled. "Hello, Mrs. Guthrie."

She glanced at him from beneath her eyelashes, a gentle blush coloring her cheeks.

Heather pulled her into an embrace, and Hayden stepped forward to shake his hand.

"Congratulations, Roady. I guess this makes us brothers-in-law."

"Guess you're right."

Morgan stood silent.

"I have some papers for all of you to sign back at my desk," Reverend Crittlestick said. "I'll be back there when you're ready."

"What're your plans?" Hayden asked, and everyone became quiet. Sally resembled a deer looking down the barrel of a gun.

"I spoke with Flood this morning before I left the ranch. We're going to stay upstairs in the ranch house until I figure out where to settle. He and Claire are eager for the company." He turned to Sally. "That is, if you're agreeable."

She worried her bottom lip. "At the McCutcheons'?"

He nodded. "That's where I work."

"That's very kind of them." She smoothed the front of her dress that was already perfectly pressed. "Are you sure they won't mind? I'd hate to put them out."

Looking down into her face, her statement just confirmed how little they knew about each other. Flood and Claire considered him a son. He was grateful for their loyalty—and love. He knew only too well, from Flood's visits to the bunkhouse every few days, how quiet the main house had grown now that everyone had moved out. Roady was sure their invitation was sincere. It would work, at least until he could figure out another place for them to live. They'd been excited when he told them he and Sally were getting married. He'd made them promise to keep it to themselves, not knowing if she'd get cold feet this morning and back out. Most likely, Luke was going to be madder than a hornet when he heard he'd been left out of the wedding.

"Sure, I'm sure. They wouldn't have said so if they didn't mean it."

"Oh."

That didn't sound happy.

Heather placed her arm around Sally's shoulder, and pulled her close.

"I brought the buckboard from the ranch," Roady said. "So we can collect your things at the Klinkners'."

Morgan straightened. "You expect her to move in today? Maybe she'd like a little time to get used to your idea."

Was he missing something? They were married, weren't they? Sally was the one who'd done the asking. "Only if she wants to. Sally?"

She slipped her hand into Roady's, causing a spark of awareness to shoot up his arm when her palm touched his. "Morgan, stop being such a grouch. Of course I want to." Sally's smile looked a little stiff to be real, but her sister and brother had bought it—for now.

Chapter Thirty-Eight

Sally moved nervously around the upstairs bedroom of the McCutcheon ranch, her insides a bundle of nerves. She'd already unpacked her trunk, having placed her garments into the chest of drawers and in the wardrobe. *I wonder how long we'll have to live here.* It wasn't that she wasn't grateful, because she was. What concerned her was imposing on the McCutcheons on the spur of the moment—as well as the large bed in the middle of the room. What would transpire there was never far from her thoughts.

The moment their vows had been spoken, she'd felt like a noose had been dropped over her head. That her life had just changed, and not for the better. How could she even think such a thing after all Roady had done to help her? First in the mountains, and a second time when she placed her life in the palms of his hands. And he'd done it without question, or the condemnation she had expected. For the most part, her dilemma had been solved.

Sally took a deep breath and soothed her thoughts. Time—she had to give it time. Settle into a routine. Get to know Roady. Right now, everything felt new and strange.

Someone tapped on the pinewood door.

"Come in."

Roady opened the door but remained where he stood, his demeanor hesitant. His confident grin was gone, replaced by uncertainty. He held his hat in his fingers.

"Well, don't just stand there, silly, come in." She tried to sound carefree and happy.

When he was close enough, she reached out and took the hat from his hands. "I promise to be a good wife to you, Roady. I'll do everything in my power to repay you for what you've done. I'll make you very happy, you'll see."

Her smile slipped away. She was babbling, and from the look on his face, making him uncomfortable. She needed to make him understand she realized the enormity of what he'd done for her. "Even if this isn't a real marriage, I plan to—I mean, it's a real marriage, just different. I can't imagine what—"

He touched his finger to her lips. "Shhh." His face held compassion, not the censure she deserved.

She closed her eyes and drew in a breath. When she opened them, his smile was back.

"Important matters call, Mrs. Guthrie. Claire would like to give us a celebration supper. The whole family, including the ranch hands. Tonight. I told her I best speak with you first."

A dinner? Celebrating how I finagled Roady into my problems and saddled him with a wife and child he'd never asked for?

She couldn't think of anything she'd like less. "Is that what you want?"

He shrugged in his boyish way she was coming to know. "Don't make much difference to me, Sally. Decisions of parties and such are usually up to the gals."

When she smiled at the way he said *gals*, his brows drew down. Seemed she wasn't the only one feeling sensitive today.

"She also said if you'd rather not, that was fine too. It wouldn't hurt her feelings a bit. She wants what you want."

"I think I'd rather not make a big commotion out of things. It's very kind of Mrs. McCutcheon to want to do it, but..." She shrugged. "I hope she doesn't mind."

"She won't mind at all. I feel the same way as you about just taking it easy."

The hat crease in his thick brown hair caught her eye. Tomorrow he'd go back to work, riding and ranching. She'd be here in the house. Doing what?

He turned and went back into the hall, then returned with an armful of shirts and some unmentionables.

"Your things?"

He nodded. "Claire said if we wanted to spread out a little, we were welcome to use two rooms up here. I thought I'd put my things across the way in Mark's old bedroom. How'd you feel about that?"

He was really trying, and for that she respected him all the more. Still, the mood was so formal. She wished they could get back to the easy feel between them she'd felt in the cabin, especially when they'd sat for hours playing checkers.

"Actually, that's a good idea. Then we won't be so cramped." Again, her eyes strayed to the bed of their own volition. She wished they'd talked a little more about what he expected from the marriage when he'd agreed to marry her. It was unsettling not to know.

Without saying another word, he crossed the hall, and she watched through the open door as he hung his garments in the wardrobe and stuffed the rest into some drawers.

"Do you have anything else?"

"A few pants at the laundry in Y Knot. But other than my saddle, bridle, lariat, and guns, this is it. I left my firearms and such in the bunkhouse. Thought you'd like that better." He motioned to her trunk. "If you have everything put away, I can take that out for you."

"Yes, all put away. Thank you."

He noticed her notebook on the top of the highboy. She should have made sure she'd put it out of sight.

"What's that?"

When he reached for it, she sprang forward and clutched it to her chest. "Nothing."

His eyebrow arched. "Seems like something to me."

The very least she owed him was honesty. "It's a manuscript I've been working on. A novel. I hope you don't mind, but I don't let anyone see it. You know, it's not very good."

"You mean you're writing a book?" His tone was pure disbelief.

Used to be writing a book. Since the happenstance with Mr. Greenstein, she hadn't been able to add a single word. She'd tried. Sat looking at the paper, pen in hand, but…nothing.

Back in St. Louis, she used to write one page every day. If not that, even just a few sentences. She'd never been at a loss before, her mind an endless birthing ground of exciting possibilities and dreams. Now when she sat down to write, her head felt like a barren, dead field, unfit for even the smallest idea to grow.

"Yes, a book."

He looked genuinely interested, not teasing like her brothers had been when they'd caught her red-handed in the attic of their home.

Roady's eyes strayed to the notebook and then back to her face. "Well, good luck. I've never met an author before, and now I've gone and married one."

Unwelcome heat crept into her cheeks. "I'm not an author yet."

"You will be," he said as he muscled her trunk up to his shoulder. "I have faith in you."

She couldn't deny the happy warm feelings his words created.

He stopped at the door and turned back. "Are you planning to come down and say hello? The news has spread, and the ranch hands who haven't met you yet are anxious to remedy that."

It was only one o'clock in the afternoon. She needed to get out there with a smile on her face. "Actually, I was just reaching for my hat when you came in. I'd like to go for a walk. Would that be all right?"

"Only if I get to escort you," he said, and then winked. "And don't forget a wrap. The snow may be practically gone, but the temperature is still a mite nippy."

"Same as this morning?" She raised her brows teasingly.

The color of his face deepened, and then his chuckle made her smile. "Yep, just the same as that, I reckon."

She positioned her hat on her head and went about tying the ribbons beneath her chin. "Then I shall be sure to wear my coat."

Chapter Thirty-Nine

Fifteen minutes later, Roady felt like a pretty darn lucky man. His and Sally's marriage might not have had a typical beginning, but that didn't mean they couldn't make it into something worth having. He glanced sideways and took a quick peek at his bride holding his arm as they walked along. Why, she suited him in every way possible. There wasn't a thing he would change about her if he could. Well, there was one, and it was a pretty big one. The feelings she had for the man who'd jilted her. Those kinds of sentiments weren't easy to throw off. She was hurting.

They toured the ranch yard, him pointing out interesting things like the corral full of horses, the red and black chickens—some with ten to twelve chicks scampering behind in a cloud of peeps and chirps—and the barn with its earthy smells. Esperanza's herb and vegetable garden, mostly gone to seed.

Sally smiled and took note of each thing as if it were as interesting as Niagara Falls. Her enthusiasm was infectious. They were getting closer to the bunkhouse where his friends waited, their patience withering up. Out of respect, they kept their distance until he was ready to present her. When he knew they couldn't stand the suspense a second longer, he ushered her over.

"Gentlemen, I'd like you to meet my wife, Mrs. Sally Guthrie." It was the first time he'd put the two names together, and satisfaction warmed in his belly. He couldn't help but smile as the color in Sally's cheeks deepened. He patted the hand that rested in the crook of his arm.

"Ma'am," they said in unison.

"I'm delighted to meet you, gentlemen," she replied. "Roady has told me a lot about you."

They mumbled and looked back and forth, probably wondering what secrets he'd divulged. He almost laughed.

"Welcome ta the Heart of the Mountains, Miss Sally. I'm Lucky, the cook. If ya need anything a'tall, you jist come to me. I can solve any problem you might have. Knock on the bunkhouse door, night or day. Don't matter. We're here ta help." He glanced around at the men. "Ain't that right, boys?"

They nodded their agreement.

Sally smiled. "Thank you, Lucky, I'll remember that."

"Any problems Mrs. Guthrie may have," Roady said drily, "I reckon she'll bring to her husband first. But thanks anyway, boys." He pointed from left to right. "That's Smokey, Uncle Pete, and Pedro. You know Francis, and the new hand, Shad Petty. There are a few men out with the herd, but I won't burden you now with their handles just yet."

Roady felt his smile fade. Shad's gaze took Sally in from head to toe. Roady remembered the dance they'd shared at the social just last night.

She glanced up at him, excitement lighting her features. "If it's all right, I'd love to see inside the bunkhouse. Living in St. Louis, I used to read stories about cowboys all the time."

"Sure thing, come on in," Lucky all but blurted, holding the door open wide. "It's been a while since we had female company come ta call."

The men stood back, and Roady had no choice but to usher Sally through the funnel of men. Lucky usually ran a pretty tight ship, but earlier, when Roady had returned for his belongings and told them the news, the cook had every hand who wasn't out ranching pick up, clean up, and polish away. The place was shipshape.

Sally stopped just inside the long, rectangular-shaped building, and the men filed in behind her. She gazed around excitedly. "Oh, this is…very nice. And warm."

The fireplace glowed on this end of the room, as well as a fire in the stove on the other end. There was always something cooking, as well as a full pot of coffee, and today was no exception. Men ate a lot, and Lucky was always prepared. The nicely made beds looked inviting. The lantern in the middle of the polished table glowed a peaceful welcome.

Roady gulped. The bunkhouse had been his home for years. He never thought he'd miss the place once he moved out, but that was a fact he was just coming to know. He led Sally to the cot that was near the fireplace and closest to the front door. "This was my bunk over here."

The doodads he'd had hung on the wall over his head were now in his duffel bag, cleared away in case someone else wanted this bed. Earlier he'd stripped off his sheets and put them into a hamper on the back porch. Whoever the laundry chore fell to next week would be responsible for washing them, as well as the rest of the fellows'. No one liked laundry duty, but as a reward, they had extra time off on Monday, and got to choose what they'd like for that Sunday's dessert.

Sally glanced at him and smiled, taking in the area that had been his for years. She stopped to read aloud the list of bunkhouse rules hanging over the fireplace.

"No using the Lord's name in vain. No drinking to excess. Be polite and courteous to others. Put your dirty dishes into the wash bucket yourself. If you can't settle a dispute, take it to Lucky. Absolutely no fighting!"

Finished, she glanced around. "Good words to live by. Who's that young boy?" She pointed all the way to the end of the room, where Hickory stood at attention by his cot as Lucky had schooled him when it came to respecting women. He had the bed closest to Lucky's private room, alongside the stove, sink, and pump. Francis's bed was next to his.

His hand on the small of her back, Roady urged her forward. "Come on, I'll introduce you."

As they approached, Hickory stashed something in his pocket. His long hair was tied back with a leather strip, and his blue eyes took in Sally and then the group. "Howdy," he said. "I guess you're Roady's new wife."

Sally laughed softly. "I guess I am. Who're you?"

"I'm the new hand," Hickory said in all seriousness. "Just hired on 'bout five days ago. My name's Hickory, and I'm from Waterloo."

Sally's face softened. As if the rest of the men faded from her attention, she stepped forward and put out her hand, taking his small one in her own. "I'm pleased to make your acquaintance, Hickory. I passed through Waterloo on my journey here. You have a nice town."

"It can be. This is nice too, though. I'm only in the bunkhouse now because it's Sunday. Usually you can find me in the barn, tendin' the horses."

"Oh?"

He nodded. "I do whatever Francis tells me—feed 'em, water 'em, or clean the stalls after he takes the horses out to the corral. But once I learn ta ride, I'll be goin' out to the cattle, just like the rest of the boys."

A reverent silence hung over the bunkhouse. It was as if each man held his breath, watching the interplay. Roady didn't understand it, or could explain it. Whatever it was, he liked it a lot.

"What about your schooling?"

Hickory chuckled and glanced over at Roady, his lips pursed in consternation. "Girls are always so worried about readin' and such." He reached under his pillow and pulled out a slate, his face glowing with pride. "I'm gettin' caught up with my letters and numbers. Once I am, I'll ride into town with Colton and the rest and go ta school. Maybe by next year."

Wearing an impressed expression, Sally nodded. "I'm glad to hear that. If you find any time on your hands, come find me. I have a book you just might like." When he didn't answer, she went on, "I like your long hair." She turned him with a gentle hand on his small shoulder, taking in the long ponytail. "A man who knows his own mind."

Hickory's chest puffed out. "It's where I get my strength." He lifted an arm and made a muscle that didn't quite appear.

"You know the story of Samson and Delilah?"

A blush crept up into his cheeks, but still he nodded. "I do. A friend of mine told it to me. I liked it."

Her gaze was warm and loving. "I like it too, Hickory. I'm so happy that we're now friends."

The sounds of someone entering the bunkhouse broke the spell.

Roady turned to find Luke in the doorway. Their gazes locked. "I'll be right back, Sally," he said, wondering what he was going to tell Luke. They had few secrets between them, and Roady liked it that way. But seeing as Sally was his wife, he'd not betray her confidence.

"I'll take over the grand tour," Lucky said. "Come right this way, Miss Sally. I'd like to show ya where the real work happens." He stepped the few paces over to the black metal cooking stove and opened the door.

As Roady headed out, Luke turned, and they both exited the bunkhouse in silence. They walked a good distance, where they wouldn't be overheard. Luke stopped and then glanced back at the bunkhouse, as if trying to decide how to begin.

"Ike rode by the house and told us the news. You and Heather's sister up and married today after church." There was no spoken question, but it was there in his eyes, and he waited.

"That's right."

Luke's brows fell. "That's all you're gonna say? That's right? It's not hard to put two and two together."

Heat rushed into Roady's face. "Something wrong with us getting hitched?"

"That's not what I'm saying—and you know it."

Luke's irritated tone irked Roady further. "Then what *are* you saying, Luke? I'm just a dumb cowpoke. You have to spell it out for me."

Luke jammed his fingers through his hair, then looked around. "With what I'm thinking, the time you spent in the hunting cabin together, I guess I just didn't expect you to take advantage of a situation."

Roady silently counted to five. This galled him to high heaven, especially coming from Luke. "Tell me, Luke, what's better—doing the right thing for the wrong reason, or doing the wrong thing for the right reason?"

They stared at each other.

Roady shook his head. "Thought so. In my mind, they're one and the same. So, it'd be best if you quit your soul-searching, do-gooding, and watching out for everyone's best interest, and just trust me and wish me good luck."

Some men had exited the building, and Sally stood watching from the front porch. Roady smiled at her. "I have to go."

"You're right, Roady," Luke said. "Congratulations. Faith and I are very happy for you and Sally."

"Thank you." Roady gave him a sincere glance, hoping he knew what he'd gotten himself into. "I'm sure you are."

Chapter Forty

"Is everything all right?" Sally asked, concerned at the seriousness of Roady's expression as he walked back toward the bunkhouse. She'd met Luke McCutcheon briefly in town with his brothers during the week while she was shopping with Heather. She had remembered seeing them at the telegraph office in Waterloo the day she'd boarded the stage for Y Knot.

If the brothers remembered her, they didn't make it known. They were nice, and she looked forward to meeting their wives. Roady had said he and Luke were very close friends. Now it seemed that he and Roady had come to words.

"Sure, darlin', everything's fine," he said, his smile not quite as cheerful as a moment ago.

The use of the endearment surprised her. She didn't expect Roady to say or do things he didn't feel, regardless that the word had brought a nice tingly feeling and a smile to her lips. It felt good to be someone's darling.

He stepped onto the porch of the bunkhouse and took one of her hands.

Shad Petty came out the door, holding a guitar. He sat on a stool while the other men gathered around and pulled up chairs of their own, or leaned on a rail. He strummed a few chords, looking plenty pleased with himself.

"What are you in the disposition for, boys?" he asked.

Roady frowned and muttered something she couldn't hear. She wanted to help. "Can we walk out to the pasture and see some of the cattle?"

His smile returned. "Sure we can. Right this way."

Seemed Shad's music grew louder as they walked down the road that led to the ranch. If she didn't know better, she'd think he was trying to keep her attention.

"It's a little bit of a walk," Roady said, somewhat distracted. He was probably still thinking about his friend and the words they'd exchanged. She felt certain it had to do with her. "But there're some pretty things to see along the way."

He stopped, bent over, and lifted her hem.

She jumped back. "What?"

He chuckled good-heartedly. "Easy now, I'm just checking your footwear. There's a short hill ahead to climb."

She stuck her foot out for his inspection. "I can climb anything you can," she said, the warm sunshine seeping through her coat and melting away her insecurities. "Just lead the way."

Roady reminded her of her brother Samuel, who considered himself an outdoorsman and loved to hike. Samuel would disappear into the hills as much as the job, or the brothers, allowed. Sally liked to hike, as well.

"The bunkhouse surprised me. It's much nicer than I pictured. Cleaner too. I expected saddles lying around everywhere, bridles, stuff like that."

His smile was back, and for that, she was pleased. "Those are kept in the barn. But I'm glad you like it. Honestly, the good condition of everything was because of you. Lucky has had the men sweeping and cleaning for the last hour. But most times, it's not bad at all."

They were approaching a good-sized trail leading off the dirt road. "Here's where we turn. The lookout isn't much farther. You holding up?"

She laughed. Did he think she couldn't take a walk? "I'm fine, Roady. I enjoy walking." His tall body close to her side was comforting. He was the only one on earth who knew her secret, and there wasn't a doubt in her mind that it was safe with him.

The trail started a gradual incline. After a few minutes of a steady uphill climb, Sally found it difficult to catch her breath.

"You need a break?"

"No, I'm still fine. Are we almost there?"

"We are. Just over that rise."

Roady climbed up first, then reached for her hand and pulled her onto a small plateau. An endless pasture, dotted with cattle, extended as far as the eye could see.

Sally sucked in a breath. "It's beautiful, Roady. I can't believe I'm actually on a real live working cattle ranch. It gives me this really wonderful feeling inside. I like it."

His sudden laughter stirred up a few hidden quail in the scrub. "You better believe it, darlin'. And you're married to a real live cowboy. I hope that suits you."

There it was again—that word. He'd said it so easily, she couldn't tell how he really felt.

"I'm glad we came for this walk, so we can talk." Being alone like this presented the perfect opportunity to discuss a few things that they hadn't been able to before.

He looked at her and his brows rose. He motioned to a nearby log, and they both took a seat.

"What do you want to talk about?"

"Lots of things, really. First of all, how did your talk with Morgan go? I haven't had a chance to ask. He looked rather grumpy in church. And all he said to me was congratulations. I've been wondering all day."

"It went about as good as a talk like that could go. A sudden wedding with someone you barely know usually only means one thing. But I assured him that wasn't the case with us." Roady swiped a hand across his face. "I don't think he believed me, because he let me know exactly what he thought of me. And it wasn't pretty."

"I'm sorry."

Roady had been watching the cattle, but now his head whipped around so fast she almost gasped. "Don't *you* be sorry," he said. "Ain't nothing he won't get over."

"What exactly did you tell him?"

"Just that we were getting hitched, and that we wanted his blessing since you don't have a pa no more. When he tried to fill in what I wasn't saying, I set him straight."

Relief washed through Sally. The most important thing to her was that this child be accepted and loved. She didn't want anyone to know the circumstances of the violent conception that haunted her. And now everyone would believe the baby was Roady's. Her heart swelled. "Thank you so much."

His mouth tilted up, and an amused expression crinkled the corners of his eyes. "For setting Morgan straight?"

She laughed, feeling a portion of her cares melt away. "Yes, for setting Morgan straight. And everything else."

"Once the babe is born, pretty doggone early in most people's minds, they'll all remember back and start counting, friend and family alike. I just don't want—"

"I know that's true," she interrupted. "But I can't worry over something I can't control. I didn't share the truth with

Heather. I wasn't sure if I was going to or not when the time came, and then a feeling so strong assured me that keeping it just between us was best." She looked into his eyes. "No one knows except me and you. They won't have a choice but to accept the baby as yours. Is that okay with you?"

He swallowed, then trained his gaze back on the cattle grazing in the pasture. "It *is* mine...now," he said gruffly. "If I'm going to raise the child, I'll consider the tadpole my son or daughter."

Overcome with relief, and a good measure of joy, Sally couldn't stop herself from taking his hand into her own. She brought it to her lips while closing her eyes. She kissed the back of his fingers and thought how good the warm roughness felt. Her heart swelled painfully, and she knew now if she uttered even one word, she'd burst out in grateful tears. A small strangled sound worked its way up her throat.

"Hey, hey," he whispered. "None of this now. Everything is going to be just fine."

He scooted nearer her on the log and placed his arm around her back. His tone, low and serious, was one she'd never heard before. She tried to control her reaction when he circled her with one arm, wanting to relax. Yet when he gently laid her head on his shoulder with his other hand, she was sure he'd felt her stiffen. As much as she wanted to react differently, she couldn't.

"You want me to stay back from work tomorrow? I'm sure the McCutcheons wouldn't mind if I took one more day off, under the circumstances."

The last thing she wanted to do was disrupt his schedule, or any of the McCutcheons, any more than she already had. Feeling better, she sat up. "No. I'll be fine." She took the hanky from her pocket and dried the few tears that had escaped.

His eyes roamed her face, but he didn't try to help. "What will you do?"

"I don't know yet, but I'll think of something."

"If you'd like to go into town, or to Heather's, I'm sure I could arrange that without much trouble. Francis is usually available for things like that."

Even though her emotions were still on the raw side, she reached over and patted his arm. He seemed to like that, for he looked at her hand and then up into her eyes. "No, please don't bother. I'll probably take a walk in the morning, and perhaps write a little on my novel. Or maybe I'll see if Esperanza will let me help her in the kitchen. I love to cook. Ever since I was a young girl, I find it hard to leave the cooking to others. There are plenty of ways for me to occupy my time."

His smile was back. "You're still a young girl. And a very pretty one, I might add."

She felt her face heat and had to look away, unable to hold his gaze. "Hardly."

"Now don't you start fibbing or I'll not be able to believe you when you tell me how handsome I am."

Sally couldn't stop herself from giggling. The expression her laughter produced on Roady's face made her chuckle all the harder. It felt good, brought up memories of home when she'd had to endure Travis and Samuel or another of her brothers' teasing.

The sun broke through some clouds to warm her face. Hopefulness sprouted and took hold. She understood why Heather loved Montana. From the corner of her eye, Roady just watched and smiled, not seeming eager to do or say anything at all.

She turned to him after she took control of her laughter. "Roady, you've never told me much about your family, and where you're from."

He nodded, but seemed hesitant. Sorrow moved across his eyes. "That's because there's not much to tell." His tone made her think it was a closed subject.

"I'd really like to know, but only if you're willing." She waited, the sounds and smells of the Western scenery healing her a little more. "Roady?"

He finally looked at her. "You're a persistent one, if nothing else."

She shot him her no-nonsense look. "You have no idea."

"Uh-oh," he responded, the smile on his face not quite reaching his eyes. "First off, I don't have many roots, if that's what you're hoping for. No history, no nothing. Any days worth anything have been spent here, with the McCutcheons."

"I see."

"Well, it ain't as bad as all that."

"I'm sorry. I didn't mean to sound so sad. Lots of people don't have family, per se."

His crooked brow said he didn't believe that for a second. "I don't remember my ma, so I guess she died when I was a young'un. My pa was a peddler. We never had a real home that I can remember. I ran away when I was old enough, looking for a better life."

How heartbreaking. Growing up, her family had barely scraped by, but at least they'd had a place to live that was cozy and warm. Most importantly, they'd had each other. "Do you have any siblings?"

"None that I know of."

She didn't like his sad expression. "Well, now you have Morgan and Heather, as well as all my other brothers and sisters." She wanted to cheer him up. "And just think, you'll never have a tussle over the family fortune when the time comes."

It took a moment for her words to sink in, but when they did, he laughed, a deep, rich sound making her happy for her efforts. "Truer words were never spoken."

She patted his arm again and decided to change the subject. "What's your middle name?"

"You sure know how to hurt a man."

"Roady? Tell me."

"Melhoff."

She blinked. She'd never heard that used for a middle name before. It was so out of character for his Western demeanor.

"But that's not common knowledge around these parts," he said, giving her the eye. "Particularly at the ranch, and especially at the bunkhouse."

"I see. Did you ever think that Melhoff might be your mother's maiden name? It sounds like a surname to me, and using a mother's name to keep it in the family is a common practice when naming a child. Perhaps you do have some roots, after all."

She saw his visible gulp, making it evident he had not considered that before. She'd moved him by the possibility of a link to family he knew nothing about. Whatever she could do for him, she was more than happy to oblige. She prayed she was correct, and that perhaps she'd be able to look into it further.

"No, I hadn't. But now that you mention it..."

She stood, very happy over the progress they'd made getting to know each other. She took his hand and pulled him to his feet.

"I guess we're going?"

She nodded. "We've been out here some time. I don't want to fuel everyone's imaginations. Get them talking."

He stretched, then nodded, seeming to take every inch of her in with his eyes. "Them?"

"You know, the ranch hands."

"Darlin', you have enough on your plate without worrying over the cowhands. Leave that mangy pack of jackals to me."

Sally got the distinct impression there were other reasons her new husband didn't want her thinking about the men in the bunkhouse, but she'd never say. It felt nice to be protected, and desired as well. Always involved with her books and studies, she'd never really had a beau before, just Timmy Tinehouse, a skinny neighborhood boy who'd dogged her steps.

She settled into step next to Roady's side, feeling very small with her hand tenderly wrapped inside his warm one. Soon it would be suppertime, and then they'd retire upstairs, *alone*.

Their first night as husband and wife.

She pushed her unsettled thoughts aside. She'd not ruin this perfectly wonderful afternoon with worries that might never transpire. Surely Roady would be a gentleman, even if they had gotten married. Thoughts of Mr. Greenstein made her shiver.

Roady glanced down into her face, seeming perfectly content to walk along in silence. "Cold?"

"Just a little," she fibbed. A strange new frost had gathered inside when she contemplated what getting married really meant in the true sense of the word.

Chapter Forty-One

Roady had noticed something about Sally on their walk out to the lookout point. She liked to touch him, but didn't like it when he touched her. She stiffened up, withdrew. It had been the same when he'd kissed her in the church, and on the ride down from the cabin. She put up with it, but that was all.

Almost back into the ranch yard, they heard several horses coming their way. Mark, Luke, and Matt rode up and stopped before them in the middle of the road. The McCutcheon brothers quickly dismounted and removed their hats.

"Mrs. Guthrie, congratulations on your wedding this morning," Luke offered. He put out his hand to Sally, and when she took it, he pulled her gently into an embrace. "Welcome to the family." His eyes met Roady's.

Roady wasn't holding any grudges, and let that show in his gaze. Anyone would be surprised at his and Sally's actions today.

Sally stepped back, her face bright red. "Thank you, Mr. McCutcheon. I appreciate that. Your whole family has been very gracious to me." She glanced at Roady and smiled. "And to Roady, as well. I hope someday we will be able to repay you."

"No need to repay anyone," Matthew said, taking his turn to hug her. "We think of Roady as another brother. All our wives"—he gestured between them—"are looking forward to getting acquainted."

"That's right," Mark added. "Amy said she's planning to stop by soon with Cinder and say hello. That is, if you have some time."

Sally laughed, and Roady couldn't hold back his smile.

"Time is all I have." She tipped her head. "I look forward to meeting her, as well as your young daughter."

Roady put his hand to Sally's back. "We best be going, fellas. We'll see you later."

The men waited until he and Sally were a few feet away before they mounted up and continued on.

Roady and Sally were almost back to the ranch when he got a prickly feeling on the back of his neck, as if they were being watched. He didn't say anything to Sally, just slowed their pace, and began to clandestinely glance here and there as if he were enjoying the scenery. He'd almost given up when from behind one of the tall ponderosa pines, he saw a flash of blue, the same color of the shirt little Hickory wore. A moment later, the breeze picked up several strands of his long hair, betraying his hiding place. The boy didn't even know he'd been seen.

Relieved it wasn't anything more serious, Roady led her back in front of the house. "What would you like to do now? There's still several hours before suppertime."

"I think I'd like to take a short nap. I didn't sleep much last night."

He tweaked her nose. "I guess not. Actually, I didn't either."

"After that, I'll freshen up and change my dress."

He glanced down, still in awe at what a beautiful wife he'd landed. "I like that dress plenty." As long as she kept blushing like that, he'd keep doling out the compliments.

The ranch house door opened and Mrs. McCutcheon came forward, a warm smile on her face. "There you two are. I've been trying to be patient for your return, but now I'm glad you're here. I know you don't want a large party tonight for supper, but I still want to make it something you'll remember." She looped her arm through Sally's. "Roady, you're just going to have to relinquish her for a little while so we can discuss a menu with Esperanza. I promise not to keep her for too long."

Sally looked completely relaxed with Mrs. McCutcheon, and for that, he was happy. "I was just going into the bunkhouse to work on next month's schedule. You two ladies take all the time you need." Roady sent a warm, thankful nod to Mrs. McCutcheon.

Mrs. McCutcheon sent him back a secretive wink. "What's your favorite, Roady? Chocolate or vanilla?"

His eyes lit up. "Either one feeds my sweet tooth just the same. You sure know how to get a man's attention."

Mrs. McCutcheon hustled Sally away, the older woman's arm around his wife's waist. She called over her shoulder, "That's absolutely correct, Roady Guthrie. This isn't *my* first rodeo."

By seven o'clock in the evening, after a sumptuous meal and then a warm bath, Sally finished her preparations for bed in the large, too-quiet bedroom.

It had only been the four of them for dinner, which suited Sally just fine. Mr. and Mrs. McCutcheon did most of the talking, regaling her and Roady with stories of how they'd met and courted.

Sally couldn't ever remember laughing so much. Esperanza slipped quietly in and out of the romantic candlelit room. The maid brought out lovely china dishes filled with pot roast served in its own juices, along with blackened carrots, beans, onions, and mashed potatoes.

When Sally thought she couldn't eat another bite, the plates had been whisked away and replaced with a beautiful white cake flavored with almond, reminding her of the Italian cake her mother made on Christmas Eve. The evening was perfect.

Whenever she looked up, she found Roady's gaze from across the table, his eyes filled to overflowing with emotion. She hoped she wouldn't let him down when the time came. All through the meal, she'd prepared herself for what was to come. She'd not disappoint him. She owed him. He didn't know how her circumstances came about, and he wasn't going to either. That was one evil she wouldn't share—ever.

A soft knock sounded on her closed bedroom door, and Sally pulled her robe protectively around her. "Yes?"

"It's me," Roady said in a low voice. "Mind if I come in?"

She gulped and looked at the bed. She wasn't ready for that; no sir, not at all. "Please do," she found herself saying, slipping into the only chair, a plush-looking wingback in the corner of the room.

The door opened slowly. Roady stepped in and quickly closed it behind him, leaning back. He looked a little nervous himself. Still dressed in the same pants he'd had on earlier, he'd unbuttoned his shirt to his undershirt, which hugged his muscled chest. His socks, darned in several places, made her think of the cabin, when he'd made her put on his extras to keep her feet warm. He looked as if he'd just washed up, because the skin of his face glistened in the lamplight, and his hair waved softly on his head.

His gaze slipped around the room, then landed on the bed. "I'll be right back."

Within a second, she heard a bump, and then he appeared back in the hall, the chair from his room gripped awkwardly in his arms. He grunted and inched forward. Sally jumped up and ran to assist.

He motioned with his head. "You stay back. I've got this."

It took some doing to get the chunky furniture through the door by himself. With a thump, he set it next to hers, and sucked in a deep breath. "Almost as bad as a wrangly steer that's decided it ain't gonna be branded."

Throwing her a casual smile, he made himself comfortable in the chair, and laced his fingers together. He placed them in his lap. "How was the bath?"

Sally snuggled deeper into her chair. "It was lovely, thank you."

"Good," he finally replied when she looked into his eyes. The word was drawn out, as if he was searching for his next sentence. He was nervous, considering the flutter of his heartbeat at the base of his throat.

She fingered the tie of her robe. "Have the McCutcheons turned in?"

"Don't know. I haven't seen hide nor hair since they left after supper for a buggy ride."

His eyes were fascinating, warm with a hint of humor deep inside. "What did you do while I was bathing?"

His brow arched as if he thought her question intriguing. "I went to see what the boys were eating in the bunkhouse."

Of course, he would. He probably missed his friends. "What was it?"

"Sunday night is usually either chicken and dumplings or a pork roast."

Sally relaxed into the chair, thinking his eyes could charm a horse right out of its harness. "Pork roast on a cattle ranch?"

"Sure. Lucky likes to mix things up, so we won't complain. He's real good about that. Tonight was pork with all the fixings." He cleared his throat. "Flood and I got a chance to talk before he and the missus headed out." His gaze sought hers, once again bringing heat to her face. "He's offered us a nice piece of land for next to nothing. It has an old cabin that we could live in until next year when we built something a mite larger. Don't know how you'd feel about that. I'd be close enough to continue working here at the ranch."

A home. She sat forward in excitement. A real home to call her own. "How nice of him. What do you think?"

"We'd be crazy to turn down such a generous offer." He leaned toward her as well, eagerness lighting his eyes. "I know the place. It has a pretty little spot to build. Used to have a barn and corral, but those have fallen down. The place is pretty darn rustic, though. Not much more than the hunting cabin."

"Just think, we'll be able to invite Heather and Hayden, as well as Morgan and June over for supper!" Her voice climbed several octaves, and she gripped the sides of the chair to keep from jumping up and down. She never expected to have a place to call her own. She owed Roady so much. He'd taken her uncertain future and turned it into something wonderful.

Suddenly her smile faded. "Do we have the means to build a house? I'd think that would be very expensive."

She almost expected the chuckle before he let one out. "Living in the bunkhouse all these years has allowed me to save most of my pay. I have the means, so don't you worry about a thing." He stood.

She stood too, disappointment rippling through her. "Are you leaving?" They had plans to make.

"I am. It's been a long day for both of us." He smiled and pointed to her midsection. "All three of us." He shrugged, a pleased expression on his face. "Anyway, I'm about as tuckered as a jack three steps in front of a wolf. If you don't mind, I'll sleep across the hall where I can stretch out."

They remained standing in silence so long she grew uncomfortable. Was he was waiting for something? Maybe an invitation to stay?

He rubbed the back of his neck and glanced around the room. Finally he said, "Good night, Sally. Sleep tight." He reached for the doorknob.

"Good night, Roady," she said, gazing into his soft, inviting eyes. What was he thinking when he looked at her like that? "Thank you again for everything."

The light in his eyes dimmed, but only for a second, and then he was gone.

Chapter Forty-Two

Early the next morning, feeling like he'd been rode hard and put away wet, Roady declined Mrs. McCutcheon's offer of coffee and breakfast. Since he hadn't seen Sally, and didn't even know if she was awake, he'd rather eat with the men in the bunkhouse.

Halfway across the yard, he met Brandon and Charity riding in. He hoped he didn't look as disconcerted as he felt. Spending his wedding night alone, across the hall from his wife, was something he could get over. He'd give Sally time to get acquainted. Time to grow some affection for him. That was, if she ever got over the other man she'd made a baby with. The way she kept thanking Roady for marrying her, as if he'd just escorted her across a busy street, was the worst of all. She thought of him as a friend, but he wanted her love.

"Congratulations, Roady!" Charity called, her face all smiles. She and Brandon dismounted.

He nodded at her. "Morning, Charity. Brandon."

"We heard the wonderful news!" Charity gave him a full-on hug. "Is Sally awake? I'd like to say hello to the new Mrs. Guthrie. Get to know her. Not many women, in my way of thinking, are good enough for our Roady Guthrie."

She meant it to be nice, but her words only made him feel worse, and he glanced away. Ranch hands milled around the bunkhouse porch, coffee cups in hand. Francis hurried out the door toward the barn.

"It's barely five thirty," he said as he turned his attention back to them, hoping Charity didn't go looking for Sally and find both beds disturbed. That was nobody's business but theirs. He'd done his best to put the covers back all nice and proper, but after the night he'd had staring at the ceiling and worrying over their future, he wasn't in the mood for housekeeping. "When I left the room, she was still fast asleep." *My room, anyway.* "But your mother is in there having coffee."

"Thanks." She glanced at Brandon. "I'll see you later."

"Trouble?" Roady asked after Charity had disappeared inside. "It's awfully early for a social call."

"No. I have a few things to pass by Luke, and thought I'd get a jump on my day. When Charity heard where I was headed, she decided to tag along and visit her mother—even if it is the crack of dawn."

Roady nodded, all too eager to get away from everything. His horse and miles and miles of open range sounded like what he needed now more than anything. "Then I'll be going in for some grub."

As he stepped into the bunkhouse, the familiar aroma of breakfast wrapped around Roady like a familiar blanket. This was where he belonged. The men who weren't out with the cattle, or asleep having just gotten off night watch at three, looked up at him from the table. Without saying as much as hello, Roady pulled out his normal chair and sat.

Silence all but engulfed him.

"Trouble in paradise?" Shad stuffed a whole strip of bacon into his mouth. His look innocent, he chewed thoughtfully, then glanced at Smokey, Ike, and Pedro, all seated at the table. Hickory was there, as well.

"Monday's a work day the last time I checked," Roady replied, keeping his tone neutral.

Lucky limped over from the stove and poured coffee into his cup.

When no one else jumped on the let's-tease-Roady-about-his-fake-marriage bandwagon, Shad chuckled and forked in some flapjacks.

Ike wiped his mouth and chin with his napkin. "Got word yesterday that a big ol' grizzly was spotted out back of the foothills."

Roady's head snapped up. He'd been buttering the plateful of flapjacks Lucky had just set in front of him. "Behemoth?"

"Don't know."

A hot jab of guilt pricked his gut, just like it always did when he thought of the poor soul he could have saved if he'd have reacted sooner. "Where?"

"'Bout twenty miles beyond Pine Grove. He ambled in and tore up a homestead pretty good. No one was hurt."

"Stock?"

Ike shook his head.

Hickory, finished with his breakfast, hopped out of his chair and took his plate over to Lucky. The cook scraped some nonexistent crumbs from the blue-and-white dish into the slop pail, and then placed it into the wash bucket of hot water. "You be sure ta make your bed before you step a foot out that door."

The boy nodded. He went to his bunk, flipped his blanket over his pillow, and then stopped at Roady's chair on his way out.

Roady glanced at the boy over his coffee rim. "Need something?"

"Francis told me Punk used ta be your horse."

Roady set his cup in his saucer. "That's right." *He's been retired for more years than I can remember.*

"Well, he's *mine* now. And I get ta keep him in the barn. Just thought I'd tell ya, in case ya saw me ridin' him and wondered."

The boy's puffed-out chest was impossible to miss. His eyes reminded Roady of two bright stars. "I appreciate that. I'll stop in and take a look at him when I have a moment."

Hickory nodded. "Not this mornin', though. I'm ridin' into town with Francis. Ta pick up some supplies and such. Second time this week."

"Won't you need the wagon for that?"

"Yeah, but I'm ridin' Punk alongside."

Roady wished he felt the boy's enthusiasm. "I'm sure he'll like getting out."

Hickory nodded again and hurried out the door.

Roady stared at the empty doorway and his shoulders slumped. *If all of life could just be that easy.*

A deep sadness gripped Amy. She'd waited for days for Cade to come back out to the ranch and meet Mark. When Brandon mentioned that he'd seen him in town, she'd been relieved he hadn't moved on, and expected him to return. But he hadn't. The days passed, and still no Cade.

I need to go into Y Knot myself and find him. He probably feels uneasy after our words the night he arrived.

"Something on your mind, sweetheart?" Mark said, coming down the stairs as he worked the few remaining buttons on his vest. Finished, he went to the stove and poured himself a cup of coffee, then took a seat at the table. "Looks like you lost your best friend."

After his return from Waterloo, Amy had told Mark exactly what had happened and how she'd thought the worst of her brother when he'd appeared on their doorstep. How guilty she felt for her suspicions. That he might be wanted by the law. She didn't want any secrets between her and Mark. Their marriage had had a rocky start, and she wasn't willing to let anything or anyone mess that up ever again.

"I'm just thinking about Cade." She used a spatula to put Mark's eggs onto his plate. "And why he hasn't come back out to the ranch to meet you. I'd like to speak with him, find out more about our younger brother, Alister. Make Cade feel more welcome than I did the first time he was here."

"You'll get that chance. I heard he's taken a few odd jobs around town, as well as working off room and board at Lou and Drit's. I'm sure he's just trying to keep busy. To make you proud."

Amy set a plate of food in front of Mark, then placed her hand on his shoulders while he salted his eggs. "That's wonderful. If you see him or Brandon, please relay the message I'm waiting on another visit. And if he doesn't come back soon, I'll be forced to go into town myself and search him out."

Mark chuckled. "I'll do just that. I'm anxious to finally meet this long-lost brother-in-law of mine."

Hearing Cinder calling from her room, Amy pulled back. Mark was right. Cade was just trying to get his life in order. Maybe put down some roots here, where they could actually have a relationship again. Hope pushed away the uncertainties that kept sabotaging her good thoughts and intentions.

She would only think the best of him. Her brother hadn't done a thing to prove otherwise.

Chapter Forty-Three

Three thirty in the afternoon came and went. Sally closed her copy of *Pride and Prejudice* and glanced out the living room window for the tenth time, wondering what was taking Roady so long to get in from his shift. Embarrassed she knew so little about her new husband, she'd been forced to set up watch by the window, hoping to see him return. This morning she'd heard him stirring, but nerves had kept her from crossing the hall to say good morning. Now that a whole day had passed, she realized how much she missed being with him.

Flood stepped through the door and hung his Stetson on a peg. When Sally stood, he looked over, surprise on his face.

"Good afternoon, Mrs. Guthrie. I didn't see you there." His warm smile put her at ease. "I see you're having a little quiet time to yourself."

The politeness of these Western men was refreshing. "Hello, Mr. McCutcheon." She tried for an air of poised sophistication but feared she looked exactly as she felt—hesitant and sad. "I've been watching for Roady. Can you tell me when he usually gets done with work?"

Understanding crossed his face. He thought her a lovesick new wife, when in reality she'd been heartsick all day after her long first night as Roady's wife.

"If he's out with the herd, he usually rides in around three. Then he spends some time in the bunkhouse going over the boys' schedule." He glanced at the clock on the wall. "I'm surprised he's not back yet."

She glanced outside. "Thank you. I'll work on my virtue of patience. Heather says it could use some shining up."

Mixed up more now than ever, she sort of wished Mr. McCutcheon would leave. Then she could let down her pretense, maybe take a walk outside and meet Roady at the barn.

Mr. McCutcheon came farther into the room. "Actually, Mrs. Guthrie, I'm glad we have this chance to speak candidly." His shirt showed signs of hard work, and there was a smudge of dirt on his temple. "I'm sure you've heard how long Roady's been with us here on the ranch, and how valuable he is to our operation. I can tell you, every word of praise you've heard is true."

His sincerity touched her.

"He's a good rancher," Mr. McCutcheon went on, "and knows the animals through and through. But I'm not sure you quite know how we feel about him as a person, as a part of our family. Claire and I consider him our fifth son, actually sixth, now that Brandon and Charity have married. He's very dear to us. Now to you, that might sound a mite strange to say about an employee—but it's not at all. As you get to know him better, you'll come to understand fully for yourself." A smile finally broke out on the older man's face. "We couldn't be more pleased that he's found a wife of his own. A very lovely one at that."

Sally didn't know how to respond. She barely knew Roady. From their time at the cabin together and his kind ways, she could understand exactly what Mr. McCutcheon was saying.

Still, a shiver of dread crept up her back. How would the McCutcheons feel if they knew Roady had married her to help her out of a difficult situation? She swallowed. That for all practical purposes, they had a marriage in name only, and he accepted a baby fathered by another man?

"Thank you for sharing that with me, Mr. McCutcheon."

"And just so you know—I, for one, do know that love at first sight is real. The second Claire opened the door to me during a whiteout with gale-force winds and I looked into her eyes, I knew at that very moment she was the woman for me. That I'd spend the rest of my life with her. The short time you and Roady have known each other doesn't bother me one little bit."

He shrugged, then turned and headed for the stairs.

Feeling sick inside, Sally returned to the window. Francis, the young cowhand, was on his way toward the house. When he knocked, Mr. McCutcheon halted on the staircase and turned around. "Come in," he called.

By the time Francis stepped in, Mr. McCutcheon had returned to the entry. Francis removed his hat.

"Around two this afternoon, Roady set out for a bear that was spotted in the foothills after Shad relieved him. Lucky wanted me to let Mrs. Guthrie know so she wouldn't fret when he didn't show up."

Flood made a sound deep in his throat. "Him and that bear!"

Sally stiffened. Hadn't he just come back from a couple of weeks of bear hunting? Why would he go out again? She searched each man's face, looking for clues.

Mr. McCutcheon looked at her, then back at the messenger. "Thanks for letting us know, Francis."

With a nod, Francis left, and Mr. McCutcheon started back for the stairs. "No need to worry, Sally," he offered from halfway up. "He'll be back soon."

As Roady's boss turned the hall corner, she rushed for the ranch house door. She pulled it open, lifted her skirt so she wouldn't trip, and dashed out to catch up with Francis before he disappeared into the bunkhouse.

"Francis, wait!"

He turned, blinking several times in surprise.

Sally gathered herself and took a deep breath. "It sounded like this was something Roady did often. Can you tell me why?" she asked, but it was as clear as the nose on his face he didn't want to. "Please. I want to understand."

"Him and that bear, if it's the same one he's been after, go way back. He hunts for him every year, vowing to kill him."

"That bear?"

Francis nodded, then took a fleeting glance at the bunkhouse, as if he could wish himself inside away from questioning females. "Behemoth. A grizzly with a history around Y Knot and farther on too. Kills stock, ruins things. He's big. It's going to take a lot of bullets to bring him down."

More than just a shiver streaked up her back. She swallowed. "Why would that be something special to Roady? There is more to this story that you aren't saying."

"Yes, ma'am. A long time ago, when Roady was out riding herd, he heard a few gunshots. Thinkin' someone was huntin', he didn't give it much nevermind. When the rifle reports came again, he did ride out, but it was too late. Some poor soul had been mauled to death by Behemoth. Roady tried to save him, but there was no stoppin' that grizzly once he tasted blood."

Francis stopped and looked off, as if the thought of that beast was just too much. "By the end, there weren't much left of the fellow 'cept his rifle. I guess Roady feels responsible. He took it really hard, still does. No one could ever figure out who the man was, but Roady kept the Winchester and vowed to someday settle the score."

This was much more than Sally had expected. When Roady had spoken about it in the mountains, he'd made it sound so matter-of-fact, not something personal. A wave of dizziness threatened to topple her.

"Darn it all. I've done gone and run my mouth. Don't worry, Mrs. Guthrie. Roady's no fool. He ain't gonna get himself killed now that he has a wife here waitin' on him." The shake of his head added to his conviction. "No, sir, he ain't. He'll come ridin' in sometime after midnight, if I had to guess."

A white-hot fist of fear took hold of her heart and twisted. Had her new husband gone in search of that horrible beast again because he'd felt bad about their wedding night? When they'd said good night, she'd seen an unreadable expression cross his eyes, something she couldn't put her finger on. Was it sadness? Regret? After all he'd done and given up for her and her baby, she hadn't even invited him to stay with her on their wedding night.

Shame gripped her. If he was hurt, she'd never forgive herself. If she could just have one more chance. Sally glanced up the empty trail, heartsick. Would she ever see him again?

Chapter Forty-Four

Roady rode into the ranch yard a little after one in the morning, the full moon lighting his way. While the big house was dark, the lantern on the bunkhouse porch put out a soft golden glow.

He dismounted, led Fiddlin' Dee into the barn, unsaddled her in the dark, then took some time to rub her down. He'd come upon bear scat and some tracks, a large grizzly with a mangled front paw, his first sign of the bear in three years. It had to be Behemoth. But other than that—nothing.

Once he had his mare stabled, he stepped out of the barn into the moonlight and stopped, unsettled emotions rolling around inside him. He was dirty and needed to wash.

At the outside washstand on the far side of the bunkhouse, he stripped to his waist and doused himself liberally, and quickly, with ice-cold water from the pump. He lathered, rinsed, and toweled off, putting his shirt back on as fast as possible.

With jittery insides, he slipped inside the house making little noise, and made his way up the staircase. He stopped in the hallway. Sally would be asleep. The whole house was dead quiet.

Turning the handle to Mark's room, he went inside, too exhausted to worry about anything for a moment longer. The soft pillow and clean sheets flitted through his mind. He stripped off his pants and shirt and climbed under the covers in his unmentionables. Taking a deep breath into his lungs, he tried to ignore the gnawing of his hungry belly.

A small sound by the door caught his ear, then a light tap. "Roady, can I come in?"

Sally?

Shocked, Roady bolted up to a sitting position, and stared across the dark room as if it were Behemoth himself come to call.

Another small tap. When the squeak of the doorknob said she was indeed coming in, he grasped the still-cool sheet and pulled it up over his chest. From the moonlight softly flowing in through the bedroom window, he could see her hesitantly standing by the door, waiting for an invitation.

"I was worried," she finally said in a small voice. She inched forward a step or two.

"Sorry about that. If I don't act quickly when there's a sighting, any leads go cold quick."

"Behemoth?"

It was evident someone had filled her in on his history with the grizzly. Sally was dressed in her nightclothes, with the same wrap she'd had on last night, tightly cinched at her waist. Along with that, she had a quilt wrapped around her shoulders to keep her warm. Her hair, released from any constraint, looked soft.

"May I come in?" she said on a breathy whisper.

"'Course." He'd get up, but in his state of undress, that wasn't possible. He glanced at the chair in the corner, but instead she went around to the other side of the bed and patted it with her hand.

"Do you mind if I sit here, so we can talk without waking everyone else up too?"

He was no prude, but a moment of uncertainty crossed his mind. He hadn't mentally prepared himself for this moment, if indeed the moment he'd been hoping for had arrived. "Need help climbing up? This bed's a mite taller than the one in your room."

She shook her head, sending her mass of hair moving this way and that, then scrambled up. He waited patiently as she settled, wondering what had prompted this change from last night.

"Comfy?"

She nodded.

"Would you like me to light a lamp?"

"I don't need one if you don't."

He felt a small smile play around his lips as she gazed innocently at him from her side of the bed. "Well, this is nice," he said, a bit embarrassed with the statement that had slipped out unintended. He wriggled into the pillow behind his back on the headboard, and loosened his grip on the sheet just a tiny bit.

She nodded. "Yes, yes it is."

Now that she was here, it seemed she didn't know what to do. Problem was, he didn't know her intentions, so he was in no way going to jump in and get his hands slapped. Time was on his side. It seemed his day away had done the trick.

"Did you get any supper?"

"Out on the trail?" He chuckled quietly. "No, I didn't. My gut thinks my throat's been cut."

She grimaced.

"Sorry. Just a saying the cowboys have."

Her gaze darted to the door. "If you'd like, Roady, I can go get you something from the kitchen. I'm sure there are leftovers from tonight."

No way was he letting her out of his sight. This was worth five days on the trail with no grub. "Oh no. I'm fine till morning." He relaxed his hand and let it fall between them on the quilt. "Are you intending to stay here all night? 'Cause if you are, I'd bet you'd be a sight more comfortable if you got under these covers where it's nice and warm. I'll be sure to stay on my side."

He hoped he wasn't pushing too hard. He'd be disappointed as all get-out if she decided to go back to her own room now. Several silent moments crept by.

"Okay, I think I will."

He didn't try to help, just let her snuggle down in on the other side of the bed.

"That's better," he said, cupping his hands around his mouth as if to be heard from so far away.

She smiled.

"Was there something specific you wanted to talk about?" He let his eyelids droop and wiped a hand across his face, feeling anything but sleepy. "I'm so bushed, I can hardly keep my eyes open."

He heard her sigh, her head on the pillow now the only thing he could see. She was so small, she hardly made a lump in the bedcovers.

"This bed is much more comfortable than mine," she said very softly.

He scrunched down into the covers himself, staying on his back. "I'm happy to share. And if you have a mind, my chest makes a good pillow too."

She didn't respond. Maybe he'd gone too far. He turned to see her eyes closed and her body relaxed in the throes of a deep sleep.

By golly, his new wife had gumption. More than he had, to be sure. He'd been nursing his sore feelings tonight, wondering what this marriage held in store for him. Gazing up at the beams over his head, he marveled at what a difference twenty-four hours could make.

Chapter Forty-Five

Sally awakened slowly to the delicious aroma of bacon. She stretched and reached out her hand, then froze, suddenly remembering whose bed she was in. Her face flamed as she recalled her oh-so-bold actions from last night. Had she really gone to Roady's room uninvited and crawled into his bed? And slept with him the entire night? Unable to keep a smile from her face, she peeked open one eye and looked across to her husband's side of the bed, hoping beyond hope he was still there.

Disappointment enveloped her. Roady had already gone to work. He was an early riser, as were all of the folks at the McCutcheon ranch.

Scrambling out of the bed, she tiptoed to the door and pressed her ear against the chilly wood. For some reason, she felt embarrassed about being caught in Roady's room—not that anyone but her knew that it belonged to Roady, but still. Hearing only silence, she cracked open the door. Seeing the coast was clear, she dashed across the hall.

Once in her own room, she dressed quickly. She wanted to speak with him before he rode out for the day. She needed to see his smile, hear the warmth of his voice. Layering on her garments had never seemed so arduous. Relieved to find the rooms below deserted, she crossed to the front door, pulled it open, and stepped out into the chilliness of the early morning mountain air.

A few men saddling up outside the bunkhouse glanced her way. She didn't see her husband among them. She casually strolled toward the barn. As she approached, a cat darted out from the dark interior and skidded to a stop in front of her. It meowed and rubbed against her leg. That was when she heard a voice coming from within the structure.

"His coat sure looks good, Hickory. I can see you've been brushing him plenty. Good for you."

She'd recognize Roady's easygoing tone anywhere. A little thrill of excitement fluttered in her tummy, and she fisted her trembling hands. Stepping through the doorway, she stopped and let her eyes adjust to the dim light.

Halfway up a stall door, Hickory hung by his elbows as he gazed at a shaggy brown horse inside. Roady stood next to the boy, a piece of hay dangling out of the corner of his mouth. Both turned at the same time.

Roady snagged her gaze and held it. "Good morning, Mrs. Guthrie." He came forward with extended hands, palms up. He'd shaved away the whiskers from last night and looked rested, his eyes soft and warm. She had no option but to place her palms in the center of his.

"Good morning," she replied, trying to sound composed when in actuality, her heart thumped painfully in her chest. Reflex almost made her pull her hands away when they touched his, but she resisted the impulse. An unfamiliar tingle sparked up her arms. She gathered her wits and asked, "How did you sleep?"

"About as good as a man possibly can—after his wife sneaks into his room to cuddle up." He said the second half of the sentence very softly, with his back to the boy. He chuckled when the black cat leaped to the top of the rail next to him and meowed loudly in his face.

Hickory let go with one arm and swung around to watch them as he dangled from the side of the stall door, one toe stuck in a lower crack.

Sally's hands warmed, still held protectively in his. "I wanted to catch you before you rode off."

"I'm glad."

Her cheeks warmed. "Are you going bear hunting again today when you're through with work?"

He nonchalantly let go of her hands, but kept hold of her gaze. "I don't think I will. I'd rather take the buggy and show you the place Flood has offered us. See if it suits you. After that, I thought we'd go into town for a quiet supper out."

Hickory's face lit up. "Can I go too?"

Sally felt a void in her heart when Roady turned to the boy.

"That's for Luke to say, not me," Roady said. "I'm sure you'll have chores that'll need tending."

Grumbling, Hickory climbed over the gate into the stall with the horse.

Sally reached out and scratched the patiently waiting cat. "I'd love to see the property, but I'm sure anything that suits you will suit me just fine." She was all too aware of his proximity. "Do you think we might be able to visit Heather as well?"

"That was my intention, but now you spoiled the surprise. Also wondered if you'd like to send a telegram to your mother in St. Louis. Tell her about the wedding."

Sally had given that idea a great deal of thought. "I think a letter would be better. If a telegram arrives saying I've married, she'll be shocked. I wouldn't have the opportunity to explain things properly. I'll write a letter today."

She'd almost forgotten about the boy in the stall until she heard him murmuring to the horse.

Roady reached in and gave the old gelding a pat on the neck. "I'd best get going." His gaze touched her lips briefly, but he didn't make a move to kiss her.

"Of course." She glanced into the stall to see the boy's thin arms around the horse's neck as the animal munched on a mouthful of hay. "See you later, Hickory."

The boy looked up and nodded. Sally preceded Roady to the barn door, where her new husband nodded and gave her a wink.

Watching him walk away was like a cloud covering the sun. She missed his warmth already.

The day couldn't pass quickly enough for Roady. He went about his duties as usual, while his mind was back in the house with his wife.

His wife. His wife who had been bold enough to come into his room last night and climb into his bed. He'd had to keep the shock off his face when he finally realized her intention. He'd lain awake most the night listening to her sleep, thinking about building the house and the baby to come. Anything to distract him from the fact that she was only an arm's reach away.

Was it possible she wasn't hurting as bad as he'd thought she was over losing the man she loved? It was all so confusing. One moment she was warm and receptive, and the next, it was as if she wanted to pull away. Like this morning in the barn. He hadn't missed her knee-jerk reaction to his touch.

Mystified, Roady pulled his handkerchief from his pocket, wiped his brow, and then slipped the wire snips into his back pocket. She was like a skittish filly, unsure and wary. He'd go as slow as she needed, and hope someday she would give him a chance to fill the other man's boots.

Ike and Smokey stopped what they were doing and reached for their canteens.

"You heading in?" Smokey asked.

Roady nodded. "Thought I would. Only a short strip of fence yet to mend. Nothing you two can't handle on your own. Unless you need my help." He glanced at the others, praying they'd say no. If he hurried, he'd have time to bathe before taking Sally to town.

"Don't think a thing of it," Ike said, screwing the cap on and hanging the canteen back on the fence post. "I'd be anxious too if I had a pretty little wife waitin' for me. Isn't that right, Smokey?"

Smokey grunted, then spit a long string of tobacco juice to the ground. He wiped his mouth with the back of his sleeve. "You bet your new Christmas unmentionables I would. I'd been gone an hour ago."

Roady laughed and headed for his horse. "In that case, consider me gone."

An hour later, Roady drew the buggy to a halt at the fork in the road. "That's the road to Y Knot. And all that," he said with a gesture, "would be the new building site and ranch yard for the barn and some corrals." He moved his arm from left to right as he spoke, giving Sally a nice view of his strong profile. She liked it when he went without his hat.

He swiveled to the side and pointed to the small one-room cabin that had captured Sally's attention since it came into view. There were several old corrals barely standing, but not much else. "There's where we would live until we build, or add on. Would you like to get out and take a look around?"

Excitement zipped through her. "Yes!"

He set the brake, hopped out, and then extended his hand to help her to the ground from his side. He grabbed the hammer on the floorboard of the buggy he'd brought along. "Being a woman, I'm sure you'd like to go see the cabin first."

She nodded, barely able to contain her eagerness.

They walked along in silence. Sally admired the view. Pines and oaks dotted the gently rolling land suitable for pasture. Not far away was a good-sized river. She liked it—no, she *loved* it! This was the start of her new future. A feeling of awe almost moved her to tears.

"The land is beautiful, Roady," she said, taking it all in. "I can envision so much. It feels promising, and gives me a contented feeling. All the good things that make life worth living."

He nodded. "I know what you mean."

She smiled up into his face. "The location is much closer to the ranch than I anticipated."

"That's one of the things I like the most. Just like the other wives, you're only a short ride away."

Wife. That was still so hard for her to believe. The thought of consummating the vows brought her a surge of warmth, but the delicious tingle was chased away by the pain she remembered from the attack. She swallowed. "And it's on the way to town."

"It couldn't get much better." With the claw end of the hammer, he pried off the rough-hewn board nailed over the cabin's weathered door. "Let me go in first, make sure there's no critter waiting to scare you." He pushed open the door and went in.

She bounced up and down on her toes. "Hurry, Roady, I can't wait!"

He appeared back at the door, an expectant look in his eyes.

"What?"

Without saying a thing, he bent and scooped her up, carrying her across the threshold. Setting her on her feet before she had time to object, he gave her a stern look. "Like I said, not much more than the hunting cabin. You sure you'd like living out here—alone? It ain't St. Louis, you know."

His gaze felt like a caress. "I'll like it just fine." She glanced around, taking in a potbellied stove, a sink with a pump, three windows, and a loft. She'd seen an outhouse behind as they'd approached.

He chuckled. "It certainly ain't like the McCutcheons' house. Until the baby arrives, it might get awfully lonely when I'm gone."

"I'll take up knitting."

Roady went back out on the small porch and she followed, looking up to see what had caught his attention. His stormy, green-eyed gaze didn't miss a thing, and right now he'd spotted a hawk way off in the sky.

"It won't be easy at first," he added. "That's east, where the sun rises, so that way is—"

"West?"

He laughed, and she warmed again as he seemed to take her measure. "Forgot you were a smarty-pants. Let's get going, I'm starved."

When they turned, she stopped him with a touch to his forearm. "Mr. McCutcheon isn't giving us the land, is he?"

"Nope, he's not. He wanted to, but I insisted on paying it off over time. Like I mentioned before, he's making the deal impossible to say no. And I'm no fool to pass up a chance to own a piece of this fine acreage. Why?"

"I don't know. I just wondered about..." She gazed down at her hands, feeling rather silly.

"Being beholden? I don't blame you, I don't want that neither. But even if we did take the land as a gift—which we're not—I wouldn't feel beholden. You need to get used to being a part of this family. Taking care of each other is how we do things."

Overwhelmed, Sally looked away and started back to the buggy. How wrong she'd been about Roady. She'd thought she was settling for someone who could help her out of a jam, when in all reality, she wasn't good enough for him. He was strong, good, and honest. He'd done so much and hadn't asked for anything in return. She could tell he was holding back from her, being polite. He'd never professed any love to her by any means, although he was very kind and supportive.

Could he grow to love her? How would he feel once the baby arrived? A shiver raced through her as she considered her still-uncertain future. Sally resolutely clung to her faith, which had only failed her once. Even so, God would look out for her—she hoped.

Chapter Forty-Six

It was almost six o'clock by the time Roady steered the buggy around the corner into Y Knot. Merchants puttered here and there, swept boardwalks, and began pulling down window blinds. Pride for having such a beautiful wife filled him as Sally sat at his side, absorbed in the sights.

"Not quite St. Louis," he said, his deep curiosity about what she thought of the town getting the better of him. He wanted her to like it more than he dared admit. "I'd fancy it's a mite boring for a big-city news reporter like yourself."

Sally shot him a surprised look. "No, not at all. I love how quaint everything appears. And I told you before, I'm *not* a news reporter. I just did special-interest articles now and then."

He shrugged and hid his smile.

"Roady, since you mentioned being hungry, I'm not opposed to eating first, and then heading to the lumberyard for a visit with Heather and Hayden. They don't know we're coming, and they might already have supper on the table. It would be impolite to intrude."

The buggy hit a hole, jostling their knees together. "That sounds good to me. I worked up a hefty appetite today repairing the fence line, one that's been eating away at my belt buckle since noon. But only if you're sure you don't mind—because I can wait." He glanced at her hopefully, praying she didn't change her mind. He wasn't joking about the pain in his empty belly.

"Not at all. Truth be known, I'm hungry myself."

"Then we'll stop right here at the Biscuit Barrel."

Roady parked the conveyance and helped Sally down. Just as he pulled open the door to the café, he heard someone call his name. He turned to see Mr. Lichtenstein, owner of the mercantile, hurrying his way. The German's round face glowed red. He still wore his white work apron and had a pencil stuck behind his ear.

Roady glanced at Sally and shrugged.

"Mr. and Mrs. Guthrie," Mr. Lichtenstein said, pushing his glasses up the bridge of his straight nose once he was before them. "I'm glad you've come to town. Saves me a trip out to the ranch—or sheriff's office."

"Sheriff's office?" Roady asked. "What's this about?"

The shopkeeper's face didn't give anything away. "Yes, the sheriff's office. I don't choose to get others in trouble vith the law if it can be helped."

Roady turned to Sally. "Would you like to wait for me inside where it's warmer?"

She shook her head. Her eyes were dark with worry, her skin as perfect as a pearl. How easy it was when they were like this—playing husband and wife—to forget she was pining for another man, one whose connection would never go away because of the child she carried.

"Go on," he said. "You've piqued our curiosity, Mr. Lichtenstein."

Shaking with indignation, the merchant handed over a piece of paper. "A list of merchants who have suffered a loss of some kind in the past veek. Problems started when Luke McCutcheon brought that miscreant home with him from Vaterloo."

Sally warmed his back as she glanced over his shoulder at the list. Mr. Herrick, owner of the leather shop, was missing a hole punch. Mr. Lichtenstein, a pocketknife and grain scoop. Berta May, three skeins of embroidery thread and a spool of expensive lace. A small keepsake clock from the Hitching Post Saloon that had sat on the back shelf for the past fifteen years. A dictionary belonging to Mr. Tracy, the telegraph operator, and a whole chokecherry pie, straight out of the oven at the Biscuit Barrel.

Roady straightened. "Proves right here that Hickory ain't the culprit, Mr. Lichtenstein. It says a clock from the saloon."

Mr. Lichtenstein harrumphed triumphantly. "Francis frequents the saloon every time he's in town—sometimes the boy goes in vith him. Other times, Hickory is left unattended. He's been seen at each and every one of these establishments. Luke McCutcheon is responsible for him. The businessmen of Y Knot are villing to look the other vay if the boy returns the things he's taken, after vich, he's stays *out* of Y Knot."

Folding the paper, Roady slipped it into his front pocket. Things didn't look good for Hickory. "I'll be sure to give this to Luke, Mr. Lichtenstein."

"Poor Hickory," Sally said before lifting a fork of pot roast to her mouth. She chewed and swallowed. "He's so young. What'll happen to him after you give the note to Luke?"

Roady used his napkin, glancing at the few other diners in the toasty-warm café. "That's hard to say. The McCutcheons follow the line of the law directly. So does Brandon Crawford, sheriff of Y Knot. You met Brandon yet?"

She nodded, enjoying the easy way of conversing she and Roady had developed. She watched how his fingers flexed on the stem of his fork, causing a warm goodness to spread through her chest. "I have. The week I spent with Heather at the Klinkners was one of many, many introductions." She laughed, remembering her panic over the coming baby, and marveled now at how relaxed she felt having supper across from her new husband in this cute café. "We had little else to do but come into town, where Heather showed me around."

"More like showed you off."

Her gaze flew to his as a small laugh escaped. "I guess. In any case, I've met most of Y Knot's business owners."

"Then you know he's newly married to Charity McCutcheon, Luke's younger sister. Brandon's not going to like the boy's pilfering one little bit. Hopefully the situation will get straightened out without bringing Brandon into it."

Again, she nodded.

"Don't worry about the boy. Things have a way of working themselves out." The green of his eyes deepened. "Tell me how you spent your day. Did you write the letter to your mother?"

Satisfied from the perfectly seasoned meat and other fixings, Sally set her fork in her plate. "I did." She patted her reticule on the chair beside her. "I have it right here ready to post."

Roady quirked a brow. "What did you say?"

Sticking to their decision to keep the baby completely secret until they announced it as their own, Sally held to the facts of her marriage that made her happy. And she *was* happy. She gave a small laugh. "Well, I'm sure they're all going to be completely flabbergasted, but I told Mother I'd met an amazing man. A man who'd saved my life, and one I wanted to spend the rest of my days with."

Roady's fork stilled in midair. His gaze grew intense, searching. It seemed to reach to the bottom of her soul, creating a giddy happiness. His expression thrilled her and was a bit scary at the same time. Like playing with fire, yet knowing how badly what it might lead to could burn.

Chapter Forty-Seven

Roady rested the tines of his fork on his plate. "You said all that?"

"I did." She took a sip from her water glass.

He cleared his throat, then casually pushed a carrot around on his plate. "What else?"

"I told her about the land and the cabin, and that you worked for a really wonderful family that I'm coming to love. I said I'm close enough to see Heather and Morgan often, and that Montana is the land of God. So beautiful it steals my breath when I least expect it."

He'd taken another bite, which he chewed slowly. Finished, he pushed back his chair, his eyes actually glistening. "I-I can see why you're a writer, Sally. That was real pretty."

Enjoying his attention, and moved deeply he seemed to be affected by her disclosure, she added, "And I said that when she writes me back to address her letter to Mrs. Roady Guthrie, and I'd be sure to get it."

He swiped at his eye. Looked around, then again at her face. "Did you get time to work on your novel?"

She had. After Amy and Cinder had gone home, she'd gathered her pen and notebook with the intention of writing a whole page. She'd walked out to the lookout, hoping the view would inspire her muse to return.

"I tried, but nothing came to mind."

"Nothing?" Lines of concern formed between his brows, but he seemed to have recovered from his sentimentality about the letter. "That's too bad. What's it about? The story, I mean."

Was he teasing? Her brothers never took her writing earnestly, making her the brunt of good-natured, brotherly type jokes.

Roady reached out, and she thought he intended to take her hand that rested on the edge of her side of the table. Instead, he lowered his arm and fingered the silver top of the saltshaker halfway between them. "I'm genuinely interested. But you don't have to tell me if you don't want to."

The timbre of his voice reminded her of warm syrup. She forced her heart out onto a limb. If she wanted honesty and trust from him, she needed to give him the same. "It's about a young woman named Adela Brown. She's a country girl who is forced to move to a large city and fend for herself after both her parents die from scarlet fever." Sally had never shared this much of her story with anyone. She lifted a shoulder and sat a little straighter.

His brows rose. "Sounds interesting. What happens?"

"Adela, a proficient cook, and skilled in the ways to keep a proper home, takes the only job she can find as a servant for an elderly woman who is confined to her bed, and who Adela comes to love. Her employer has a nephew who lives on the other side of the city. The only problem is he's—"

Sally's sentence was cut short by a young couple who came through the door on a gust of chilly air. As soon as the woman saw Roady, her eyes lit up in surprise. She hurried over, followed by her tall, lanky escort who had removed his hat and held it in his fingers. The woman had a healthy head of curly blond hair, and Sally could see she was in the family way.

"You're Sally!" she said, stopping in front of their table. "I'm Evie Holcomb, your sister's friend. I was the first mail-order bride to come to Y Knot—right before Heather."

Roady stood and held out his hand. "Good to see you, Chance. It's been a while."

Sally stood too and hugged Evie. "Of course you're Evie. I should have recognized you from Heather's description—and your messages in her letters. She's told me so much about you."

Evie turned and gazed up at her tall husband. "This is my husband, Chance Holcomb." One couldn't miss the affection in her voice.

Sally smiled at the handsome cowboy, whose soft brown hair was combed neatly for a night out. "I'm pleased to make your acquaintance."

Chance Holcomb dipped his chin in response and smiled.

Sally glanced down at Evie's small tummy protruding in front of her. A strong kinship swirled within. "How're you feeling?" she asked. "Heather wrote to me the day you found out you were expecting."

Evie giggled. "Better now that the morning sickness has passed."

Sally's face burned, and she sneaked a quick glance at Roady.

Roady pulled out one of the vacant chairs. "I believe these two empty seats have your names on 'em."

Evie's smile faded and she said in a concerned voice, "We shouldn't. You're newlyweds."

Roady motioned for her to sit. "That's the best reason of all. We've just about finished our supper, but I'm not leaving without a piece of pie."

Evie all but glowed. "Dessert is what we came in for. I crave pie all the time, and Chance is so good to indulge me." She got comfortable, then leaned forward. "I want to hear all about the stagecoach accident and the snowstorm. Heather told me some, but I'm sure it's better coming from you. What an unbelievable story to tell your children about how you met your own true love. It's remarkable."

Sally felt Roady's gaze on her face. She couldn't help but look up into his eyes. There was understanding there—and something else. A small smile played around his chiseled lips.

"I couldn't agree more, Evie," he said, his voice low and conspiratorial. "Sally'll make a wonderful mother—when the time comes. She's brave and strong. And determined."

Sally wondered why Roady would think her brave. He even had the audacity to wink. Everyone at the table saw it and laughed, them thinking one thing, and her knowing Roady meant another.

Chapter Forty-Eight

Roady emptied his pockets onto the highboy in his bedroom, intending to speak with Luke first thing in the morning about Hickory. Spending time with Chance and Evie in the café, and then making a short visit to see Sally's sister at the lumber mill, they'd returned home much later than he'd planned. The house was quiet, and Sally was doing whatever it was women did before turning in. He wondered if he could expect another late-night visit. Last night had him hopeful, but was she ready for him to take their relationship to a deeper level?

In a quandary, he paused at the window. This bedroom faced away from the front and bunkhouse, and looked out over pastureland and rolling hills. Far off, the moon was just topping the mountains.

Darn if he hadn't gone and lost the rest of his heart to his wife. That wouldn't be a problem in the least if she wasn't pining for the father of her baby. Slowly, he unbuttoned his shirt as he gazed up at the stars. Stripping it off, he tossed it onto a chair, leaving him in his undershirt. What did the future hold? He'd signed on to this marriage knowing it might take time to win Sally's heart. Working with animals every day, he knew how to be patient. But to love a woman who might never return his feelings? That would be pure hell. Sure, they were friends, and that was growing stronger every day. But lovers?

He took off his pants, and they followed the path of his shirt. Good thing he'd bought new unmentionables not that long ago.

Knock, knock.

He turned. The muscles in his stomach clenched, and he felt as vulnerable as a day-old calf. What would she do if he tried to kiss her? Sleeping in the same room made him want to rush things. He picked up a wool throw blanket off the chair and wrapped it around his waist. "Come in," he called in a quiet voice.

Sally stepped in and closed the door behind her. Dressed in her nightclothes and all smiles, she was clearly not thinking along the same lines as he was. Her eyebrow arched at his funny outfit. She came right up to the window and stood next to him. "All dark, nothing to see."

He smiled, feeling silly. "I was looking at the stars."

Sally sighed longingly. "It's so pretty. Takes some getting used to."

"What?" He knew she meant the stars, but the beauty of her face as she gazed out the window moved his soul.

"The darkness and the stars. The sky in St. Louis was never this bright. I love it here."

Her sincere tone made his heart catch. "Do you, Sally?"

She turned from the window, a strange look in her eyes. "I thought you knew. I said so in the café tonight."

"Not really. You said it was beautiful." It would be so easy right now to fold her into his arms and carry her over to the bed. Show her just how much she meant to him. Was tonight the night? Would there ever be a night? "I only know you've a great big hurt deep inside that keeps you from me. That makes me sad."

Surprised, she took a small step back. The easy feel in the room dissolved. Perhaps the thought of loving him was enough to make her breath come out in little spurts of fear. To her credit, she held his gaze. He'd never been this candid with her. Platitudes about the future—*their future*—yes. But true, gritty pain, that was something he'd kept to himself.

Angry for probably scaring her off with his impatience, he turned, lit a candle by his bedside, and blew out the lantern. He pulled down the quilt, completely aware that she hadn't moved a muscle and was watching his every move.

"You want more?" She'd said it so quietly that he almost missed it in his pursuit to discard the blanket at just the right time as he climbed under the cover so she wouldn't be shocked by his cotton-covered derriere.

Of course he wanted her. She must know that by now. "I'd be lying if I said no."

If he thought his words would move her into action, he'd been wrong. He couldn't have misread her that completely during supper and the buggy ride home. She'd sat close to his side and chatted away happily, even flirted a little. She'd laughed and touched his arm ten times, if not once. Now the color had drained from her face as if she were facing a death sentence. If he got out of bed and touched her, she'd pull away.

At a loss and unsure what to do, he murmured, "It's okay. Don't mind me."

Instead of leaving, as he thought, she circled the bed and pulled back the covers. Discarding her robe, she climbed up under the quilt. He couldn't tell what she was thinking, but he knew what he hoped for. She scooted toward him.

"Sally, you don't have to do this. There's plenty of time to get acquainted. No need to rush into something that makes you uncomfortable." He was rambling, too nervous to admit her proximity was intoxicating. He felt as if he'd just downed a full tumbler of whiskey.

She slowly snuggled next to his side and laid her head on his chest, just above the hand she'd placed there a moment before. He kept his hands at his side and let her relax. Several minutes passed.

"Sally?"

He felt her move.

"Yes?"

He looked down at the woman, his wife, resting on his chest. "I'm not sure what you want me to do." He longed to touch her, enfold her in his arms, or stroke her beautiful hair that covered her shoulders. He longed to do so many things, but knew she would cringe away, her heart aching for another man. Who was he? And what was he like? What had he done to so completely capture Sally's heart to where she'd give herself to him?

"I want you to kiss me."

The second she said the words he felt her stiffen, even though she tried to hide it, which was mighty strange. "You sure?"

"Yes."

He pulled out of her embrace and scooted down until they were face-to-face, her warm breath tickling his cheek. "You sure?" he repeated, feeling more than his share of shy.

She nodded and closed her eyes.

Roady gently pressed his lips to hers, but made no other move to hold her. Her lips were warm and soft. When she didn't move, didn't even breathe, he pulled away and waited for her to open her eyes.

Her lashes fluttered and then her eyes opened, the soft glow of the candle making it possible for him to see the wave of emotion deep inside her. They were still facing each other, but he was far enough back to see her lips tremble, then one corner pull up into a small smile.

He smiled back. "Did you like that?"

She nodded.

Encouraged, he inched closer, but kept the kiss light. She didn't respond, but neither did she pull away. Her lips were sweeter than any he remembered, and he fought to keep his desires in check. He carefully brought one arm over her body and touched her nightgown in the middle of her back.

The moment she felt his touch, she froze. An instant later, after two jerky breaths, she bolted up and threw off his arm. "Good night, Roady," she all but gasped.

Before he could ask what he'd done wrong, Sally slipped out of bed and ran to the door. When it clicked shut, something in his heart cracked and a gripping pain rushed out. He stared at the door, confused.

Chapter Forty-Nine

Straining, Hickory hefted the pitchfork full of heavy manure and dumped it into the wheelbarrow he'd placed in the doorway of the stall. This was the last of it. Soon Lucky would ring the supper bell, calling them in to wash up.

Taking a break, he stretched his back muscles, then wiped his brow with his handkerchief. He liked it here. The men were nice, the bunkhouse warm, but best of all, the meals the boss provided were delicious. Three squares every day, come rain or shine. No more digging through the trash or trying to sleep with a belly gnawing from the inside out. Why, he was sure he'd gained five pounds in the few days he'd been here. Working wasn't bad at all when one knew there'd be something hot and filling when the day was over.

Before going back to his chore, Hickory took a minute to scratch Whiskers under her chin. The barn cat had taken to him, and followed his every step. A wisp of sadness pulled his lips down. He remembered how his ma used to love cats, and any that came to their door looking for a handout ended up staying. How he missed her, and Pa, and his sister Lucy. Whiskers mewed, and Hickory blinked away the moisture from his eyes. Ma would be happy he was learning to read and write. He had a long way to go, but he'd make her proud, wherever she was.

"There you are!"

At the sound of the deep voice, Hickory jerked his hand away from the cat as if he were doing something wrong. "Howdy, Luke. You lookin' for me?"

Luke came down the barn aisle, his tall frame making the cat scamper away. "Sure am. Thought you were with Francis, but found out otherwise. How're you doing?"

"Fine."

"You cleaning stalls today?"

"Sure."

Luke came in and looked around, inspecting his work. He nodded his approval. "How's Punk working out? Did you ride him today?"

Hickory liked the way Luke treated him like an equal, not like a little orphaned kid to scorn and kick around. "Sure did. I rode out to the back pasture and helped Smokey bring in some heifers."

Luke gazed at him so long, he began to get nervous. "I'm real proud of you, Hickory. You've taken to ranching like a duck does to water. I hope you like it here."

"Sure, I like it here." Hickory kept his eyes from narrowing. Something was up. Luke was fishing. The man who had snatched him out of his hand-to-mouth existence in Waterloo crossed his arms and leaned back against the stall divider.

"Good as the next place, I guess," he added. He hadn't meant to sound surly, but the notion things were about to go wrong had pricked his stomach the moment Luke asked how he liked living on the ranch.

Luke's brows drew together. His lips pursed. "That's all? Are the men giving you a hard time?"

Hickory shook his head, feeling sheepish over his churlish manner. Maybe he was wrong; it wouldn't be the first time. "Naw, everyone's real nice."

Luke's smile chased away Hickory's concern. "That's good to hear. Francis said you listen real well. He only asks you once, and the job gets done. I like that in a man."

Hickory could feel it coming. He hadn't been wrong…

"How do you like Y Knot? I heard you've been there a time or two."

Whiskers trotted into the stall and rubbed against Hickory's leg. "Like it fine."

"What'd you do, the last trip in?"

This time Hickory did narrow his eyes. He'd been questioned enough times by the sheriff in Waterloo to know when he was under suspicion for some infraction. "Just whatever Francis asked me to do. Fetch a horse from the livery, drop something by the sewing shop for Mrs. McCutcheon, go to the mercantile… I don't know." He looked down at the cat. "Lots of things."

Hickory's insides frosted up like a December morning. He'd never outrun his past. He would always be a no-account to everyone, no matter how much they said different. Angry now, he swung around on Luke. "Why? What am I being blamed for now?"

"I never said that."

"Didn't have to. I know what's up and what's down. I ain't no baby to tippy-toe around. Come on and spit out what you come here ta say!"

"All right, I will. Some merchants have had several items turn up missing."

"And you think *I* took 'em."

"Don't put words in my mouth, Hickory. I'm just asking."

"Are you askin' the other men, or just me?"

Luke glanced away.

Heat rushed to Hickory's face. "Yeah, I didn't think so. Just so you know, I ain't never stole nothin' from any store in Y Knot! Go search my bunk if ya don't believe me." A jab of guilt made him glance away from the tall cowboy who'd taken him under his wing. The lump in his pocket felt like a rattlesnake ready to strike.

Luke straightened. When he reached out, Hickory ducked under his arm and around the wheelbarrow before Luke could stop him.

"Wait up, Hickory," Luke called.

"Can't," Hickory hollered back over his shoulder. "I have work ta do. Lucky's ringin' the supper bell right now, and I got Punk and the other horses ta bring in and feed." He hastened his speed out the back door of the barn.

Once out of sight, he dashed the moisture from his eyes. So much for fitting in. Or making a new start. There would never be a new beginning for him.

Chapter Fifty

Roady reclined in a well-worn chair in front of the bunkhouse hearth, the easy goodness of his old life soothing away the tensions in his head and heart. A clanking racket from the sink as Lucky washed the dishes while Hickory dried them kept him from falling asleep. The hearty meal of steak and potatoes, combined with an endless night of restlessness, had his eyelids drooping. The evening shift had already gone out, and Smokey, Ike, and Pedro were playing cards at the table.

It might not have been right, but earlier in the day Roady sent word to Sally by way of Francis that he had work to go over with Luke, and was taking supper in the bunkhouse with the men. After last night, he couldn't face her yet. He'd risen even earlier than normal and had practically snuck out of the house, feeling silly and guilty over his perfectly natural feelings of wanting his wife. He didn't like to speculate that his marriage to Sally had been a mistake. Yet her reaction when he'd kissed her was proof enough that her heart still belonged to the baby's father in St. Louis—no matter how hard she tried to act different. The scoundrel might be out of her sight, but he was anything but out of her mind or heart.

Shad ambled over in his socks and lit his pipe by means of a straw in the fireplace. He took a few puffs, then tossed the burning stubble into the flames. He looked at Roady from the corner of his eye. The questions would start any second.

"I'm surprised you're still here, Roady."

"I'm waiting on Luke. Have a few things to go over."

Shad lowered himself into the opposite chair and stuck his feet out toward the flame. He took a puff from his pipe and let the smoke ease between his lips and up toward the open rafters. "How are—"

"Just fine."

Shad's brow arched, then he took another draw. "I supposed you noticed, I moved my things to your old bunk. Didn't think you'd mind."

Impossible to stop his gaze from darting to the bed that had been his for years, he lifted one shoulder. "'Course not." He stood, antsy to get business taken care of and then... He shrugged into his jacket. "Think I'll get some air while I wait on Luke."

Shad nodded. "See ya in the mornin'."

Roady stepped outside the bunkhouse. At the porch railing, he stopped and grasped it firmly, looking through the darkness at the big house. By now, supper would be finished. Flood would be sitting in his brown leather chair, having a brandy by the fire, Claire reading by his side. That was when he and Sally usually said their good-nights and spent time in her room talking.

His chest squeezed.

Her upstairs window was dark. What was she doing? Was she thinking about him?

A horse trotted up through the darkness. It halted and Luke dismounted. His friend glanced over at him, his eyes widening slightly at the sight of Roady waiting outside.

"Roady?" Luke tied his reins and moseyed over. "Hope I didn't keep you waiting. Dawn had a lot of things to tell her ma and me. Mostly about Holly and Cinder, and the mud pies they baked today and tried to feed to the chickens." He chuckled. "That girl keeps me going."

"I'll bet." Roady nonchalantly leaned a shoulder to a post. "I was flabbergasted today when you brought up skipping the spring cattle drive this coming year. We're concerned with the drought and the possible lack of feed, but I don't think that's going to be that serious of a problem."

Luke gave him a long look, then lowered himself into one of the porch chairs. "Is that what's on your mind? Because if it is, I don't see the importance of discussing it tonight."

Defensive, Roady scowled. He dragged up a chair and sat, bracing his arms across his knees. Seemed no one was taking him seriously these days. "When better to get prepared?"

"Tomorrow morning over coffee."

Roady rubbed a hand over his face. His gritty eyes stung. Luke was right. Evening was time for rest. Luke should be home with Faith and his children. And he should be upstairs with...

"Roady?"

The lantern behind Luke's head cast his face in shadow, making it impossible to read his friend's eyes.

Luke had the audacity to chuckle. "You remember what you told me way back in the day when I was torn up over Faith, and the fact that she was holding back from me?"

Roady grunted.

"You said I should try some sweet talk. That a little sweet talk went a long way with a woman. You were right as rain on that one."

Roady just sat there, recalling that day as they pushed the herd down the Valley of Flowers. Felt like a lifetime ago. How did Luke know he was torn up over Sally, and what had become of their non-marriage?

"I'm saying the same to you right now. Sally certainly is pretty enough, and sweet tempered. Any man in his right mind would have no problem at all—"

"Who's to say I'm not sweet-talking her already?"

Luke glanced around skeptically as if someone else had joined their conversation. "Me?" He stretched out his legs and crossed his ankles. "If you *were* sweet-talking her, you'd be upstairs doing it now, instead of out in the cold night air jawing about the lack of rain and cattle drives."

Roady stared off into the dark night. He couldn't divulge what was really bothering him. He had to work this out on his own. "I appreciate your advice."

"It's actually your own."

"I'll keep that in mind."

Luke pulled his legs in and leaned forward, lowering his voice. "If you need to talk, you know where to find me. On another subject, I spoke with Hickory. He guessed right away something was up. I don't know what to believe. Even though everything points to him and he acted guilty as hell, my gut says he's not the culprit."

"Hope you're right. The town won't put up with him for long if he is stealing things."

"Neither will we. Guess I'll have to tell Francis to leave him behind the next time he goes into town, until we get to the bottom of it."

Roady nodded and then stood. He shouldn't have called Luke out. He'd have to get through this predicament with Sally on his own. She liked to write. That must mean she liked to read as well. Maybe it would be easier for him to jot down some of his feelings on paper and give it to her.

Luke slapped him on his shoulder. "There's always some adjusting to do. Give it time." He mounted up and rode off.

Sally gazed out her bedroom window, the darkness of the night not easing her mind at all. Where was Roady? Supper in the bunkhouse must be over. Was he staying away on purpose?

Rubbing her temples, she wished the headache she'd had all day would go away. She missed him, wanted to be a wife to him, but was too ashamed to divulge the real reason why she rebuffed even his tiniest show of affection.

That terrifying day in the newspaper storage room was always ready to catch her up, crush her spirit. Her breathing came fast even now, and her heart pounded out of control. How ugly. Surely, Roady would be repulsed if he knew the truth. He'd think she'd wanted it, that she'd dallied with a married man. Would he still desire her after she told him everything?

The strange thing was, she did desire Roady, wanted his kisses, but the moment she felt his arms closing around her, her insides screamed out in protest. An insurmountable fear gripped her entire body and the pain she'd experienced came rushing back, robbing her of life-giving air and every sane thought in her head.

A soft knock sounded.

Roady!

Happiness blossomed as Sally rushed to the door. Opening it, she found a concerned Mrs. McCutcheon.

"Sally, is something wrong? You were very quiet at supper, and you stayed in your room most of the day. I had hoped when Roady showed up, your smile would return. But he hasn't." The older woman's eyes filled with empathy. "It helps to share your troubles, one woman to another."

"I just had some letters to write today," she said softly, sorry for the fib. It would be so easy to confide in Mrs. McCutcheon, who'd been so warm and accepting. The older woman's advice would mean so much. Confused, Sally held her tongue. "I'm sure he'll be in shortly."

Mrs. McCutcheon smiled. "You're most likely right. That boy's a very hard worker. Never puts off until tomorrow what he can do today." She tipped her head. "How did you like the cabin? Flood said you went to see it yesterday."

The sound of Mrs. McCutcheon's calming voice soothed Sally, and she opened the door wider for her to enter. She didn't want to be left alone with her agitated thoughts. "Won't you come in for a few minutes? It does feel nice to talk." She gestured to the chairs she and Roady usually shared at this time of the evening.

Once they were comfortable, Sally said, "I loved the beautiful rolling land, and the cabin is perfect. The minute I saw it, I knew we could be happy there. It's cozy and charming. We'll make do. And when…"

"When a baby comes along," Mrs. McCutcheon filled in for her when she paused, "he can add on, or even build a new home, if that's your desire. You know, that was our first home."

Sally's face heated. *Does she know? Can she tell my waistband is snug?*

"Flood's and mine. When we first married. Matthew and Mark were born there."

Sally gasped. "I didn't know. We can't take it—it wouldn't be right."

Mrs. McCutcheon reached over and covered Sally's hand with her own. "I can't think of anything that would be more fitting. The place has been vacant far too long. We had so many wonderful times there, and shared so much love." She patted Sally's hand once and then sat back. "It makes me happy to know love will be alive in those four walls again. Laughter—and maybe even some tears too, since no marriage is without all emotions." The older woman's compassionate gaze held her own. "Life is not about rules, Sally, but relationships. I see a very sweet one growing between you and Roady every day. Anything of value takes time."

A knock on the door brought both women to their feet. Mrs. McCutcheon smiled, then gave her a brief hug. "I'll be going," she whispered.

Roady's eyes widened when Sally opened the door and he saw Mrs. McCutcheon. A dark line of scarlet started at his neck and quickly climbed his face.

"There you are, Roady," Mrs. McCutcheon said. "I hope your business with Luke went well."

He nodded, then shifted his weight from one foot to the other. "It did."

"Good night, then. I'm sure Flood is wondering where I've made off to." She hurried down the hall toward the stairs. After she turned the corner, Roady's gaze swung back to Sally and their eyes met.

Chapter Fifty-One

Sally couldn't move. It was as if her feet were encased in quicksand, and she couldn't move an inch even if she'd wanted to. The guarded look in Roady's eyes made her want to weep. She remembered just a few days ago after the wedding, here in this same room, crossing the floor and boldly taking his hat from his hands. She'd smiled, even flirted.

Roady cleared his throat. "Just wanted to tell you good night."

His words, as soft as a bunny's fur, sliced her to the quick. He was through with her. He didn't understand. How could he? "But it's only eight o'clock. Can you sit a spell so we can talk?"

He shook his head, the hat he held turning in his hands. "Been a long day, and I'm about asleep on my feet. Before I go, though, have you given more thought to buying the cabin? I wanted to make sure you're sure."

"The cabin?"

"Yes. Do you still want to live there?" Lines rimmed his eyes, and he looked exhausted. "If that's your intention, starting tomorrow, I'll take Ike and Pedro with me and we'll get the place cleaned up and the fences put to right in a handful of days." He glanced toward the window for a few moments, then back at her. "Just wanted to be sure you hadn't changed your mind."

Did he want her to change her mind? Did he want her to go back to St. Louis and forget the day he'd ever laid eyes on her?

"Sally?"

"I'm sure, Roady."

He dipped his chin and started backing toward the door. "Fine then."

She wished he'd stay. If only she had the courage and fortitude to tell him how she'd ended up with child. Maybe then he'd understand why it was so difficult for her to let herself go.

"That's good enough for me. Sleep well." He pulled the door closed.

She listened to him go into his room, and imagined him stripping down and climbing into the large, fluffy bed. Her heart ached. How had things gotten so mixed up?

Chapter Fifty-Two

The next two weeks that came and went were the longest of Sally's life. Each day she thought Roady would come to tell her the cabin was ready—that it was time to move in. Hopefully the change would improve their relationship, and they could find their way back to the easy friendship they'd discovered in the hunting cabin.

Instead, he stayed out late, worked himself to the bone, missed most dinners, and always went to bed early, claiming he was exhausted. His teasing smile was gone. He treated her with respect, but kept her at arm's length.

The two weeks had also changed her figure. She'd begun leaving the top button on her skirts undone for comfort, but feared that if she didn't get out of the ranch house soon, Mrs. McCutcheon would notice her thickening waist. This morning after breakfast, she planned to hitch a ride into town with Francis. She would seek out Heather for a much-needed visit, and buy some fabric from Berta May so she could discreetly let out the waistband of at least one skirt.

Dressed and ready for the day, she discovered a note that had been slipped under her bedroom door as she was about to leave. She picked it up and opened the paper with trembling hands.

Roady.

Her heartbeat quickened.

My Dearest Sally,

I am not one for writing so please forgive my simple verse. I had hopes I could win your heart from the man you still love in St. Louis, but I think that is not the case. Now that I have lost my heart to you, I find it difficult to be around you and not show you any affection—which you appear to strongly dislike. I do not think I can live a life of a marriage in name only. In truth, these last two weeks have brought me to despair. Now that the baby has a name, maybe I should go away and make this easier for us both.

On the other hand, if you could only find room in your heart to give us a chance, we might find contentment in our union. I do not want to rush you, but maybe I could help you forget him.

Your loving husband, Roady.

Sally didn't even know tears had formed until one landed on her hand. Dashing them away, she stared at the note. Roady thought she *loved* Mr. Greenstein? Nothing could be further from the truth! She despised her former boss, and prayed she'd never see his face ever again.

The hopelessness written between the lines was enough to drop Sally to her knees. She needed to find Roady, to talk to him and explain, no matter how dirty or embarrassed it made her feel. No matter how incriminating the truth sounded. Folding the paper, she placed it under her personal items in the bureau and hurried out the door.

Outside, the ranch yard was a buzz of activity. Men ran to the corral, haltering two or three horses at a time and bringing them out. One hand galloped off while shouting something to Francis, who was hurrying out of the barn with his horse. He mounted up and rode off.

Fear tightening her chest, Sally picked up the hem of her skirt and hurried toward the bunkhouse. No one paid her any mind. Finally, she saw Hickory lugging a saddle over to the hitching rail where his horse stood. She ran his way.

"What's going on? Where is everyone going?"

Hickory turned around. "After the grizzly everyone keeps talkin' about."

Two more hands rode out in a cloud of dust.

"But why is it so important now?" She didn't understand the urgency, when in the past it was mostly Roady who wanted the bear.

"Sheriff from Pine Grove said a farmer took Behemoth on when the grizzly broke into his smokehouse. Shot him a few times, but then the bear mauled him real bad, enough to—" Hickory closed his mouth and pointed to the sky. "Bear's mad with pain, Miss Sally, and tearing into anythin' in his path. They intend ta kill it afore it kills any more people."

Wounded? In pain? "Where's Roady?"

"Bein' he was workin' on the cabin, he got the message first. Him and Pedro went after the bear, and Ike rode back here ta tell us."

"No!" In his present frame of mind, Roady was liable to do something stupid, take chances—get himself killed. Could she saddle a horse and find him herself? In a panic, her gaze darted around as more men rode out, rifles in hand. She needed to tell him how she felt, what really happened.

Shad Petty burst out of the bunkhouse door. At the hitching post, he grabbed his horse's reins and swung into the saddle.

This was her only chance. She waved her hands over her head. "Mr. Petty! Mr. Petty!" she shouted over and over above the cacophony.

Already halfway turned, he reined up, then trotted up to her side. His horse chomped at the bit and threw its head, eager to follow the other horses. "Mrs. Guthrie?"

She clutched the bottom length of his chaps to be sure he didn't gallop off.

He smiled. "If you're worried about your husband, don't be. He'll be fine."

"You're wrong! He's upset with me. He'll take undue chances with his life. Please, if you can, you have to tell him…"

What? How on earth can I convey what's in my heart through this cowboy?

"Mrs. Guthrie, I need to go! Time is of the essence!"

It was now or never. Roady's life could depend on it. "Tell him—" She stared into Shad's face. "Tell him I love him! And always have since the time we met. There's no one else in my heart."

The cowboy cocked his brow and his eyes opened wide. "You *sure* you want me to tell him all that? He'll wonder why I know so much about you."

She gave the long fringe of his chaps a jerk so he'd know she was serious. "*Please*, Mr. Petty, it's very important to tell him! Exactly what I said. Can you remember?"

"You love him," he mumbled, as if embarrassed. "Only him, no one else."

"Yes! Tell him, please!"

He nodded, pulled his hat down over his eyes, and took off like a bullet.

Sally glanced around. The place was deserted. All the ranch hands were gone, even Hickory.

Chapter Fifty-Three

Bent over Fiddlin' Dee's neck, Roady gave his horse her head as they galloped toward Pine Grove. The wind felt good in his face. Pedro was a horse length behind. They'd need to slow up soon so the animals could catch their breath.

Hearing a shout, Roady looked back under his arm.

"Lame!" Pedro shouted, slowing his horse to a trot, then stopping. "Good luck, *amigo*!"

Roady lifted his hat off his head, and gave a sweeping wave. When he looked again, Pedro and his horse were already fifty yards behind him, and growing smaller by the second.

Roady slowed to a lope, letting his mare catch her breath. The Blanchard farm came into view. It looked deserted, no one in sight. Too bad about the old man. Mrs. Blanchard must already be in town with a gaggle of women to care for her in her hour of grief.

Damn! If he'd killed the grizzly the first time, she'd not be a widow today. He was just as responsible for Mr. Blanchard's death as the bear. This was *his* fault—but he would right it today.

Determined, he slowed further and passed the quiet farm at a walk. He'd need his horse's legs fresh, if called for. Past the farm, where the trees thickened, he picked up the bear's trail. A spot of blood on a leaf directed him in the unobvious direction. *You're smart, Behemoth, but I'm smarter.*

The deeper Roady went, the darker the forest became. Nervous energy made him pull his rifle out of its leather scabbard and check the chamber. He rode along quietly, his heartbeat quickening as he spotted some tracks where the leaves were damp. The hunt had just begun.

Several hours passed. By now, others must be out here too. He hoped everyone had the good sense to see what they had in their sights before pulling the trigger.

Frustrated, Roady slipped his rifle back into its scabbard. The last sign, some fur rubbed into the bark of a pine, he'd spotted some time ago. Just like all the years before, it seemed the grizzly had the power to disappear into thin air.

A deep chill settled inside. A fleeting thought of Sally made him smile, but that faded away all too quickly. Did she see his note? What did she think?

He came to a stream that flowed between two towering embankments. He followed it for a while, the path easier for Fiddlin' Dee to navigate. Even though he was unprepared to camp, Roady was determined to stay out as long as it took to find the wounded animal.

A scrambling sound reached his ears. Curious, he turned his horse and scaled the steep bank. Once on top, he had a good view of the terrain below. He stilled, listening.

The sound came again, a growl so deep it might be mistaken for a rumble of thunder. A tingle of fear crept up Roady's spine, and his horse pranced nervously. He pulled out his rifle and cautiously proceeded forward across the top of the highland plateau.

A whimpering sound mingled with the occasional growl. What could that be? Roady moved at a trot when the land and rock permitted, but weaving through the dense foliage and pines made that difficult. He halted abruptly when the land cut away.

Two hundred feet below, the massive brown bear sat on his haunches, his head low, and the silver tips of his fur glittering like rainfall.

"There you are, you son of a gun," Roady hissed to himself. "I've got you now."

He took aim. From this height and distance, making a direct hit to the grizzly's heart would be next to impossible. Best not injure him more than he already was. He lowered his Winchester and descended the mountain, picking his way slowly through the trees. When his mare stepped on a dry branch, a loud snap echoed through the air.

The bear looked up and saw him coming, but didn't appear concerned in the least. Bright red blood stained his shoulder and several other places on his back from the altercation with Mr. Blanchard. Maybe the animal was tired of running, and knew his end was near. His weary gaze held Roady's.

Empathy burned in his chest. *We've been through a lot, you and me. You've been a worthy opponent.* A twist of regret for things bygone as well as the job he had to do weighed heavy. *It's time to put our past to rest.*

With a belabored groan and clamping of teeth, Behemoth stood. He threw back his massive head and let out a snarl that would make anyone in their right mind turn and run. Roady's mare spun a quarter circle before he knew what she was about.

Get it done! He's suffering!

A little less distance between him and his target would ensure a cleaner shot—under the grizzly's foreleg and through his heart. A fast death.

Descending the incline a few more steps, Roady lifted his rifle and took aim.

Behemoth charged.

Fiddlin' Dee reared up on her hind legs and fell over backward on the uneven, leaf-strewn terrain. Roady pulled up his legs and rolled, gun in hand, as the mare scrambled to her feet and galloped off. Lifting his rifle, he squeezed off a shot. A vision of Sally, laughing at something he'd said, flashed in his mind only to be replaced by a deep, heartburning regret.

Undeterred, the bear made fast work of the ground between them.

A projectile whizzed through the air and caught the bear square on the nose. The animal skidded to a halt and shook his head, snarling as he lowered it to rub his nose on his foreleg. His head came up at the exact moment Roady spotted Hickory, halfway up a tree. Winding up, the boy flung another rock, his precise aim hitting Behemoth on the top of the skull. Roady now forgotten, the snarling bear changed course and headed for the tree holding the boy.

Roady ran forward. He dropped to a knee and took aim, knowing a shot to the bear's backside would not kill the grizzly, but it might distract him.

He pulled the trigger. A volley of shots rang out, surprising him.

It was one heartbeat before the bear fell. His sides heaved and a long shuddering breath whistled from his mouth.

Roady stood, regret burning his lungs. *It's done.*

He glanced around, wondering about the shots. Shad and Luke rode out from the trees, their rifles in hand, followed closely by Brandon, who led Punk.

Roady sucked in a deep breath, savoring a moment of relief. Hickory was still alive—and so was he. "I'm mighty happy to see you men."

Luke pushed up the brim of his hat. "We're pretty relieved to see you two, as well."

Shad rode forward and looked Roady in the eye. "And I think you're gonna be even happier when ya hear what I have to say."

Chapter Fifty-Four

"Sit down and rest yer feet, missy," Lucky said for the fortieth time since Sally had knocked on the bunkhouse door and asked to wait inside with him. "You've about wore yerself a trail around this room. Yer makin' me dizzy."

Sally sighed and looked away. Mrs. McCutcheon had ridden into Y Knot to assist with Mrs. Blanchard, but Sally had chosen to wait here for the men. "I can't, Lucky. Not until I know Roady and the others are safe. I should have taken ahold of Hickory the moment I saw him saddling his horse! I'm such a fool." A black fear had grabbed her the minute she discovered he'd followed the men.

"That boy's resourceful. He'll be all right."

Noon had come and gone, and now it was almost five o'clock. If anything happened to Roady or Hickory, she'd never forgive herself.

"You must be famished," the cook said, his voice steeped in compassion. "At least have a piece of this chocolate cake I made fer supper. The boys won't mind if there's a slice missin'. It'll take yer mind off what's goin' on."

Sally stopped to gaze at the cook. She liked Lucky a great deal; he reminded her of her pa. A surge of homesickness clutched her insides, threatening to bring tears.

The older man rushed forward as fast as his limp allowed. He took her by her shoulders and directed her over to the fireplace. "I insist you sit! I can see yer on the verge of waterworks." He encouraged her gently into one of the leather chairs. "Don't you move a muscle until you drink a cup of the tea I have brewin'."

She opened her mouth to protest, but snapped it closed when he gave her his no-nonsense evil eye.

Back at the stove, he rattled around for a minute or two, then returned with a large mug of peppermint tea. "Don't you say a word till you finish the whole cup."

Sally took a deep whiff and let the aromatic steam settle her nerves. The first sip was hot. And good. She closed her eyes.

Please, God, let all the men return safely. Keep Roady safe. Watch over Hickory.

A bittersweet kaleidoscope of memories of Roady passed through her mind. She felt a smile tug at her lips when she thought of the good-hearted gentleness of her husband. It brought a peace to her heart. She'd just relaxed into the memory of them standing side by side in the hunting cabin's candlelight, shoulders almost touching, when a shout from outside made her eyes snap open.

Startled, she set her cup down and followed Lucky to the door.

The men were back! They galloped into the ranch yard, whooping and hollering and carrying on like a bunch of wild Indians. Sally searched for any sign of Roady—or Hickory. They weren't there! Had something happened? Surely, the mood of the men would be different if they'd lost two of their own.

Sally hurried out into the middle of the horses, unconcerned for her safety. She saw Morgan and Hayden, but when she spotted the McCutcheon brothers, as well as Mr. McCutcheon, Brandon Crawford, and Francis, she went straight over. "Where's Roady?" she asked Luke. "And Hickory?"

The smile on Luke's face widened. "Punk can't quite keep up with the rest of us anymore. They'll be along shortly."

She turned toward the way the men had come. When she saw Roady and Hickory round the bend in a slow lope, she wanted to cry with joy. Roady saw her and galloped forward, then slid to a stop. He swung out of the saddle and gathered Sally into an embrace. When his lips found hers, Sally's knee-jerk reaction to pull away flashed through her but she fought it like a tigress, doing her best to relax in his arms.

Laughter sounded. She pulled back and looked at all the smiling men sitting their horses that had circled around. Shad Petty had the widest grin of all.

"Mrs. Guthrie, I gave Roady your message."

She felt her face go hot.

"He sure did, sweetheart," Roady agreed. "But not until we'd gathered up just about every ranch hand that works here, and a few of the townspeople as well."

Chuckles rippled through the men. Some were red faced, where others just looked overly sentimental. Smokey actually swiped at his eye.

She glanced up into Roady's face. "Well, I'm glad he did. Then no one has cause to think I love anyone but you."

When Roady's eyes widened, she went up on tiptoe and placed a soft kiss to his mouth. "I love you," she whispered softly against his lips. "No one but you."

A horse racing into the yard broke up the circle of men. Jack Jones slid to a halt.

"Where is he?" he called out in a loud voice as he dismounted. "Where's the boy?"

Soon after a buggy followed with Mr. Lichtenstein, Berta May, and Mr. Herrick, the leather shop owner.

Berta May leaped from the still-rocking buggy and hurried over to Flood's side. "I told Jack he should wait until after the funeral for Mr. Blanchard to bring up this unpleasant business, but he wouldn't listen!"

Brandon stepped forward, angry lines marring his normally handsome face. "What's this about, Jack?"

Mr. Lichtenstein and Mr. Herrick glared from the buggy. "Berta May speaks the truth!" Mr. Herrick said at the top of his scratchy old voice. "Once Jack found out there'd been another theft in my store, there was no stoppin' him from coming out here and confrontin' the boy! We followed him out as fast as we could."

"I fired you a month ago!" Brandon's voice was hard as steel. "What business do you have with these townspeople?"

A stricken-looking Berta May raised her reticule threateningly. "Jack Jones, come over here right now so I can smack you!"

Mr. Lichtenstein, now out of the buggy, shuffled to Berta May's side. "The deputy told us that vas just a ruse so he could find the shoplifter that's been plaguing our businesses."

"What are you talking about? What shoplifter?" An angry-faced Brandon stared into the German's face. "No one has reported a thing to me."

"That is my fault, Sheriff. I didn't want to get the child in trouble, so I went straight to Luke McCutcheon, since he vas the one who brought the boy to Y Knot. He said he'd take care of it. I hadn't heard a thing until Jack came around and said he was getting close."

Jack puffed out his chest, not backing down one iota. "He's right! It's the kid." He glanced around. "The boy is guilty as sin. I'm breakin' this case, then you'll have to hire me back."

"I don't have to do anything," Brandon said, then shot an angry glare at Luke that promised they'd discuss this later. He started for the bunkhouse.

Sally dropped Roady's hand and ran to the front of the crowd that was marching toward the bunkhouse behind the sheriff. Spotting Hickory sitting quietly on his bunk, she ran to him and threw her arm around his thin shoulders. As the others came close, Hickory stood, and so did Sally.

Luke shouldered through the men to stand next to Brandon. "Hickory," he began. "In light of your very brave act of valor this afternoon, saving Roady from that charging bear—"

Sally gasped and pulled Hickory closer.

Luke's face held concern. "I have to ask you another question. I'm sorry."

The room was dead quiet. Lucky stood next to Luke and Brandon, his face a mass of worried lines.

"You told me before you'd never stolen anything from the shops in Y Knot, and I believed you. Do you still stand by that statement?"

Chapter Fifty-Five

Hickory swallowed. Whatever he said, it wouldn't be enough. They'd never believe him. What was the use in trying?

"Hickory?" Brandon went down on one knee and looked into his eyes.

"I ain't never stole nothin' from a shop in Y Knot. Not before, and not now."

Jack pushed to the front. "He's lying!"

Brandon stood.

Instantly, Hickory's face flashed hot. He took a step toward his accuser. "I'm not!"

The large sheriff spun and grabbed Jack Jones by his shirt collar. "I'm arresting you, Jack," he said, almost seething. "For impersonating a deputy." He shoved the man away. "Now, keep your mouth shut!"

Sally's arm across his back felt good, supportive, and gave Hickory courage. "I know who did, though." He was embarrassed how shaky his voice sounded in front of all these people.

"Go on," Sally encouraged.

He shrugged.

Brandon and Luke nodded. "You need to speak up now, son," Luke said. "Tell everything you know."

Hickory swept the room with a quick gaze. Every man leaned forward, waiting to hear what he had to say. Even the townspeople looked like they hoped he gave them the name of the real culprit. "I'm not sure if he's the one who took everything, but when I was in the store"—he glanced at the stout German man—"the man in front of me palmed a pocketknife and stole it."

"If you believe this little beggar," Jack hollered, "you're bigger fools than I thought!"

The moment the words were out of the ex-deputy's mouth, Pedro grasped Jack's arm and shoved it up behind his back, making him gasp in pain. "No more from you, *gringo*!"

"Why didn't you report it?" Luke asked.

Hickory shrugged. "It'd be my word against his. And no one believes a kid, especially an orphan." He'd hate to leave this ranch, he really would. "I wasn't willin' ta chance it."

"I believe you," Sally said.

Luke exchanged a look with Brandon. "And we do too. Is that fella here among us?"

Hickory dragged his gaze from the floorboards and looked around. He shook his head. "No, he don't work out here. I seen him a time or two in town, but never at the ranch."

The room came alive with talking, the spectators trying to figure out who the guilty party might be.

Jack glared, still unconvinced. "Check his pockets! Around his bed!"

Lucky drew up tall, an iron skillet still dangling in his hand. He pointed it at Jack's face. "There ain't nothin' hid in my bunkhouse! If there was, I'd know."

It was time to come completely clean. After which, he'd pack his duffel and make his way back to Waterloo. Maybe stay a day with Mrs. Mary Margaret while he figured out what his next step should be. She'd be glad to see him.

Digging in his pocket, he pulled out the orchid pin he'd lifted from the thief and had since kept with him at all times. He held out his hand for all to see. "I did take this, but not from some store."

Everyone craned their necks to get a glimpse of what he held. Roady nodded encouragement from his spot next to Luke.

Hickory went on. "I saw the man take the knife. While he hid it in one hand, he dug for his money with his other ta pay for somethin' else he was buyin'. The pin came out with the money and fell onto the counter. The way he picked it up real quick, I could tell he'd stolen it—just like he was stealin' the pocketknife. I lifted it from his trouser pocket when he wasn't lookin'."

Hickory looked straight at Brandon to make his final point. "You just can't trust a fella who don't look ya in the eye."

Brandon straightened. "Cade Morrow."

Mark stepped forward from behind Luke and said, "Amy's brother? Let me see that." He examined the brooch. "This is Amy's. I gave it to her for her birthday. Just yesterday she asked if I'd seen it anywhere."

"Hickory ain't been out ta Mark and Amy's," Francis said. "I know that for a fact. He's like my little shadow."

"Cade Morrow's been in my establishment more times than I can count," Mr. Lichtenstein said. "I never thought—"

"And mine too," Berta May added. "He was there the day I discovered my expensive lace gone. The same day Hickory picked up some things I'd made for Mrs. McCutcheon. I remember because Mr. Morrow looked at it for a really long

time. He said he was thinking of a birthday present for Amy."
She looked ashamed when she sought Hickory's gaze.

"He's been in my place plenty." Mr. Herrick's hangdog face
made Hickory reach out and touch his arm.

Brandon turned on Jack. "When was the last time you saw
Cade Morrow?"

"Two nights ago," Jack said with less bravado. "In the
saloon. Said he didn't like Y Knot and was headin' out."

"Good job, Jones," the sheriff said with disdain, then
turned back to him. "Well, Hickory, I guess you saved Amy
McCutcheon's jewelry for her. If her brother still had it now, it
would be long gone." He crooked a brow, and the stern
intensity of his gaze almost made Hickory squirm. "You won't
be taking anything else from anyone ever again. Am I correct
with my assumption?"

Hickory straightened, shocked at the turn of events. A
giddiness whispered through his heart, along with a deep
gratitude as he looked up into Luke McCutcheon's eyes. No, it
was more than that, more like the love he used to feel when
his pa carried him around on his shoulders that settled inside
his soul.

Brandon Crawford cleared his throat. "Hickory?"

"No, sir, Sheriff! Never, *ever* again! You have my word."

Brandon grasped his shoulder and smiled. "That's good
enough for me."

Chapter Fifty-Six

Roady paced around Sally's bedroom feeling like a caged coyote. A lantern glowed on the highboy, and the coverlet was turned back. Sally had hardly eaten a bite at supper, then claimed she needed a hot bath after the endless nerve-racking day. He'd taken the opportunity to use the tub from the bunkhouse and take a bath of his own.

After the ruckus with Hickory, Brandon took Jack and the rest of the Y Knot citizens back to town, determined to teach Jack a lesson by locking him up for a good long time. The ranch hands had smiled and nodded as Roady had walked away with Sally holding his arm. He wondered if any of them guessed that this would be his real wedding night. Let the silly, smiling ranch hands think what they would.

The bedroom door clicked open. Sally came in and set her toiletries on the highboy, then turned to search out his gaze. "You bathed as well?"

He nodded. "Thought it only fitting."

She stepped into his arms, tipped her head up, and kissed his neck, surprising the heck out of him. "I'm glad. You smell nice." She leaned back and smiled up into his face, looking prettier than Easter morning.

He played with a damp wisp of hair on her temple, still gun-shy to take her completely into his arms. "You smell nice too." The bed was directly behind him. Was she waiting for him to scoop her up into his arms? Something inside told him to let her set the pace.

"Roady, there's something I need to tell you. I should have told you the night we talked at the social in town."

"You mean the night before we married?"

She nodded. A flicker of apprehension moved across her eyes.

"You can tell me anything, Sally."

She pulled out of his arms and crossed her own. He wondered if she knew her stance held him at arm's length. The tip of her tongue slipped out, wetting her lips, and then she swallowed. He wanted in the worst way to ease away the line pulling her brows together in worry.

"Until I read your note," she said softly, "I never stopped to consider what you thought about how my baby was conceived."

He waited.

She reached out a hand, but then let it fall to her side. "It's not what you think. Not at all. What I told Shad Petty is the absolute truth. I was never in love with the baby's father. In fact, I feel the opposite. I loathe him."

Loathe him?

"He's someone I considered a friend, until the day he took liberties."

Took liberties? Against her will?

Shocked, Roady cut his gaze to the darkened window. What was she saying? Took liberties?

Had she been—

Now everything made perfect sense. A groan slipped from his lips. He remembered her shaky reaction in the cabin when they'd been playing checkers and he'd asked her about her boss. He should have figured it out sooner. Fury ripped through his heart. Someday the culprit would pay for hurting her. Roady would make sure of that. It might not happen this month, or even this year, but he would go to St. Louis to exact a portion of the pain that man had caused his sweet girl.

For now, he had more important things to do. He reached for her, needing to hold her, but she stepped back.

Understandable. He dropped his hands to his sides. "What happened? Why didn't you tell anyone?"

Again she hugged herself, then lowered her eyes.

"Look at me, Sally. It's okay."

Her gaze came up and found his, grasping it as if it were her lifeline. "He was married. Somehow, I must have given him the wrong idea. I must have done something to lead him on, make him think—" Tears swam in her eyes. "I don't know, I just don't know. I've gone over it a thousand times in my mind. I knew his wife, and liked her. His children too. One day he just pushed me down and—"

She gagged, unable to go on.

"Shhh, darlin', don't cry," he managed to get past his constricted throat. The horror and pain she'd endured gutted him. "It wasn't your fault. I know you. *You* know you. You'd never even think of such a thing. The blame lies at his door." *The snake!* "Don't for one minute think anything else."

He wanted to hold her in the worst way. "Can we sit down?" he said, gesturing to the chairs. "Or cuddle up on the bed? I'll just hold you, nothing more. You have my word on that."

She came into his arms then and let loose a tempest of tears. He held her racking body as she let all her pain gush out. She balled his shirt into her fists and held on as wave after wave of grief rocked her soul. She cried until her tears soaked through his shirt and there were none left.

When her legs buckled, Roady scooped her up into his arms and laid her on the bed, covered her with the blankets, and then scooted in beside her.

"Shhh, darlin'," he crooned, slowly stroking her hair as her head pillowed on his chest. "Shhh now, sweetheart. You're gonna be okay, I promise. No one will ever hurt you again. I'll make sure of that. You have my word."

Chapter Fifty-Seven

Two weeks flew by in the blink of an eye. Sally inspected her supper table carefully, then turned to scrutinize the rest of her cozy home. Her gaze meandered the room, stopping on the rifle Roady had mounted over the fireplace. Satisfied everything was in order, she hurried out onto the new porch. The view of the expansive pasture and the river that cut through the property always brought a jolt of happiness.

Stepping off, Sally picked up her skirt and started for the new barn the townsfolk helped them raise. "Roady," she called at the wide-open doors. "You in here?"

"Up in the loft."

She placed her hands on her hips and gazed up. "That bath water won't stay hot forever." She tried to sound irritated, but the sight of her husband, especially with a few pieces of hay in his tousled hair, made that next to impossible. He knew how to work that dangerous smile of his. "It's already five o'clock. Our guests will arrive before you have time to clean up."

He descended the ladder, his approach reminding her of a tiger she'd seen once in the St. Louis zoo.

"Too bad you're already in your good dress," he said, hungrily looking her up and down as he approached. The tease stopped one inch in front of her, his soiled clothes in contrast to her pretty blue dress.

"Yes, too bad." She arched a brow. "But your lips look impeccably clean."

Leaning in, he kissed her, long and sweet. Heat pooled in her belly, and she marveled how perfectly things had turned out. It was still so hard to believe.

He pulled back and searched her eyes. He must have found the answer to his unspoken question because he laughed, then warmed her further with a smile. "So, did you get any writing done on your novel this afternoon? When I left, you were in deep concentration, bent over your notebook."

"I did! Five pages. Sometimes my pen can't keep up with my mind."

He laughed again, looking curious. "Have you written about me yet?"

Embarrassed, because indeed, she had a difficult time thinking of anything else when she escaped into her imaginary world of heroes and heroines. "Never! I'm keeping you all to myself."

She took his hand and pulled him toward the house. "Now, come on. I don't want Heather and June to see you in such a state."

"What about Hayden and Morgan?"

She giggled. "I'm sure they've seen worse."

Almost to the house, Sally stopped. "Look." She pointed up at the fluffy, rosy-hued clouds that filled the endless sky. "Is that the same hawk we saw before?"

He followed her gaze. "Most likely. I discovered a nest in the stand of pines behind the barn. I'm sure it's one of the pair. If we're lucky, come spring, we'll be able to see some chicks as they lose their down and learn to fly."

A moment passed. "What do you think everyone will say when we make our announcement tonight? Will they believe the baby is ours?"

He took a moment to wholeheartedly consider her question as his gaze touched every part of her face. "Without a doubt. Because the little rascal *is* our baby, and no one will tell us otherwise."

Filled with emotion, Sally turned into his arms and buried her face in his chest.

"Hey, hey," he said as he tried to pull away. "I don't want to get you dirty."

"I love you so much, Roady. When I think of everything that's transpired since leaving St. Louis, it's difficult to believe. Finding that hunting cabin was the best thing that ever happened to me." When she pulled back and looked up into his eyes, she saw her love returned tenfold. "I can't live without you, my love. I hope you know that."

He cupped her face between his warm palms, his lips hovering just above hers. "Don't worry, darlin'. You'll never have to."

ACKNOWLEDGMENTS

As I began the adventure of creating a new story for the McCutcheon Family Series, I wondered what Roady Guthrie had in store for me. He's been with the series from as far back as the fourth chapter of the first book, MONTANA DAWN, looking out for his loved ones, giving advice, and generally making me laugh. His big heart and good sense have made him one of my favorite characters. In essence, I love him as much as I do Luke, and that is saying a lot. You may think it strange for an author to fall in love with his or her heroes and heroines, but that is the case, at least with me. Because of my deep affection for him, Roady's story had to be worthy or nothing at all. Needless to say, I think this book may be my favorite to date.

Sincere appreciation goes to my critique partners for all their help, even when they had their own deadlines to meet: Leslie Lynch and Sandy Loyd. To Pam Berehulke, of Bulletproof Editing, for making this book shine. To my ever-loyal friend and beta reader Kandice Hutton. And, of course, to my wonderful family, whose support of all my endeavors keeps me sane. I appreciate you all so much!

And, as always, deep heartfelt thanks and gratitude go to my lovely readers, who keep clamoring for more McCutcheons! Without you, I couldn't do what I love, so, in essence, you are the steam that runs this ship. Always know, I love you very much.

About the Author

Caroline Fyffe was born in Waco, Texas, the first of many towns she would call home during her father's career with the US Air Force. A horse aficionado from an early age, she earned a Bachelor of Arts in communications from California State University-Chico before launching what would become a twenty-year career as an equine photographer. She began writing fiction to pass the time during long days in the show arena, channeling her love of horses and the Old West into a series of Western historicals. Her debut novel, *Where the Wind Blows*, won the Romance Writers of America's prestigious Golden Heart Award as well as the Wisconsin RWA's Write Touch Readers' Award. She and her husband have two grown sons and live in the Pacific Northwest.

Sign up for Caroline's newsletter: www.carolinefyffe.com
See her Equine Photography: www.carolinefyffephoto.com
LIKE her FaceBook Author Page:
Facebook.com/CarolineFyffe
Twitter: @carolinefyffe
Write to her at: caroline@carolinefyffe.com

61677105R00190

Made in the USA
Lexington, KY
17 March 2017